ISBN-13: 978-1-62086-986-4
CPSIA Code: PRB0215A
Library of Congress Control Number: 2015900797

Printed in the United States

www.TripleCrownDreams.com
www.mascotbooks.com

BOOK ONE
TRIPLE CROWN TRILOGY

THE CALM BEFORE THE STORM

KIMBERLY CAMPBELL

In memory of Our Saint Ed, a Thoroughbred with a lot of heart, who had nine lives.

Acknowledgements

Everything happens for a reason. That is my mantra and how this book came to be. The details and experiences outlined in The Calm Before the Storm *would not have been possible to write about if it weren't for certain individuals who helped support me along the way.*

A chance introduction one summer afternoon at the barn to Naren Aryal, CEO of Mascot Books, led me down the path to pursue publishing The Calm Before the Storm. *I appreciate all of the support and feedback Naren, and his editors, Meghan Reynolds and Hannah Wagner, have provided me.*

My first experience at the Kentucky Derby was on May 4, 2013 and will never be forgotten. Through the hospitality of Mark and Jennifer Lamkin, my husband and I were able to tour the backside of Churchill Downs, watch the Kentucky Oaks from an owner's box, and cheer the horses down the homestretch on Derby day.

I am grateful to Larry Doyle of KatieRich Farms for showing me around the grounds of the Keeneland Auction, as well as providing details of his experiences within the racing industry.

Sue Kenney of Sagamore Farm has been my cheerleader along the way, reading the story as it developed and providing valuable feedback.

Terri Young, my sister and riding instructor, helped me brainstorm during my riding lessons when I needed to work through scenes I was developing in the book.

A special thank you to my mom, Elsa Bonstein (an author herself) who spent hours providing me counsel as I pursued my dream of writing this story; and my dad, who not only is my mom's editor and proofreader, but now has a daughter who requests his help in reading through the details.

And lastly, I am grateful for my husband, Kelly, and our children, Connor, Carter, and Codie, who support me on my journey with our horses and my sometimes crazy ideas, like writing a book.

"The blood runs hot in the Thoroughbred and their courage runs deep. In the best of them, pride is limitless. This is their heritage and they carry it like a banner. What they have, they use."

- C. W. Anderson

Prologue

In the world of horse racing, the Kentucky Derby is the most sought after prize in the sport. Run on the first Saturday in May, the build up to the Derby mesmerizes the world, as each candidate is dissected, its team of people interviewed, and the odds of winning established. Derby stories are famous, from the feel-good story to the heartbreaking one.

The Derby is restricted to three-year-old Thoroughbreds, regardless of gender. A colt, a filly, a gelding: it doesn't matter. As of 2014, with the running of the one hundred and fortieth Derby, only nine geldings and three fillies have won it. Over one hundred and fifty thousand people squeeze into the grandstand at Churchill Downs in Louisville, Kentucky to cheer for the favorite or root for the longshot.

There is no standard recipe for success for winning the Derby. Those involved in training horses debate the merits of how often a horse should run to be prepared for the race. Donau won the Derby in 1910 after having made forty-one starts as a two-year-old, while Apollo won the Derby in 1882, without having raced as a two-year-old at all. Anything can happen in the Derby.

The race is considered the most exciting two minutes in sports. Generally, horses who win the race finish with a mark just over two minutes. The record, one of only three sub-two minute times ever recorded, is held by Secretariat at 1:59 2/5 when he won the 1973 Derby.

A win at the Kentucky Derby has eluded some of the finest horsemen, the wealthiest businessmen, and the hardest working individuals in the racing industry, both in the United States and internationally. In a sport with so many variables, it is nearly impossible to find a sure thing. A lot can happen in two minutes. After all is said and done, after everyone else gives everything they can, it comes down to what the horse wants. The will to win runs deep. A horse that is racing for the fun of it, and for the ones he loves, can make impossible things suddenly seem quite possible.

Bloodlines of Courage

Mr. George Shilling was obsessed with Genuine Risk. From the moment she became the second filly to win the Kentucky Derby, he was smitten. He followed her racing career closely, keeping a notebook to track her races, times, and her workouts. He knew she was the one.

In 1980, Genuine Risk burst onto the three-year-old racing scene. A filly had not won the Kentucky Derby since 1915, the year Regret won it, the first filly to do so. The theory was that female horses - fillies - were not capable of beating the boys, the big burly colts whose times and teams were dissected each year leading up to the Triple Crown. The crown jewels that every racehorse owner, trainer, and jockey dreamed of winning - the Kentucky Derby, the Preakness, and the Belmont.

Genuine Risk was the first filly to finish in the money in each of the Triple Crown races. After winning the Kentucky Derby, she finished second in the Preakness and second in the Belmont. Some argued she would have won the Preakness if she hadn't been whipped in the face by the jockey on the eventual winner. Mr. Shilling watched her in each of those races, with a close eye. He had big plans for her.

Genuine Risk continued to race into her fourth year. One morning at the end of the summer, she got loose in the backstretch and ran into a fire hydrant, which caused a career-ending knee injury. She finished with a spectacular record of ten wins in fifteen races, never finishing worse than third. Mr. Shilling was heartbroken over the end of her racing career, but he knew that her contribution to the world of horse racing was far from over.

Anticipation was high for her as a broodmare. Her first mating was to be with the great Secretariat, the winner of the Triple Crown in 1973. It would be the first-ever breeding of two winners of the Kentucky Derby.

Alas, her success as a broodmare was not to be. This first mating with Secretariat resulted in a still-born foal. She was bred a second time to Secretariat without success. Over a period of seventeen years, Genuine Risk only gave birth to two foals, neither of which raced. In 1993, Genuine Reward was born, sired by the stallion, Rahy. After an unsuccessful attempt at racing, he was retired to stud, and Mr. Shilling lost track of him. A second colt, Count Our Blessing, born in 1996, was subsequently gelded and lived out his life as a show horse under the name Westley. The decision had been made that if the colts couldn't race up to the level of their heritage, then they would be placed in careers where they could be successful.

Through it all, Mr. Shilling watched and waited. He was perplexed by Genuine Risk's lack of success in the breeding shed. It seemed a shame that one of the most successful racing fillies in history could not produce any offspring. However, the same could be said for Secretariat, the most famous racehorse of the century, whose direct offspring did not come close to reaching the levels of his success on the racetrack. Mr. Shilling still had hope.

Mr. Shilling contemplated an idea to track down the whereabouts of her colt, Genuine Reward.

The horse racing community is quite small, considering the patience and money it takes to be a part of the sport; Genuine Risk had been retired to a farm just about an hour away from Shilling's Grand Oak Farm. There were a few active Thoroughbred farms left in Virginia, and the owners of the farms were all close friends.

Mr. Shilling was invited to a small get-together with several horse owners over the Thanksgiving holidays at the farm where Genuine Risk resided. It was the chance he had been waiting for, to finally put his plans into action.

He had kept his interest in Genuine Risk and her offspring a well-guarded secret, afraid his friends would think he was crazy. Upon arrival at the farm, instead of heading to the front door, Mr. Shilling went out to the barn. He walked quietly over to one of the only occupied stalls.

"Hello, Little Lady," he called out.

The big chestnut head with the long white blaze turned to look at him. She walked over to the door and took the peppermint from Mr. Shilling's extended hand. At the age of thirty, Genuine Risk still had a majestic air about her. Mr. Shilling stroked her neck as he spoke,

"I've got big plans for one of your kiddos. Yes ma'am. We are not going to let your bloodline fade into the wind. I promise you that." Genuine Risk stood quietly, enjoying the attention, and let out a contented sigh.

"What are you doing out here, George?" Remy Holloway walked up from the direction of the house.

"I could ask you the same question," George turned away from the mare and gave Remy a big hug. Remy, a family name, short for Remington, had been a part of the racing community almost as long as George. She and her husband used to have a larger operation, but had reduced their team over the years. They enjoyed traveling and maintaining their racing operations had taken its toll, both emotionally and financially. However, they still enjoyed getting together with the close friends they had made throughout the years.

"I saw your car in the driveway and I know you have a habit of haunting old barns."

"Am I that predictable?" he asked, turning back to Genuine Risk.

"Come inside, George. There's a party going on," she smiled.

"You know I am not one for big parties and crowds," he was trying to work up his nerve. There was no way he could ask what he wanted to in front of all the people in the house. Now was a perfect opportunity to get everything out in the open.

"I know, George. But they're a necessary evil when it comes to the horse racing industry." They both laughed and Remy walked up to Genuine Risk and patted her gently.

"Five more minutes in the barn, then I'll go back with you," George said. Remy continued to pet her horse, a thoughtful look on her face.

"She's getting old, George," she said.

"I know."

He stood quietly aside while owner and mare had their moment together. There wouldn't be many of those moments left. George cleared his throat. The time had finally come. He dove into the deep end.

"Remy?"

"Yes, George?" She looked over at him, pulled out of her thoughts and memories.

"Do you by chance know where Genuine Risk's colt, Genuine Reward, is?" he asked sheepishly. Remy eyed him. She knew George was one of the most accomplished breeders in the state. She paused before answering him,

"George Shilling, what do you have up your sleeve?" He looked over at Genuine Risk. She gazed back at him with soft, big, brown eyes.

"Remy, I want to breed one of my mares to Genuine Reward." There he said it, out loud. Remy continued to stroke her mare's neck.

"You know her line hasn't had any success on the track, George."

"Of course, I know that," George replied, his years of waiting and researching were culminating in these few minutes. "It's taken me a long time to research. You know me, I don't make decisions quickly. I need to take time to ponder and find the right mates. I have one now, Storm Minstrel. I would like to breed her to Genuine Reward."

Remy smiled. George Shilling's methodical ways made him a

successful breeder.

"He's in Wyoming, George. His owner keeps me up to date on him. I like to tell Genny what her baby is doing." Remy began to turn, "Come on inside to the party, and I will get her name and phone number for you." She gave Genny one last pat and kiss on the nose, looped her arm through George's, and they both walked over to the house.

Genuine Risk watched them go, holding her head high with all the authority of a champion.

Though it was nothing like his own, Mr. Shilling loved this beautiful farm, with its expansive fields and great oak trees that shaded the grounds. The main driveway was asphalt, but everything else was dirt. It was easier on the horses.

Mr. Shilling was full of sheer joy. Genuine Reward was the next piece of the puzzle. He'd been waiting for a long time for the pieces to start falling into place. He'd spent countless hours combing over pedigrees and family lines, and he was confident that he was about to produce nothing short of a force of nature.

Before he left the party, Mr. Shilling decided to pay one last visit to Genuine Risk.

"I'm betting it all on you." He looked deeply into the horse's eyes and it was as if he was seeing the future. All of his doubts melted away. Genuine Risk nodded her head once, and Shilling knew that everything he had hoped for was about to come to pass. He left the farm that night with a new sense of purpose.

The next day, he wasted no time calling up the owners of Genuine Reward. He was pleasantly surprised at how easy it was for him to get them to agree to the match. Shilling wasn't one to throw his name around, but he had this time, and before he knew it, he was signing all the paperwork necessary for the breeding.

The broodmare herd at Grand Oak Farm was Mr. Shilling's life's work, and his pride and joy. There were several nice candidates to mate with Genuine Reward, but Mr. Shilling had only one in mind – his favorite mare, Storm Minstrel, or "Minnie," as he liked to call her.

She may not have had the reputation of his other broodmares, but she had the bloodlines that he was looking for – her dad was Storm Cat, who descended from the great Secretariat and her mom descended from Pleasant Colony, winner of the Kentucky Derby and Preakness, the year after Genuine Risk, in 1981.They were horses that reflected the qualities throughout their careers that he was looking for.

Mr. Shilling had spent his life studying and establishing bloodlines and researching the different qualities of each foal born on his farm. The elusive traits that couldn't be predicted were those that made for the greatest racehorse - heart, courage, and desire. Those were the traits that helped a horse overcome adversity; during times of stress, they could reach deep down within their souls and overcome great challenges.

Like the Vanderbilts, Hancocks, and Wrights before him, Mr. Shilling was interested in forming a breeding dynasty. He was a student of the old ways of breeding: keeping his herd intact, racing the babies, and then keeping them in retirement by incorporating them into his breeding shed to pass along their traits to the next line of winners. His ways weren't commonplace anymore. At most other places, racehorses are raced maybe through their three year old season and shortly afterwards they are retired and syndicated for breeding, all before they have truly proven themselves as a great racehorse with bloodlines to match. Mr. Shilling was adamant about having a horse prove himself for several years before incorporating them into his breeding stock.

Genuine Reward, though not a success at racing, was proving himself to be a great success in the world of polo ponies. He had sired many talented, well-known horses in the sport. Polo ponies had to be smart and quick, with a lot of stamina, which meant that Genuine Reward was passing on his dam's traits to his offspring. It was time to bring her bloodline back to the track.

Mr. Shilling made plans to take Minnie to Wyoming to be bred. Artificial insemination was out of the question; foals conceived that way are not allowed to race, and that would defeat the whole purpose. Mr. Shilling would leave Minnie in Wyoming with Genuine Reward until it was confirmed that she was in foal, and then he would bring her home and wait for the foal that had been almost twenty years in the making, his life's work.

The call couldn't come fast enough.

Rolling Thunder

Grand Oak Farm sat in the foothills of the Shenandoah Mountains, in the lazy, small town of Gordonsville, Virginia. Over 2000 acres of rolling hills, home to some of the best Thoroughbred bloodstock that Virginia had ever seen.

The farm was set on the northern most border of the town, in what amounted to a forest. Big, tall trees surrounded the property and littered the grounds in the areas that hadn't been cleared out for the horses. There was a river not too far off, and the wind often brought the sound of rushing water to the farm. The scenery was beautiful, and the atmosphere was relaxing for the horses. The farm was out of the way, so there were never many visitors, but it was close enough to the town center for the locals to know and respect Mr. Shilling.

It wasn't uncommon to see Mr. Shilling riding around the hillside on one of the retired racehorses from his farm. He liked to ride each of them when he could, just to make sure they were getting enough exercise. Many weekend nights, the town's people would find Mr. Shilling at the local restaurant describing one of his horses, a race he had won, or a birth he had witnessed. A crowd would gather and more often than not, everyone wound up with a drink in their hand, courtesy of Mr. Shilling.

Mr. Shilling was an avid breeder, always looking to improve his bloodstock. His operation was rare these days, as he not only bred his horses, but also raced them. Many of the modern farms were just breeding establishments, and the babies were sold at auction once they were old enough. Over the years, Mr. Shilling had had several winners, and he had been voted Top Breeder in Virginia many times.

It had been several months since Storm Minstrel had come back to Grand Oak, baby on the way. Mr. Shilling made sure she had everything she needed. He put his best people in charge of her care. Whatever the time, whatever the weather, she was Mr. Shilling's priority, and his patience was about to pay off.

Thick clouds hung low, heavy with the raindrops that had yet to fall. The sun had just set and a chill rose in the air. Joshua Nelson, the breeding manager, stood outside the door to the breeding shed, looking up at the sky; there was not a star to be seen. Josh could feel the electricity in the air. The thunder was getting closer. The mares inside were getting restless.

The broodmare barn was Josh's favorite place in the entire world. It was originally built in the 1800's, by the Irish settlers. When Mr. Shilling bought the place, it was assumed that he would tear it down, but the old man thought it would be good luck to have some of the original buildings, and he ordered that it be renovated. The outside of the barn was all original and it looked like it was still falling apart; the green paint had even been made to look like it was decaying.

The inside was a different story. Josh often used the word, "pristine" to describe the well-kept stalls and floors of the stable. The wood was polished and the equipment was kept immaculate. Josh liked to think of the barn as a symbol; from the outside, the world of horse racing was old, and a lot of people wouldn't give it a second look. From the inside, it was full of beauty, history, and tradition.

Josh walked back inside and rested his arms on the half-door of Minnie's stall. She was his only concern that evening. His gut told him that it was her night. The boss was anxious to hear about her progress.

Minnie was breathing heavily, but not yet circling her stall. Doc Weaver stood beside her, listening with a stethoscope. Josh glanced out the open barn door in time to see the sky light up with the crackle of lightning.

"Storms gettin' closer, Doc," Josh said. "It'll be a loud one, for sure."

"The storm is probably why the mare is going into labor early, Josh," said the Doc. "Glad I was able to make the rounds and stop in to check on her. She may need some help."

"Boss Shilling is sitting by his phone waiting for the call. He doesn't normally want to be disturbed with each foal being born, but he has a keen interest in this one," Josh said.

He glanced nervously out the door again, watching the storm gain speed over the Shenandoah Mountains.

"I'd say it's about time to call him, Josh." It was 12:15 am, and the calendar had rolled onto February 18. Josh grabbed his cell phone out of his jeans pocket and hit the speed dial for, "Boss Shilling," just as the first large raindrops hit the ground.

"She's ready, Boss." Josh said into the phone. He listened a few moments and hung up. "Boss is on his way. Make sure she doesn't push too early. He doesn't want to miss a minute of it!"

Minnie started circling her stall, looking to find the thickest straw to rest her big belly. The thunder cracked overhead as the storm rolled down the valley and settled on top of Grand Oak Farm. The lighting lit up the sky and was immediately followed by another loud rumble of thunder. A set of headlights could be seen racing wildly down the driveway. The initial droplets of rain turned into sheets, falling quickly to the ground. If the driver of the car hadn't known the road so well, he certainly would have careened into one of gullies on the side. The driver of the car hastily pulled up to the barn door. Mr. Shilling quickly scrambled out of the car and into the barn, his thick grey hair tossed about by the wind of the storm. He combed his fingers through it and walked quickly towards Minnie's stall.

"Grab some towels!" Doc Weaver yelled over the sound of the rain pelting the roof of the breeding barn. Minnie was now stretched fully out on her side. As Josh returned with the towels, the Boss asked,

"How's she doing, Josh?"

"Great, Mr. Shilling," Josh replied. Mr. Shilling only had eyes for his favorite mare. Storm Minstrel was big and grey, and always stood out in the crowd of horses throughout the farm. He had raised her himself and raced her until she was five, and then decided it was time for the breeding shed. She had a fine career, in racehorse terms: five wins, eleven second place finishes, and three third place finishes. Not too shabby.

Mr. Shilling had a way about him with his horses when it came to knowing if they could handle the rigors of racing. His horses didn't always return to breeding. Sometimes he found them new careers. Mr. Shilling was well-loved throughout the small town of Gordonsville and his horses could be found throughout the countryside as show horses, eventers, or even as a backyard horse for that kid that needed a friend. There were several children about town riding Mr. Shilling's horses; they actually had a club. They met on Thursdays. Mr. Shilling would often go and speak to the group, or lead trail rides, there were even occasions that he had the children to his farm for a camping trip

There were always young people on the farm, learning to work around the horses. Mr. Shilling had instituted a program when he first started out, and he allowed children to work and learn the ropes of a farm, in exchange for interacting with the horses: grooming them or leading them out to the fields. The socialization of his horses was important to Mr. Shilling and he felt interacting with horses was therapeutic for many kids during their tough growing-up years. Mr. Shilling had great success in keeping the young folk in his town interested in horses and the proper way to run a breeding and racing farm.

Once in a while, one of the children from the program, would come back to the farm seeking employment as an adult; the bug never really left their system. Mr. Shilling welcomed them back with open arms and talked with them about their overall goal in the business. If they wanted to be a jockey, he would put them in a position to learn from the best. If they wanted to be a trainer, he gave them a job that would allow them to rise in the ranks. Never was a farm more full of genuine love of horses and people than at Grand Oak.

"Hey Doc, how's she doing?" Mr. Shilling asked a second time, now directing his question to his expert vet.

"She's a trooper, Mr. Shilling. Everything is going like clockwork. Just waitin' for her to start pushing." All three men gathered together, away from the mare to allow nature to take its course. They huddled at the far wall like expectant fathers awaiting their first baby.

Mr. Shilling thought back to the day almost a year ago when he had arrived at the farm where Genuine Reward was living. As he drove down the driveway, his farm trailer behind him with Minnie inside, he saw the big chestnut with the same white blaze on his face that his mother had, out in the pasture. The horse had raised his head to watch the vehicle approach. Genuine Reward, in the flesh, was all Mr. Shilling had hoped for: deep chested, big barrel and hind-end. Genuine Reward trotted along the fence line with the vehicle, calling out to the mare inside the trailer. He had his mother's authoritative, but graceful, way about him. Shilling could see he had been right to make the trip out west.

Mr. Shilling was graciously received by Genuine Reward's owner. After introductions, Minnie was stabled in her barn. Mr. Shilling didn't stay long, as he had a business to run, but he left his trusted stable helper, Ben Kessler, with Minnie. Ben stayed in Wyoming until Minnie was confirmed in foal, and then brought her home.

Minnie lifted her head and stared at her belly. She had had three babies with no complications. The air grew thick in the stall. Minnie snorted and kicked her legs a bit: it was evident that something wasn't right this time. The men watched as Minnie kept lifting her head and looking at her middle. Doc Weaver returned to Minnie's side and rested his stethoscope against her stomach once again.

"What's going on, Doc?" asked Mr. Shilling.

With no reply from Doc Weaver, Mr. Shilling and Josh moved from their corner, back to Minnie's stall. Minnie laid her head back and, with a big groan, pushed. Josh lifted her tail out of the way, expecting to see the two front hooves of the baby foal. Doc Weaver's eyes grew concerned. He looked up at the two men and sighed.

"We may have a problem," he said. "When Minnie pushes, the foal's heartbeat slows, which leads me to believe that we may have an issue with the umbilical cord around the foal's neck." Mr. Shilling took a quick breath in.

"How can we help?" he asked.

"I'm going to have to reach up and try to unwrap the cord from around its neck. Josh, grab my gloves out of the pile of supplies in the aisle." Josh ran out of stall and into the aisle as the storm raged on overhead.

He returned with shoulder-length gloves and knelt on the other side of Minnie. Mr. Shilling moved to her head to help comfort her.

"It's okay, girl. It's just another foal trying to find its way into the world. You are a good momma." Minnie's ears pricked forward at his voice and she gave a great sigh. She trusted the man by her side. Mr. Shilling would do whatever he could to make it all okay.

At Minnie's side, Mr. Shilling couldn't help but think about his time with her. As a young horse, he used to call her over to the fence line, always with a peppermint hiding in his pocket, just for her. At the racetrack, she ran for him, knowing her job was to try and win. He was happy when she won, and stood in the winner's circle holding her bridle. He was also happy if she didn't win; there was a reason if she couldn't fight to the front. Never was a scolding word said or a whip raised. That was not his way.

Minnie closed her eyes. Doc Weaver inched the glove up his arm to the armpit and covered the glove with lubricant. With Mr. Shilling at her head and Josh holding her tail, Doc reached into Minnie's birth canal.

"I can feel the front hooves!" he yelled above the storm. He felt his way along the foal's thin legs. He felt the muzzle and head lying along the legs like they should be.

"Good news is the foal's not inverted!" Doc shouted. Under the rage of the storm, he added, "Those births don't end very well." Minnie lifted her head once again and looked at her belly. Doc Weaver felt around the foal's neck.

"Yes! Here it is. The cord is wrapped around the neck! It is not tight, but whenever she pushes, it tightens." The air around the stall was still, but not from the storm.

"Can you unwrap it?" Josh asked.

"I am feeling around. If it isn't too tangled, I may be able to un-loop it from around the head, but if there are many twists, there won't be much I can do..." Doc replied.

"Isn't there any other way? A C-section? Anything?" Mr. Shilling was doing his best to keep his voice calm, but the tremor was hard to ignore.

"If there was any other way, I promise you, I would do it. With certain other animals, the trip through the birth canal is short, and I might consider the brief lack of oxygen a non-issue, but a foal spends too much time in the birth canal to have its oxygen cut off. I don't have the tools for a C-section, and the mare is too far along to move anywhere."

"Doc, what's the bottom line here?" asked Shilling.

"I'm going to do everything I can for Minnie and the foal, but...you may need to make a decision, Mr. Shilling," Doc said, looking up. Doc had been the vet at Grand Oak for over twenty years. He knew how Mr. Shilling felt about each of his horses. He also knew that Minnie held a special place in his heart, and he knew that this foal was the one Mr. Shilling had planned for his entire life. The pressure was on.

"Doc, what do you need from me?" Josh asked. He cared about Minnie for Mr. Shilling's sake, but also for his own. He hadn't gotten to be the breeding manager by accident. Josh cared deeply about his charges, and he wasn't one to take no for an answer.

"I need you to throw on a pair of gloves and take my place here," Doc said. "There's an extra pair in my equipment bag." Josh dove for the bag, but came up empty. He knew there was a pair in the supply closet, and he ran down the isle of stalls as quickly as he could.

"What's wrong, boss?" Josh turned to see Ben coming out of one of the other stalls.

"Minnie's labor isn't going well. I need gloves!" Josh was frantically searching. Ben pulled a pair from his pocket and handed them to Josh.

"I always keep a pair on me when I work in here, just in case."

"Thanks, Ben. Come on!" They ran back down to the stall where Minnie and her foal were fighting for their lives. Ben wasn't prepared for what he found when they entered the stall.

Emergencies were rare in Mr. Shilling's breeding shed. Usually, if there was any inkling of a problem, Mr. Shilling sent the mares to Virginia Tech's Marion duPont Scott Equine Medical Center in Leesburg, Virginia, to make sure they had the best care for a successful delivery. In the nearly five years that Ben had worked at the farm, only one horse had died in labor, and only two foals hadn't survived delivery. Of course, there were other instances of stillborns and other birthing complications that led to loss of life, but that was still rare. Mr. Shilling spared no expense to keep his horses safe and healthy. Doc Weaver was the best of the best. If anyone could make this work out, it was him.

Mr. Shilling, while whispering quietly to Minnie, looked up at Ben and gave him a quick nod, before returning his focus to the mare.

Josh quickly put on the gloves Ben had given him and, kneeling next to Doc Weaver, slid his arm into the mare as well, feeling up the birth canal until he reached the foal.

"What are you gonna do, Doc?" Ben asked. He was wringing his hands for lack of something more productive to do.

"I'm going to make an incision…here, Josh, move over this way. Can you feel my hand?" Doc asked.

"Yes," Josh replied.

"Okay, I am putting some relief between the cord and the foal's neck. I need you to hold on exactly as I am." Josh felt around and replaced Doc's hand on the umbilical cord.

Doc quickly removed his arm from the mare, found the gloves that

Josh had missed, and opened his equipment bag. He took out a very large scalpel, a syringe filled with a numbing solution, and some iodine.

"Ben, grab as many towels as you can find." Ben ran down the barn aisle, grabbing towels and blankets off the stall doors.

When he returned, Doc was kneeling behind Minnie, inserting the syringe in various places to numb the area around the birth canal.

"What's the move, Doc?" asked Josh. He was tensed as if ready for a battle.

"Alright, when I say, I need you to let go of the cord, grab the legs, and pull with everything you've got. We're gonna get this foal out, and we're gonna do it quickly. Okay? Ben, please grab a towel and have it ready. As we lay the foal down, I want you to start drying it off." Ben draped a towel over his shoulder and stood out of the way and watched as the two men readied themselves for the upcoming task.

He deftly made a quick incision about a foot long, below the birth canal. Blood began spurting from the cut.

"Quick, Ben!" Doc yelled. Ben placed as many towels as he could around the vet, Josh, and the mare. Doc quickly inserted both his hands into the mare, running them up next to Josh's; at the same time, Josh inserted his other arm.

"Ready? And…pull!" Doc instructed. Josh and Doc Weaver, each holding one of the foal's front legs, leaned back, pulled the foal out of the mare and onto one of the blankets Ben had laid out. At the same time, in one motion, Doc cut the umbilical cord and clamped the end coming from the mare. The black colt breathed freely and laid next to his mom, stunned from his quick delivery into the world.

Minnie lay quietly, listening to Mr. Shilling. His voice was calming to the horse, despite its shaking. He rubbed her head and scratched her ears and tried to keep her still. It was a symbiotic relationship: the more he tried to calm her, the more her serenity and grace calmed him. He didn't know what he would do if he lost this horse. There wasn't a single person or horse that he loved more than her. She was his family, and he liked to think that he was hers.

She couldn't feel what had transpired at the other end of her body, due to the numbing medication the Doc had given to her. Prior to getting the foal out, the vet couldn't drug her, given that anything he gave her would be passed to the foal through the umbilical cord. Now that the foal was out, Doc Weaver quickly grabbed his other syringe and gave her a shot, both to sedate her and relieve any pain.

"Ben, you're up," the vet instructed.

Ben started rubbing the foal all over with the towels, doing his best to dry the foal as well as its momma would have done. Josh cleaned out its nostrils with a big rubber nasal syringe. The foal was lying on the blanket quite dazed from its entrance, and didn't object to all the attention. Meanwhile, Doc Weaver pulled the placenta out of the mare, cleaned up the wound, and began the arduous task of stitching up Minnie's incision. While he stitched, he talked,

"Mr. Shilling, Minnie will need to go to the vet hospital. The incision I made is deep, and it would be best if she was in a more sterile environment, to ensure that it doesn't get infected." Mr. Shilling nodded. He was relieved that the immediate danger was over, but they weren't out of the woods yet. He needed to make sure both of them got the very best care. The vet continued,

"I recommend that we try and get the foal to nurse immediately," Mr. Shilling nodded his understanding again.

"Doc, thank you for all you have done here tonight. You saved them, and for that, I am eternally grateful." Mr. Shilling and Doc Weaver both stood up at the same time.

Minnie made a big sigh and heaved herself up. She walked over to the foal, which was just starting to put its big gangly legs underneath his body to try and stand up himself.

"He got up on the first try, Mr. Shilling!" Ben shouted. Mr. Shilling smiled.

The Colt

It was opening day at the Keeneland yearling sale. Over 4,000 horses pass through one of the most famous auction rings in the world – a stage set for the buying and selling of some of the world's best horses by some of the most affluent people in the world. The auction runs over a fourteen-day period, where the sale price for an individual horse can be in the millions. Anyone can attend the auction, either as buyer or spectator. Thousands of horses are shipped onto the grounds. Potential buyers scan the sales catalogs and personally inspect each horse they are interested in buying.

There was excitement in the air on that particular day because the sale included the dispersal stock of George Shilling; the last great holdover of the golden age of breeding in the state of Virginia. When news spread that Mr. Shilling's horses were to be sold at Keeneland, pandemonium ensued. Everyone wanted a piece of the Shilling empire, and the who's who of the Thoroughbred racing world was in attendance, posturing for the purchase of one of the many great bloodlines now up for grabs.

A gangly colt stood in the back of his stall, his head held low to the ground, almost touching the soft, yellow straw. He was sleeping, waiting for his turn in the auction ring.

His color was that of the greyest thunder cloud: the one that appears when a storm begins to form, the blue sky being rolled over by the front edge of a puffy white cloud, followed by the darker grey of the boomer. There's a change in the atmosphere, an electric tingling in the air that denotes a bad storm and warns everyone to take cover. Yet there are some that stand there and watch it roll in, taking in the awesome power and beauty of it all.

The colt began to wake up. He stretched his head, and shook it to clear the fuzziness of sleep. His nostrils quivered and his ears pricked forward at all the activity outside his stall.

The stall door opened and a groom came to attach his lead to take him out of the stall. There was another showing, another potential purchaser that wanted to evaluate the attributes of the colt.

"Come on, big guy. We gotta wow 'em this time." The colt playfully nipped at the lead rope attached to his halter. He trusted this man.

He followed the groom willingly and stood in the row, while several people stood around him looking at his write-up while they made comments.

"He is quite gangly. Look at how his hindquarters are several inches higher than his front end," said one.

"The knees are too big and knobby. They won't hold up under the daily pounding on the track," said another.

"He doesn't exhibit much energy, probably not a competitor."

"Wonder what Mr. Shilling saw in the mating of Genuine Reward and Storm Minstrel?"

Little did they know, beneath the surface slept the thunder cloud waiting to unfurl.

Genuine Storm. Mr. Shilling had aptly named his prized colt after both his mother and father. He'd started to train the colt, but it was all kept so secret, that no one really knew what this yearling was capable of. He had the demeanor of a backyard horse, but he loved running more than anything in the world. Mr. Shilling couldn't have been more pleased with this colt: and he couldn't wait for the world to know and love his horse as much as he did. However, things happen differently than planned, sometimes, and there was a chance now that the world would never know what a masterpiece Mr. Shilling had on his hands.

Auction ring

The walk to the auction ring at Keeneland was beautiful, row after row of cinder block barns, filled with yearlings for sale. Storm walked next to his groom, Ben, his eyes taking it all in. He knew something was up, as Ben wasn't whistling his normal tunes. Ben walked quietly next to him. Head held high, the colt whinnied to some of the fillies passing by.

"Be calm, Stormy," Ben said. He was having a hard time doing his job, under the circumstances. He'd grown up in Gordonsville, he was one of the kids who worked on the farm with Mr. Shilling: he learned the basics as a child and, once he finished school, he came back and got a job on the farm, intending to move up and start his own racing farm one day.

Storm nipped at Ben's black hair, making it even messier than it already was. Ben's light eyes grazed over the happy colt as he wondered what was going to happen: not just to Storm, but to himself.

Storm tossed his head and pranced alongside his groom. Above his head arose the big black water tower and in front of him lay the oval of Keeneland racetrack. While they walked, Ben daydreamed about his days on the farm – how things had changed in such a short period of time.

****

The news was devastating to everyone. Mr. Shilling had gone to his apartment in Washington D.C. for business. On his way back to the farm, something went wrong with the electrical circuits of the helicopter, and the propellers had stopped suddenly. There was no time to make use of the parachutes stored under the seats. There were two confirmed dead in the accident: the pilot, and Mr. Shilling. The headline in the newspaper made him look like nothing more than a rich man who decided to spend the weekend at one of his different homes: "Avid Horse Racer Dies in Helicopter Crash en Route to Farm from DC Apartment."

Just thinking about it made Ben fume. The people of Gordonsville were still in mourning over the loss of their beloved patriarchal figure, but the rest of the world hardly cared. He was not married and had no heirs. No one else in his family, his brothers or sisters, knew anything about the horse business and weren't willing to continue his breeding establishment. Within a few short weeks, his siblings decided it was best to disburse the bloodstock.

Storm nudged him again. Ben was fighting now to keep his mind on the task at hand: getting Storm through this auction and to his next owner with as little incident as possible. It almost made him sick to think that, after everything Mr. Shilling went through to get this horse, another trainer was about to reap the benefits. Ben had seen enough of Storm's preliminary training to know what this colt would be capable of in the future. He'd been with Storm on the night he was born. He couldn't imagine not working with him every day.

Ben turned the feisty colt between two barns and headed toward the holding area outside of the auction presentation house. The outside pavilion was the first stop where the crowds gathered to observe the horses before they entered the inside pavilion and finally, the auction ring. Storm waited behind Royal Duke, another colt from the Shilling farm, a big bay colt that had been in the stall next to Storm. Duke had been in and out of his stall many times over the past few days, three times as much as Storm had been. He was the golden child, the colt everyone had come to see. He was the last foal of the late, great Personal Ensign and his sire was Malibu Moon.

The number on Storm's hip was starting to itch and he turned to tear it off, but Ben kept his head forward. Finally, Ben pulled him into the sales preview ring. They walked around the oval.

The crowd stood in the middle of the oval as well as around the outside. Each person surveyed the yearling they coveted. Many of the yearlings had been evaluated many times over the past few days. Pedigrees had been dissected by the blood stock agents, x-rays examined by the vets, and dispositions evaluated by the trainers. If the horses were the athletes, the owners and buyers were the scouts: they watched old footage and compared stats, all to get ready for the draft, hoping their horses would make it to the Super Bowl of horse races. Now was the time to put up the money, and try to buy a Triple Crown win. It was show time.

Storm was playfully prancing next to Ben. His head turned left and right to look at all the people.

"Look at that bay," someone clamored. "He is going to be a big colt."

"He should be, given his sire. Nice straight legs, big barrel means big lungs," another said. The crowd moved along with Duke, as he moved around the pavilion. It was like Storm didn't exist.

The yearlings moved to the walking ring in the covered arena. The area outside of the ring was crowded with the teams of people waiting for Duke to enter the auction ring. At the top of the ring, Duke was led to one side of the announcer stand and Storm was led to the other.

Duke and Storm were handed over to a showman who will take the each colt, one at a time, into the auction ring to be presented to the audience. Each showman was neatly dressed in a jacket and tie, emphasizing the importance of each of their charges. Ben stood off to the side, keeping his fingers crossed that the bidding on Duke and Storm would go well.

"Number thirty-two!" the announcer called. Duke was led through the big sliding wooden gate and disappeared from view. Storm stood still, ears picking up the noises on the other side of the door. His turn was next.

The bidding started at $50,000 and immediately jumped by $50,000 increments. $100,000, $150,000....The bidding war for one of the sons of Malibu Moon began to slow, $850,000, $860,000, $870,000. Going once, going twice, *bang* - SOLD - for $870,000! The crowd erupted! The highest priced yearling of the sale so far!

Storm was jittery; he could feel the excitement. The showman tried to calm him, but to no avail. Ben watched in nervous anticipation. The big wooden door slid open and Storm charged into the auction ring. He pulled up short, nearly crashing through the ropes surrounding the ring. Storm held his head erect and snorted through his nostrils. Ears pricked forward at the crowd, he surveyed his surroundings. All eyes were on him. The tension was building.

"Hip number thirty-three. A yearling colt by Genuine Reward out of Storm Minstrel by Storm Cat. Let's open the bidding at $50,000." The excitement of the previous sale was dying out. Storm half-reared, and the showman had a hard time keeping him within the confines of the small auction ring. Grooms work tirelessly with their horses to ensure they behave, but they never know what will truly happen until they walk into the crowded auction ring.

Not a hand went up to start the bidding. As there was no reserve on Storm, no minimum price the seller needed to get, the auctioneer could drop the bid as low as he needed to start the process.

"How about $25,000?" urged the auctioneer. He began reading from his notes. "One of the last babies bred by the great George Shilling. His dam, Storm Minstrel, had a successful racing career with winnings of almost $300,000, has two offspring in training." He kept his information on the dam's side of the pedigree as everyone knew his sire, Genuine Reward, didn't have any success at the track. Indeed this was the only Thoroughbred bred to race out of Genuine Reward. Mr. Shilling's reason for breeding this yearling was a mystery. No one wanted to take a chance on an unknown.

"$10,000?" the auctioneer continued to try and get some bid started on this colt. Storm continued to move restlessly back and forth in front of the announcer stand. Sweat began to stand out on his neck and hips. The showman used a towel to try and dry him off, but was having a hard time of it given Storm's prancing.

From the back of the house, a small movement was detected by the bid-spotter. A swollen-faced man with no neck, raised his hand. The crowd turned to look at who had bid on the colt. An audible gasp ran through the crowd. The trainer, Dale Blackston, was tipping his cap. Not a well-liked horseman, Blackston had just come off a suspension for illegal tactics while training his horses: drugs, illegal training devices. He always seemed to slip through the hands of the stewards and just push things to the brink. Everyone knew it was a matter of time before he got ejected from the sport altogether.

The auctioneer paused, hesitant to give this bid to the greasy man in the back. He'd known some of the horses that had gone home with Blackston previously, and none of them lasted long in the business once he got his hands on them.

"We have $10,000, do I now twelve?" the auctioneer urgently looked to all corners of the pavilion for a competing bid, "$10,000 going once. Going twice. Sold, for $10,000." No one clapped this time. As little faith as the crowd had in this gangly, thundercloud colt, none of them believed in Blackston's tactics. Sympathetic murmurs accompanied Storm as the showman led him from the ring and handed him back to Ben.

Storm jogged happily as Ben led him back to his stall. Ben didn't know what to do. It was one thing to know that Mr. Shilling's horses were being sold off to a bunch of strangers who didn't care about the legacy he'd built, it was another thing to see Storm sold off to the lowest bidder, who also happened to be a crook.

"This isn't fair, buddy. I'm sorry." Storm nudged Ben's pocket. "Yeah, I've got one. One for the road." Ben gave Storm a peppermint from his pocket and continued petting him, until a dark shadow loomed over them from behind. Blackston had come to claim his prize.

"Step back from my horse, boy," drawled the large man. Even in the dim light, Ben could tell that he was dirty.

"I've been the groom for this horse since he started training. Is there anything you would like to know about him?" Ben was hoping that maybe all the rumors were false and that Blackston wasn't the man everyone thought he was. Sure, he smelled worse than the stall, but some good people struggled with that, too. Abraham Lincoln probably smelled horrible. Ben looked deep into Blackston's eyes, trying to find a glimmer of goodness within the black irises. There was nothing.

"How quick does he fight back when you start to push him?" Blackston spit into the corner of the stall.

"Excuse me? No, he loves to run. We've never had to-"

"Runnin' ain't meant to be fun. It's a job, and this horse works for me now. We're gonna show him what it means to work hard. I appreciate your bond with the creature, but I'll thank you to leave me with my purchase now, son. This is where you say goodbye." Ben took one last look at Storm. What would happen to this magnificent horse? How could he keep Mr. Shilling's pride and joy from succumbing to the horrors that this man had in store for him?

Dejected, and alone, Ben left the stall, trying to ignore the anxious whinny coming from behind him.

Girls Night Out

Defeated, Charlie stood in her closet, her eyes falling over the clothes she had worn time and time again. They no longer had anything to offer her; they all held memories of her years as a wife and a mother.

"There has got to be something in here with some spark," she said to herself. She knew her time was running out; Jillian and Kate would swoop in at any moment, ready to take their friend out for a night on the town. Charlie could feel the nerves move like butterflies in her stomach, and her anxiety grew. It had been ages since she had a night out.

Charlie pressed on, desperate for something eye-catching to wear. As she shuffled through the clothes, her eyes caught a glimpse of a red frilly thing toward the back of the rack. She pushed the sweaters, the polos, and the comfortable button-downs out of the way to find an old, red-tasseled shirt.

"Oh my God," she whispered to herself, a small smile spreading across her face. The memory came back quickly...

****

"Charlie, come on! We are going to be late." Paige was Charlie's roommate in college, and they pledged the same sorority. Go Gammas!

"Paige, you can't be late to a frat party," Charlie said. She was regretting having agreed to attend the party. It was Halloween, and she hated dressing up, and she knew Paige would leave her alone the minute they walked through the door.

"If we don't leave now, all the cute guys will be taken, and I will have wasted my whole Halloween." Charlie rolled her eyes and sighed.

"Alright, I'm ready. Let's go." Charlie threw her cowboy hat onto her head and followed Paige out the door. They didn't have to walk far, the party was at the fraternity house on the same block. Before they even walked in the door, Charlie could tell that there was lots of beer, and lots of cute boys to flirt with.

True to form, Paige disappeared as soon as they set foot in the house. Charlie made her way to the keg and got a beer. She met up with some other friends and actually managed to start having a good time. There was one guy, a pledge by the looks of it, dressed up as a giant potato, and he kept having to sing Cher songs whenever a fraternity member said something to him. Charlie couldn't stop laughing about it, even when she went to the keg to get a refill.

"What's so funny, Annie?" She looked up. A cute boy wearing jeans, a t-shirt, and a nametag that said, "Buffalo Bill," was smiling down at her.

"Your lack of costume." She said, feeling a little flirty.

"But you know who I'm supposed to be. So my costume is a success, Annie, and there's nothing funny about a success story."

"I think you've mistaken me for someone else..."

"Annie Oakley, right? You've got the whole cowgirl thing going on, I figured that's who you were supposed to be."

"I guess...I hadn't really thought of being anyone in particular."

"You mean you bought all this and you didn't make a plan?"

"I already had everything I'm wearing, for your information. You can't own horses and not own the gear," Charlie replied with a smirk. The boy's eyes took her in, and Charlie suddenly felt dizzy. *Why can't I form a sentence?* she thought. Before she could gather her thoughts, he interrupted,

"Oh, I see. So you're a genuine cowgirl, then. And this is what you look like when you ride?" With a confident smile, he locked eyes with Charlie, making her head spin. Charlie searched for words and before she knew it, they seemed to be spilling out of her mouth uncontrollably.

"Hardly! You can't ride a horse looking like this! I mean, I guess you could, but it wouldn't be very comfortable, and I don't see how you could actually lift your leg to get onto the horse without ripping the pants, and–"

"I like you, Annie," he said with a grin.

Confused by his grin, Charlie retorted, "My name isn't Annie."

"My name isn't Buffalo Bill."

"It's not?" She said, pouring as much sarcasm as possible into those two words. He moved closer to her. Suddenly very self-aware, Charlie swallowed the lump in her throat, trying to remember to breathe.

"I'm Peter." He held out his hand for her to shake. She reciprocated the gesture, "And you are…?"

****

"Charlie?" a familiar voice called from downstairs. "Charlie, where are you?"

"In the closet!" she answered, shaking the memory away as she came back to reality. Her focus fell once again on her hopeless wardrobe. She felt the red tassels between her fingers. *Should I even bother trying?* she thought. *Oh and the jeans. Yeah, right.* But maybe…

Charlie had lost weight during the past year, a lot of it. Depression will do that to you. Desperate to help, Jillian and Kate hoped a night out would give Charlie a reprieve from the sad thoughts that persisted in her mind.

Charlie heard footsteps bounding up the stairs. Before she could completely pull herself together, Jillian and Kate exuberantly burst in to the room. Charlie turned and smiled feebly before turning back to her clothes. They knew her well enough to know a simple night on the town would be painful.

"Come on, Charlie! We are going to be late," said Kate. Jillian ignored Charlie's downtrodden attitude, gently shoved her aside, and took over outfit choosing duty.

"Surely there is something in here that will work," said Jillian, as she plowed through Charlie's clothes. Charlie moved to sit on the bed with Kate.

"I was kind of thinking about that red shirt," Charlie said. Jillian held it up.

"I like it!"

"It's what I was wearing the first time I met Peter."

Jillian and Kate did their best to hide their pitying looks.

"Okay, well then definitely not," said Kate.

"Also, you need to go shopping, because that was over twenty years ago," Jillian said, trying to be gentle, but also incredulous as to how anyone could own the same clothes for that long.

"We will have a good time tonight, I promise," said Kate, as she put an arm around Charlie.

"But that hair," Jillian started with a smile, "we have got to do something about it." She tugged gently on Charlie's short, plain hair. Charlie let out a sigh,

"Work your magic. How you manage to have zero bad hair days is beyond me."

"Kate, come pick out her outfit. I like that blue thing I saw at the back, but what do you think?" While Kate tore through the closet, desperately trying to piece together a worthy outfit, Jillian worked on Charlie's hair and makeup.

"How are you feeling?" asked Jillian, as she combed through Charlie's hair.

"Trying to be okay," Charlie said, forcing a smile.

"We don't have to go out. We can stay in and watch a movie or something."

"We are going out!" Kate called from the closet. Her confident footsteps traveled to the bathroom. "Charlie, I love you. But it's been forever. You have to go out sometime. You can't stay inside forever. Netflix only has so much to offer."

"Kate," Jillian warned.

"No, she's right," said Charlie. *I can do this*, she thought. "We are going out, and I will have at least a decent time!"

"That's the spirit!" said Jillian.

"It will do," said Kate, as she nodded with a smile. "Remember, we picked the casino because horse racing is going on at the same time. You can have your pick of fun!" She moved back to the closet.

As Jillian finished Charlie's hair and makeup, Kate appeared at the bathroom door.

"Okay, I found something, and you're going to protest. But you're wearing it," demanded Kate. Jillian and Charlie moved to the room, where Kate channeled her inner Vanna White to show a silver, heavily beaded, shorter-than-mid-thigh dress.

"You're joking, right?" asked Charlie.

"What? No, I'm not joking!"

"Kate, the last time I wore that was to our 1920s mixer sophomore year!"

"Yes, and you looked fabulous."

"Okay, this is ridiculous, *you* really need some new clothes and *you* need to go sit down while I pick Charlie's outfit," said Jillian, pointing to Charlie and Kate respectively. "Let's compromise." She snatched the flapper dress out of Kate's hand and moved to the closet herself.

"I still say it would have been perfect," said a defeated Kate as she moved to the bed. Charlie breathed a sigh of relief; Jillian's wardrobe choices were a bit more in line with her own. Within minutes, Jillian pulled together an outfit that was given partial approval by Kate, and a weak smile by Charlie.

Charlie stood in front of the mirror, taking in a look she hadn't seen in quite a while. A tight pair of jeans with rhinestones on the back pockets matched the big-buckled belt with plenty of bling of its own that accentuated Charlie's now tiny waist. The deep red halter top was Kate's choosing, and Charlie had visions of leaning over the craps table, showing a little cleavage. Charlie could just feel the panicked look spreading across her face. The shirt matched her dark red boots, and the outfit was complete with large hoop earrings.

"This is going to be such a blast!" exclaimed Jillian.

"Charlie, you haven't been out in months. It's time to shake off the mom image and put on the woman image," added Kate. Charlie took a deep breath,

"Okay. I guess I'm ready!"

"Let's see, we get out the door in five minutes, thirty-minute drive to Charles Town; we should be there by 8 pm," said Kate.

"Kate, relax. Everyone knows the real party doesn't start till after 9 pm," Jillian said. "Or until I get there. Even if we're late, we'll be fashionably late." Before they headed out, Jillian added a touch of lipstick to finish Charlie's look.

"I don't know if I like that, Jillian," she said.

"Sweetie, you don't know what you're talking about, okay? That's why I'm doing this for you. It's for your own good."

"I like it. It makes her look sort of mysterious," Kate said, trying to forget that her friends were throwing her whole schedule off.

"That's exactly what I was going for. Rub your lips," she ordered. "You know, I've been thinking about teaching a class at the local rec center, so that women can learn how to properly apply makeup."

"That's actually not a bad idea. You'd be a really good teacher," replied Charlie.

"I don't know...you're not actually that personable. What would happen if some older woman asked you to show her how to do a smoky eye?" asked Kate.

"I would politely tell her that a smoky eye is for women younger than her, and she'd be better off learning how to cover up her wrinkles and liver spots. So maybe you're right." They all laughed.

There was a knock at the door. "May we come in?" Skylar's voice was unsure in her request.

Charlie flung open the door and wrapped her beautiful, nine-year-old daughter in her arms. Behind Skylar, Ryan's stern eyes looked worriedly into Charlie's. At fifteen, he was beginning to look much like his father.

"Are you excited, Mom? You look sooooo different!" Skylar's chatting began. Before Charlie could get a word in, Ryan said,

"You'll be careful, right Mom? You haven't gone out without us in a long time."

"We'll take good care of her, I promise," said Jillian.

"We'll be downstairs," said Kate, as she and Jillian moved toward the door. Charlie sat on her bed with Ryan and Skylar, trying to gather the courage to leave.

"I haven't seen this shirt before, Mom. I just love it!" Skylar's excitement filled the room.

"You don't have to go out, you know," added Ryan.

Charlie smiled, "I think I do. It's time we got back to a normal life."

Worry and anger quickly grew on Ryan's face. Before he could respond, Charlie grabbed Ryan's hand and added, "Life won't ever be the same. But it's time to start living again. Your father would want that."

Charlie hugged both her children and they headed downstairs.

"Say hi to the horses for me!" yelled Skylar as the women headed out the front door, into the night. As the door closed, Charlie smiled. Skylar had inherited a love of horses from her. There is a lot that horses can teach about life: patience, grace under pressure, responsibility, poise.

After she got into the car, Charlie looked back at her house. *At least I get to be with horses tonight*, she thought, figuring the horses racing would be much more attractive than the guys at the casino. Horses would never stop being a part of her life.

Night at the Races

As they walked through the doors of the casino, Charlie was overwhelmed by the sights and sounds of wall to wall slot machines, craps tables, roulette wheels, and lucky men and women hitting the jackpot.

There seemed to be people from every walk of life within those four walls. There were the older men with trophy girls hanging on their arms as they rolled the dice, senior citizens pulling the slot handle, dwindling away their social security checks, and underage groups of girls posing off to the side, pondering their next move, wanting to have a casino experience without getting caught. The waitresses served free drinks, enticing people to bet more, while security guards eyeballed the clients sitting at the tables, making sure there was no cheating.

Charlie hadn't been to a casino in a long time. She had gone with Peter on a work trip to Las Vegas one time before they had kids and had spent some time in the casinos. She had enjoyed the celebrity shows much better than the casinos, where you couldn't tell if it was day or night. Locally, casinos had been popping up all over with the passing of new gambling regulations. The granddaddy in the area was Hollywood Casino at Charles Town Raceway in West Virginia, which was where she now found herself.

She wasn't that impressed. Sure, the furniture was nice, and there were expensive looking chandeliers lighting the place, and most of the people were wearing fancy clothes: but the air was stale, and the smoke from the smoking sections lingered over to the non-smoking areas. Really? Weren't all buildings non-smoking these days?

The carpet was an awful yellow, red, and blue pattern that was straight out of the disco area and if you looked at it long enough made you dizzy. All of the fixtures were fake gold, which lent a cheap look to the place, and made the light from the chandeliers cast glares on the backs of cards. It was, overall, just not her scene.

"Come on, Charlie, time to get busy!" Jillian felt right at home. She pulled Charlie over to the closest craps table, Kate close behind. Charlie was lost, but Jillian threw down a few twenty dollar bills and the dealer gave her the equivalent in bright blue chips. With a flip of her blond hair, and big white smile to the dealer, Jillian placed her chips at various places on the table and was handed the dice.

After watching Jillian play for a while, and taking a few turns at the roulette wheel and some slot machines, Charlie wandered away to get some fresh air. The sounds, the shouts, and the stuffy recycled air - it was all closing in on her and she was getting a bit claustrophobic. She'd had some drinks; they were free and her glass was never empty. As of late, her tolerance had dwindled due to disuse, so the alcohol had gone right to her head.

Through the back of the casino, the sign pointed, "To Racetrack." There was a path of red in the disco carpet leading the way. Charlie focused on the red and followed it out of the casino, up a flight of stairs, and out into the cool night. She inhaled deeply. The world wasn't spinning as quickly out there.

"Not your thing?" a strange voice asked. Charlie turned suddenly to find a ruggedly handsome man standing off to the side. Leaning against the railing, one side of his mouth was turned up into a sly smile. He didn't look like a serial killer, but you never can be too careful about those things, so she tried her best not to be an easy target.

"Well, you know…no, it's not." She was not doing a very good job. The wine was making her confused: or was it his smile? In any case, the combination was more than she could handle, apparently, and she ended up saying the first thing that came to her mind.

"My girlfriends wanted to get my mind off things." She hiccupped and put her hand to her mouth, embarrassed. Her brown eyes locked with bright blue ones, her voice left her, and she just stared, her hand dropping to her side. She was alone, with a man. That hadn't happened in a long time and she was at a loss for what to say next. Luckily, he didn't seem to have the same issue.

"Well, hanging with several hundred drunk people, all losing their hard earned money can certainly get your mind off, 'things.'" he laughed. His laugh came from deep within and gave her goose bumps.

Charlie shook her head to try and clear it. Suddenly, a giggle escaped her lips. If Charlie had been sober, she would have been mortified. She didn't make a habit of being out of control: she was organized, put together, and certainly did not fall prey to giggling with strange men.

"I guess. It's so boring in there though, all I wanna do is go home and talk to my horse. That's not a euphemism, by the way. I mean, I don't know if it sounded like one, or if you thought I was trying to make it one…I have a real horse. He's got hooves and everything. And I've also got kids, so I don't generally make euphemisms about horses."

Charlie stopped talking and held up a hand. He seemed very amused at her confusion and waited patiently for her to look at him again.

"I think my point was, that I love my horse. And if that wasn't my point, it should have been, because it's the truth."

"I must say, that is an excellent point to make, and you did it so…what's the word I want…eloquently." He laughed out the last word and she couldn't help but giggle again. "I, too, have real horses and I love them, as well. So I guess we have that in common."

"What else do we have in common? Do you have kids? I have two kids. I love them more than my horse, but I think that's okay," she said. At that point, there was nothing she wasn't saying. Charlie could feel her mouth moving and words coming out, but there seemed to be no way to stop them. She was embarrassed about it. In fact she said that, but he just laughed at her and took a few steps closer.

"I don't have kids. But if you really love them more than your horse, maybe I ought to have a few. It might be nice."

"You would probably have really cute kids. Usually cute guys have cute kids. It's just a fact of life, I think. Wait a second, I came out here to find the racetrack. Do you know where it is?"

"Actually, I do. I was just on the way there, myself. Would you allow me to escort you?" He held out his arm, and by that point, Charlie had forgotten all about the fact that he could be a murderer: what kind of murderer loves kids and horses? Probably the kind that lies. She took his arm and they walked over toward the racetrack. He was steering her, so she was free to just stare up at his eyes while they walked.

She felt the pounding before she heard it. The ground began to vibrate. The sound of heavy breathing. Rolling thunder. She pulled her eyes away from the sea of blue and searched for the herd of horses straining towards the finish line. Charlie held her breath.

Coming down the homestretch were eight horses bunched together, separated by only inches. On their backs the jockeys were crouched up, trying to squeeze the last bit of speed out of their mounts. Some hand rode, or waved their whips alongside, urging their horse to victory.

A racehorse can reach speeds of 35-40 miles per hour. Charlie could practically feel the wind racing by as she imagined herself a part of the race. Her fuzzy mind was taken back to her sweet sixteenth birthday, when her mom treated Charlie and her best friend to a day at the races at Monmouth Park in New Jersey. As a kid, she was horse-obsessed, particularly with Thoroughbreds.

Her entire junior high career had been a horse phase. All of her notebooks had horses on them, and she spent her recesses playing horses with her friends. She had horse posters in her room, and she slept with a horse stuffed animal named Secretariat Jr; she'd named him that because she loved Secretariat.

She could remember being eleven years old, spending months and months begging her parents for a horse. Finally, one day, Charlie's parents relented and agreed to buy her a horse, as long as she did all the work, including getting herself to and from the barn. Every day she rode her bike the two miles to the barn to take care of her horse, and she never complained. Her horse was a Thoroughbred that had been retired off the track. A spunky, grey horse that she loved dearly.

Charlie was pulled out of her reminiscing by the announcement, "and Flying Squirrel wins by a nose." The guy with his quick smile was still standing next to her, only now his eyes shone a bit brighter.

"Seems like you like this out here a bit more?"

Charlie smiled, "Yes, I really do. I had forgotten the excitement of watching horses come down the stretch. I used to go to the racetrack when I was a kid, I wanted to be a jockey so bad. I used to practice on the arms of the couch. My mom would get so mad at me because I would hop around, pretending to be on a racehorse." She laughed as the memory of her mother scolding her popped into her head.

"So what happened?"

"Are you kidding? Look at me. I grew out of my dream. Literally." Charlie pointed to her long legs. His gaze focused on her legs for a few seconds before he said anything. She blushed and she thought he noticed, because that sly smile crept back onto his face and he stepped closer to her.

"What's your name?" he asked. Somehow, the way he asked the question sounded seductive, and she blushed deeper. She was really out of practice with this whole guy thing.

"Charlie," she whispered. He was close enough that he still heard her.

"My name is Doug, pleased to make your acquaintance." He held out his hand. Charlie put out her own, and he took it in his with a firm shake.

His hand felt warm against hers, rugged but manicured at the same time. She couldn't take her eyes off his hand. She hadn't had this rush of feeling in a long time.

"I'm Charlie," she sighed back at him. It took her almost a full minute to realize she'd told him her name twice. He didn't seem to care though. He just stood there, smiling at her, making her want to tell him her name again and again so that he'd never forget it.

"How about we get a little closer for the next race?" His hand moved to the small of her back to guide her down the steps towards the racetrack. She wobbled in her high heeled boots.

"Do you come often to watch the horses race?" she asked.

"Fairly often," Doug replied. He seemed to know his way around. They walked along the asphalt and along the bottom of the clubhouse. She looked up and noticed that the restaurant was almost empty. A few elderly folk were scattered throughout the many tables.

"Something wrong?" Doug asked. She could feel the deep lines form between her eyes, which happened when she was confused.

"I don't understand why no one is here. When I went to watch horse races as a kid, the stands were packed. My 4-H club did the morning breakfast to watch the horses work out at the crack of dawn, and to tour the backstretch. It was so special. Jimmy Lasseter and I snuck away from the group and made out behind one of the stables. It was the best day."

She looked around a bit more and noticed that only about twenty people were in the expansive grandstand. They walked the concourse without having to worry about bumping into anyone, there was no one around. No one to watch those beautiful creatures run their hearts out.

"Unfortunately, the sport of kings has become virtually extinct, now just a gambling addiction for those you see here. What used to be the favorite pastime of America is slowly becoming obsolete."

They walked toward the rail of the track. Across from them was the finish line pole. The large tote board showed the odds for the next horse race.

"Do you understand the board?" Doug asked her.

"I think so. The horse with the lowest number is the favorite to win, right?" Her knowledge was rusty, because she hadn't been to the racetrack since she was a teenager: that, along with the drinks and those blue eyes… it was surprising that she remembered anything. She was really starting to want to take him behind a stable, Jimmy Lasseter style. This time would be much better, cause they wouldn't get caught by any troop leaders and her mother wouldn't get a phone call about her, "promiscuous behavior."

"Exactly. See Number Five, his odds are at 5-1, which isn't too bad. Then you have Number Ten at 2-1, he is the favorite. And then Number Two is at 50-1, he is the long shot. No one thinks he will win." A light brightened in his eyes and he smirked.

"What?" Charlie asked. He turned to look at her and once again, she found herself short of breath as she stared at his chiseled face.

"People bet on horses for all kinds of reasons. The uneducated may just look at the race program and pick a horse because they like its name or its color. The experienced horseman will look at the horse's trainer, rider, sire and dam; they will look at their workout times, and their previous racing record. Me, I look into their eyes. That is where you see if they have the will to win. The courage to overcome all obstacles: a bad start out of the gate, a horse that gets in their path, or a poor rider. The heart of a champion exists the day it starts beating. These qualities cannot be measured, they come from within. I like the Number Two horse because I saw him earlier today; his eyes told me he was the one to beat." The easy smile was there again.

Doug turned back to the rail as the post parade began for the seventh race. Charlie was speechless and touched by this man's eloquence and compassion.

The horses moved towards the starting gate and got in one at a time, all ten of them. The tension built as each horse was loaded. The handlers tried to load them quickly to decrease the time that the first horse needed to wait.

They were all in. The bell rang, the gates flew open, all ten horses lurched forward and the announcer yelled, "They're off!"

Charlie held her breath.

They moved like an engine, all forty legs ate up the ground, trying to find their position along the rail and not get boxed in. The horses raced so close together that when two were abreast you couldn't get the width of a hand between them.

As they raced by the first time, Number Five was in the lead, with the favorite, the Number Ten horse, in second. Behind them stretched the other eight horses, with the Number Two horse, the longshot, in last.

Charlie glanced sideways at Doug and he was intently watching the race unfold. They stood silently, side by side, watching the horses move along the backstretch.

Positions changed, one horse moved up as another one tired. The jockey on the Number Ten horse waited long enough. He swung him out and around the leader and into first place. Charlie could see Number Five tiring as the rest of the field moved past him - the price paid for going out the quickest. Charlie searched for Number Two, where was he within that mass of pounding flesh?

Doug hadn't moved a muscle, his eyes set on following Number Two. The horse had moved up to the middle of the pack as they made the turn for home. Charlie and Doug were so close; they could see the horses bunched together as they started their bids down the homestretch. Four horses wide, Number Two came barreling down the center of the track. Charlie grabbed at Doug's arm.

"Come on!" She yelled.

She could see the pink of their nostrils from running so hard, breathing deeply to get the most of the oxygen. Number Two strained and reached, his jockey sat quietly, knowing the horse was giving all he had. Slowly, the distance between the leader, the favorite, Number Ten, and the long shot, Number Two, closed. Three lengths, two lengths, one length - they ran as one.

With one last lurching move, as the sand from the track pelted them, the Number Two horse pulled ahead. The finish line passed above his head; he won by a nose.

Charlie let out a scream, and jumped up and down in excitement for the race. She had forgotten how thrilling it was to watch a horse race. She came back to reality and realized she still had Doug's arm in a tight grasp.

Sheepishly, Charlie let go and glanced up into his face. It was hard to read what was going on behind his eyes. He looked at her with a questioning look, shook his head as if to clear a thought, and smiled.

"Gotta go," he said. "It was a pleasure meeting you this evening, Charlie." Charlie laughed and nodded her head. Doug held out his hand again. She held the handshake longer than necessary, but it didn't seem like he minded all that much.

"Thank you for the tips," she said. Finally, Doug turned on his heel and walked down the length of track. Her eyes followed him.

Out of the double doors of the grandstand Charlie heard, "There you are!" With drinks in hand, Kate and Jillian descended upon her. She grabbed the glass of wine they brought, and downed half of it, trying to cool off from the heat of Doug's hand around hers.

She glanced back over her shoulder and saw Doug walk into the winner's circle and grab the bridle of the Number Two horse.

The Morning After

Charlie lie still. If she moved, the stars would start bursting in her head again. She had been like that for about twenty minutes now. Her body ached, particularly her head. She hadn't had a hangover in a very long time. She had the pillow over her head because even the light through her eyelids was painful. *What happened last night?* She groaned.

Through her groggy head, she heard a commotion downstairs. Charlie vaguely recognized the slamming of the front door, followed by the sound of feet running up the stairs. Her bedroom door was flung open and her daughter launched herself onto her bed. A stream of words that Charlie couldn't comprehend came out of Skylar's mouth.

"Skylar, honey, slow down, and talk quieter. What are you asking?"

"Who is the new horse in the barn, Mom? Where did he come from? He is beautiful! Can I ride him?" Skylar waited anxiously for her mother's answers, bobbing on the bed.

Charlie slowly pulled the pillow off her eyes and squinted up at her daughter. It took a moment for Charlie's eyes to focus.

"Can you stop moving please, Skylar, I don't feel that good," Charlie pleaded. Skylar continued to look at her mother with those wide green eyes so many people commented on how beautiful they were.

"Mom, did you hear me?"

Charlie pushed up on her arms, pulled Skylar close to her and tried to stop the earth from spinning. *What did she say about a new horse? What new horse?*

Charlie stopped breathing and her eyes opened wide - *What new horse? Oh my god, what did I do last night?*

****

"Let's walk over to the paddock," Charlie said to the girls, still holding tightly to her wine glass. Jillian, Kate, and Charlie walked to the oval where they saddled the horses getting ready to run the next race.

Seven horses were being walked by the grooms. There was a thin crowd watching. In the center of the oval, the trainers were giving last minute instructions to the jockeys. Jillian had brought one of the race programs out with her.

"What race are we on? Let's place a bet on one of the horses."

"It's race number eight. Look at that gorgeous bay over there," Kate chimed in, pointing to one of the horses on the far side of the ring.

They all had knowledge of horses; they'd spent many girls' weekends out horseback riding, gossiping, and working through their individual life issues. Recently, their chats had been mostly about Charlie.

Kate and Charlie huddled around Jillian, who was holding the program. It was a $7500 claiming race. In simple terms, it meant that any of the horses in the race could be bought, "claimed", for $7500. In the world of racing, this is where horses changed hands frequently, moving from owner to owner, trying to get the most out of the horse. Sometimes, rarely, there's a diamond in the rough: an under-performing horse that winds up going on to win at the stakes level, one of the big time races.

Charlie watched the horses in the paddock, wondering what their stories were. *Where were they born, how were they treated?* The horses moved onto the track for the race.

"Come on, let's go get some refills and watch from the grandstand."

Kate led the way and they settled at one of the tables in the dining room overlooking the homestretch.

"Can I get you something?" asked the waiter. Jillian spoke up. It didn't sound like she was drunk at all. Kate and Jillian had been playing games while Charlie had just been drinking: and she hadn't had dinner because she was so nervous about the night. Charlie didn't think it seemed fair: she hadn't even wanted to come to this dumb old place and now she was the only one that was going to be paying for it in the morning.

"A bottle of your most expensive Cabernet." They sat like horse-crazy little girls, watched the races, picked their favorites, and placed imaginary bets.

After watching a few more races and finishing off a couple more glasses of wine, Charlie had enough sitting, and needed to get closer to the action. There were only two races left, and she wanted to be closer to the track. She eagerly looked at the horses being led to the paddock in front of them.

Her eyes came to rest on a grey colt. He was walking quietly next to his groom, but more like a dejected quiet. Not the quiet, confident walk expected from a racing Thoroughbred. In fact, he was carrying his head low - not high and proud like the rest of the horses in the race. Charlie reached for the program.

"What race are we at?" She asked the girls. Kate looked at the board.

"It says Race Eleven." Charlie turned to Race Eleven in the program. She looked up and found the number of the grey horse - Number Four.

"What's up, Charlie?" Jillian asked. Charlie motioned to the grey colt.

"Check him out. Doesn't he look sick or sad or something?" Kate and Jillian followed the grey as he made his way down the track in front of them.

"The program says this is a $2500 claiming race for two-year-olds. For two-year-olds! He should be full of life, but just look at him! He looks so dejected. I wonder what his story is."

Charlie's heart went out to the young horse. She could feel his pain.

Many times during the past twelve months she had felt the same way this horse looked - like there was no hope. Her eyes filled with tears. They were kindred spirits, and she was going to save him.

Charlie grabbed her glass of wine and stood up from the table. She steadied herself on the back of the chair.

"Come on," she urged. Jillian and Kate stood up obediently. Charlie slipped her free arm around Jillian, with Kate on her other side, and guided her two best friends out the door and down to the paddock to get a closer look.

The viewing area of the paddock was elevated and looked down on the race participants. They searched out the grey in the field of nine horses. All the other horses were various shades of bay and chestnut. Her eyes alighted on the grey colt on the far side of the paddock. He was standing still, not jittering like the other youngsters. In fact, he looked bored with the whole thing.

Thoroughbreds are bred to race and are usually ramped up and excited by that time of the race, full of anticipation. Not that one. A burly, short man stood next to him, as well as the jockey, who wasn't much shorter. The groom holding the colt kept a tight rein, like he was anticipating the horse to bolt - hah! The horse looked like he wanted to lay down for a nap.

The horses paraded around while the jockeys received their final instructions. Charlie followed the gangly colt as he walked towards her. As he got closer, a butterfly feeling started in her belly. A cool sweat broke out on her hands. Was she getting sick from too much wine? Charlie held tight to her wine glass, afraid she would drop it over the railing.

She couldn't take her eyes off the colt and just as he passed her, he raised his head and looked right at her. Charlie took a quick breath in. The eyes. Aren't they windows into the soul? Charlie's heart went out to this sorrowful creature. One who was born to run and had no passion for it. She felt goose bumps run down her arms. The world closed in on them: it was just the grey horse, jilted and forlorn, and Charlie, drunk and depressed.

Charlie could barely breathe, and God knows she was already having a hard time thinking straight, but she knew one thing - she needed to help the colt. Somehow.

"Kate, didn't you say this was a claiming race?" She yelled. Kate jumped back, staring at Charlie like she had two heads.

"Why are you yelling?" Kate asked.

"Just look at the program. Quickly. What is the description of the race?" Charlie asked, breathing in quick beats. Kate opened the program and repeated,

"It's a $2500 claiming race for two-year-olds."

"How much time do I have till post time?" Charlie asked her.

"What's wrong, Charlie?" Jillian piped in. She had been busy ogling the jockeys as the announcer called, "Riders up!"

"I have to save him," Charlie said.

"What are you talking about? Save who?"

"The grey colt." Charlie stared at them. She knew her friends thought she was crazy. "He needs my help. I could tell. His eyes - they were so sad. He is sad, just like me. A Thoroughbred should be full of life and a love of racing. He looks like a wet rag. Something has happened to him. I have to help him. I don't know why, I just do." Time was ticking by and she needed them to support her.

"Come on," Kate finally said after a few calculated moments. Charlie looked up into Kate's shiny eyes. She alone knew the extent of the pain Charlie suffered. Kate was the only one Charlie told her deepest thoughts, during her darkest hours. She was Charlie's best friend: Charlie could tell because Kate was considering letting her put a claim on a horse after Charlie had had a bottle and a half of wine, and Kate never even stopped to tell her that she was going to regret it. That's real friendship. Or maybe Kate was too tipsy to realize what a huge decision her friend was making in such a delicate state. Either way, Kate supported Charlie like only she could.

Kate was all business. Even with several glasses of wine, she still had the ability to focus on a mission.

"What are you all doing?" Jillian piped in, right in step with her friends. Kate pushed them quickly toward one of the stewards of the track.

"How much time do we have to claim a horse in this race?" she asked.

"This race? You may be too late. The horses are almost heading out to the track for warm ups." He stated.

"Please, sir, it is important that we try. Can you tell us where to go?" Kate implored.

"Down this hall is the bookkeeper. He'll help you," he said as he held the door open. The women ran down the hall, their high heels echoing off the walls.

****

They stood outside of stall number thirty-eight, afraid to look in.

Kate had pulled it off. Her cell phone had been going a mile a minute as they ran into the bookkeeper's office. She knew someone, who knew someone, who had money on account at the track that Charlie could place the claim for the grey horse against. You couldn't just write a personal check or charge your credit card and expect to take home a horse. She would need to dig into her emergency fund for this act of craziness.

Charlie was now the proud owner of a new horse. She took a step closer and looked inside the stall.

The grey colt was standing in the back of the stall, his head hanging low. His eyes were half closed but Charlie knew he saw her.

The race was a flop which is probably why they were able to put a claim in so late. After the horses were loaded into the starting gate, the bell rang, and all the horses bolted out: well, almost all. The grey colt had stood for a few more seconds within the gate before his jockey could get him moving. The others had moved off.

It seemed like a no-brainer that the horse should take the rail for the shortest trip around the track, but the grey colt would have none of it. He stayed right in the middle of the track and no pulling or whipping by the jockey could get the horse to move any closer to the rail. He wound up passing a few of the tiring front runners in the homestretch to finish seventh out of nine.

Charlie clutched the claiming ticket in one hand and the race program in the other. She un-crumpled the page of the race the grey horse ran in, and slowly scanned it. With butterflies in her stomach, she looked up and caught the eye of the Thoroughbred before her.

"Well, Genuine Storm, it looks like you're stuck with me. Now, I just need to figure out how to get you home." Jillian moved up close to Charlie and whispered,

"Hey, isn't that the good looking guy you were talking to when we found you outside?"

Across the way, Charlie could make out Doug talking to another man in a blue cap. As if sensing she was watching him, he glanced up from his conversation. Surprise lit up his eyes, followed by a sparkle of recognition. His off-centered smile appeared as he finished up his conversation and walked over to where the girls were standing.

"Well, hello again," Doug said.

"Hi," said Charlie. Not much else came to mind as she gazed into his baby blues.

"Hi, I'm Jillian, Charlie's friend, and this is Kate. Charlie just bought this horse!" Jillian volunteered.

"You did? Well, I'll be. I didn't realize you were a crackerjack horse claimer," Doug said raising his eyebrows, looking over at Charlie.

"I'm not," she said. "But something came over me and I saw that he needed help. You know, from his eyes." Doug's smile widened.

"Really? Well, let's take a look at the champion you have acquired." He walked over to the stall and opened the door. He didn't hesitate in the least, he just walked in.

Charlie walked up behind him as he examined the grey colt. His hands were soft as they ran over the length of the horse and down his legs; the whole while, the grey colt looked very unenthused. Doug lifted his head from its resting position and opened his mouth and examined his tattoo.

Then he took a long, hard look into his eyes.

He patted the colt gently and then walked out of the stall. The three women looked anxiously at Doug, waiting to get his opinion.

"I don't see signs of physical abuse, though it's possible it happened. The way he holds himself and just stands in the back of his stall like that, I'd say he's been emotionally abused. That's something you normally see in older horses that have been run into the ground, after years on the track. I don't know that I would have advised a purchase like this, Charlie. You may not be able to do anything with a horse this beaten down."

Charlie looked around in hopes of throwing eye darts at the trainer of this beautiful, but broken creature. He must be the one at fault. Alas, there was no one around, probably because they didn't care one bit about this colt.

"Do you have a place to take him?" Doug asked, pulling Charlie out of her hatred towards whoever mistreated her new horse.

Jillian piped in, "Charlie has a four-stall barn, and only two stalls are being used, so we can take him home with us."

"In what?" the realistic Kate asked. The three girls stared at each other. They clearly hadn't thought very far along in their adventure.

"Where is your farm?" Doug asked.

Still in a bit of a fog, Charlie replied, "Leesburg, Virginia."

"Cappie, over here." Doug called to the man in the blue cap he had been talking to. Cappie had been attending to the horses in the barn across the aisle. He was a short, stocky man, with a hitch in his gate.

"You still planning on taking Joey and Pinot back to the barn tonight?" he asked, as Cappie approached.

"Yes, sir," Cappie replied.

"Would you mind taking a small detour to this young lady's farm to drop off this colt she just claimed?" He winked at Charlie as he completed his request.

"Not a problem at all, sir, the others would like the company." Cappie replied.

****

Charlie groaned loudly. Skylar was still bouncing up and down on the bed with a huge smile across her face.

The Lost Soul

Charlie grabbed her bathrobe, threw her feet into her slippers, and headed into the bathroom, Skylar close on her heels.

"Skylar, honey, can you give me a few moments to brush my teeth and use the bathroom?" She asked.

"Okay, Mom, I'll wake Ryan up and tell him all about the new horse!" Skylar exclaimed.

Charlie leaned on the sink, trying to clear her head. She grabbed three Advil, filled a glass with water and threw back the pills, in hopes her headache would pass quickly. She gulped the rest of the water and washed her face. As she looked in the mirror, she didn't recognize the person looking back at her.

A few minutes later, she walked down the stairs and into the kitchen. Ryan looked up at her with a concerned expression.

"What is Skylar talking about, Mom? Is she making this up about a new horse in the barn?"

Charlie's head was still thumping, though not as hard. She was not sure she could stand up to Ryan's inquisition of last nights' festivities. She held up a hand.

"Let's chat over a big breakfast," Charlie knew she needed to get some food in her stomach or the queasiness would follow the headache. That part of a hangover she could remember from her college days.

Years ago, she could keep up with the best of them. In college, she could go out, drink whatever, and still get up and run a 5k the next morning. After she met Peter, the late nights became movie nights, home cooking, and cocooning on the couch. After the dating-honeymoon stage ended and they would go out and tie one on, the next day had been a killer. She could be functional in the morning, but after the nausea set in, she would need to lie down for the rest of the day. Charlie could not let her kids see her like that. Food, first thing, took precedent over the new horse.

With a plate full of cheesy scrambled eggs, greasy bacon and sausage, and a pile of toast in front of each of them, Charlie told her kids about the previous night. Since Peter's passing, she had promised to always be honest with them. They had already been through so much together. Besides, Skylar had already seen the horse; it's not like Charlie could tell them the night was uneventful.

"The night started off fine. We got some drinks and started gambling a little. "

"But you hate gambling. You think it's stupid," Skylar said. Charlie tried to smile, but she felt sure it looked more like a grimace. When the whole plan for the girl's night out had been hatched, she had felt the need to ask her children's permission to go, and she told them that she thought casinos were dumb, but that it would make Jillian and Kate happy.

In reality, she was perfectly apathetic about the whole concept of gambling. On her eighteenth birthday, she used the money her grandpa sent her, to bet on a horse race. She doubled her money and then used it to get a small horseshoe tattooed on her foot: that is one thing she would not be honest with her kids about. She didn't want them thinking it was okay for them to get tattoos, just because she had one.

"Yes, well I did get bored of the gambling pretty quickly, and I ended up walking out to the track. The horse track. Not a people track. Watching people run would have been more boring than gambling."

"Mom, you're rambling," Ryan said.

"Sorry. Anyway, the girls met up with me after a while and watched some of the racing, and all of a sudden, I saw this horse. He was gorgeous, but he looked lost; kind of like…how we've all been a little lost since dad…" Ryan shoved far too many eggs into his mouth, and Skylar tore the crust off her toast. Charlie knew they understood what she meant.

"So you bought him?" Ryan finally broke the silence after he'd successfully swallowed the gigantic mouthful of food.

"There was something about the way he looked at me when he walked past that just spoke to me. I felt like I could help him, you know? I'm not sure exactly what happened to him that made him so disinterested and downtrodden, but I've been there, and I couldn't let him keep thinking that there wasn't something to look forward to."

Charlie knew she'd seen herself in the horse and she knew she'd wanted to save him from the same depression that she was going through, but it suddenly hit her that she wasn't over her despair. She was toiling daily, trying to make her life seem like it wasn't missing anything. Maybe she didn't have a right to try and save anyone. Her children were silent: but only for a moment.

"What's his name, Mom?" Skylar asked. Charlie smiled. Skylar always asked the perfect questions.

"Genuine Storm," said Charlie. "I don't know much about him, except that he is the grandson of Genuine Risk."

"The filly that won the Kentucky Derby?" Ryan asked. Charlie saw the light in his eyes blaze. He had inherited her love of Thoroughbreds. Over the years he'd read as many books as he could put his hands on, about horse racing and the winners of the Triple Crown races.

"That's the one," Charlie replied.

"Come on, let's go see how he is doing with Sarge and Hershey," Skylar said. She quickly shoved her plate aside and only half pushed in her chair as she made her way to the barn.

The barn was small, only four stalls. It had been Peter's labor of love for Charlie. He knew how much she wanted to have property and a barn to keep her own horses. For so many years, she had kept her horse at other peoples' stables and needed to drive long distances to spend time at the barn and ride Sarge. When Skylar turned five, Hershey, her pony, joined their herd. Skylar and Charlie were spending hours away from Peter and Ryan due to the drive to the barn, ride time, and return home.

After two years of the driving craziness, Skylar to riding, Ryan to basketball and hockey, a gazillion miles on the truck, and lots of gas bills, Peter offered up a change of scenery. They bought a house in the country, something Charlie never thought Peter would go for, and he undertook the task of constructing their barn.

The barn was a masterpiece, rustic wood with dark green trim. Weathered stone ran around the base of the entire building. The handles on all the doors and cabinets were silver, which was very nice against the polished wood of the stables inside. The rafters crisscrossed and zig-zagged randomly, as Peter found more places that he felt needed extra support.

It was the first place Charlie came after Peter died. A little piece of him lived on in this place, in the crooked beams that he said, "gave it character" and the squeaky door hinge that he never could remember to grease. It was Charlie's safe haven, that barn. As she approached with her children, she realized that whatever reservations she had been feeling about her drunken purchase were gone. She was at peace with everything.

The smell of the stable wafted enticingly over to her as she walked closer. There is nothing quite like the smell of a stable: it has the ability to calm the nerves and force all tension from the body. Charlie didn't know what possessed her to buy the horse, but she knew there was definitely room in her safe haven for another lost soul.

New Horse

Sarge nickered to them as they entered the barn. His head was over his stall door and he looked bright-eyed.

"Hey big fella, how's the new addition?" Charlie asked him. As if on cue, Sarge turned his head towards the stall across the aisle. Charlie had kept the half-door closed in case the new horse had any aspirations of jumping out.

Skylar was already peering through the closed half-door into the stall.

Hershey, in the stall next to Sarge, was impatiently pawing at his door, looking for the treats Skylar always brought with her. He wasn't all too happy that the attention was now on the new horse across the way.

"Mom, why does he just hide in the corner?" Skylar asked.

Ryan and Charlie walked up to the stall and Charlie opened the half door. Genuine Storm was standing in the far corner of the stall, similar to where he stood in the barn at the racetrack. His head was hanging low, but Charlie could tell he was interested, as his ears kept flickering their way.

"What's his story, Mom?" Ryan asked. He did his best to hide his curiosity, but the way he gazed at Storm gave him away. Charlie hadn't been prepared for the way Ryan's teenage years would take him away from her. She knew it was natural, and she expected it, but it still hit her like a ton of bricks, that first time he had taken his new attitude for a spin. Of course, it was just at the beginning of Peter's treatments, and Charlie was so focused on her dying husband, that her son's moodiness didn't register much after that.

Now that she was getting back into the swing of things, she could tell he was less and less the sweet little boy she'd once known, and more the grumpy man-child that wanted little from her except food and rides to "cooler places". She did her best to savor the times when their ideas of a good time were aligned.

"I don't know. It was so sad to watch him before the race, he just seemed so lifeless. He was standing the same way when we got to his barn to claim him. A man…uh…another owner I met, helped me look him over and he thinks Storm may have been abused," Charlie finished. She felt herself blushing and quickly turned her face away from the children. It wasn't a weird thing to say, so why couldn't she say it without blushing? She chanced a glance at the kids, they hadn't noticed anything, or if they had, they'd ignored it and kept their attention on the horse at the back of the stall.

"I think you did the right thing, Mom. He needed a better home," Skylar said. She'd given Hershey his treat and was now petting him absently, her eyes still on Storm. Charlie recovered her normal coloring.

"I have never done anything like this before, kids. Not sure what got into me," she said as she linked her arm into Ryan's. Ryan looked over at her and smiled.

"Mom, you haven't had much fun over the last eighteen months, either. Not that this is really getting back to normal, but it was what you wanted. So, you bought a horse. You did something for yourself. I am happy for you."

"Me too! And I'm happy for him, cause we're gonna be so good to him! Right? What are you going to do with him?" Skylar asked.

"You mean, what are we going to do with him?" Charlie asked back at her.

"Well, since he is a racehorse, he should love to run," Skylar said innocently. "Maybe we can help him learn to love it again?"

"He's only two years old," said Charlie.

"Only two? Man, I wonder what his story was before last night." Ryan said. "Mom, you have his papers, right?" *Papers, oh right*, thought Charlie. She quickly recalled an envelope that had been given to her the night before.

The driver, Cappie, had been so nice the whole drive to the farm. Charlie had ridden in the truck with him, while Kate and Jillian drove behind them.

"Too bad Kate didn't stop drinking in time to stop me from buying the horse, huh?" Charlie said as they drove along. Cappie just smiled and nodded.

Charlie had been nervous on the drive home, so she had talked a lot. Cappie was a good listener and just nodded his head as she rambled on about her evening at the track. She thought she may have talked a little too much about the moment when Doug put his hand on her back, but Cappie just smiled wider and said,

"Mr. Doug is a good man," Charlie heartily agreed with him.

When they got to the farm, he helped put the horse in the barn and made sure he had hay and water. He shook Charlie's hand. Cappie was pulling out of the driveway when he hit his brakes suddenly, and got out of the truck. He walked back to Charlie and handed her the envelope with the horse's papers that she had left on the dashboard. Along with the envelope, he handed her a business card for Shamrock Hill Farm. He winked at her and told her to call anytime if she had any questions. He knew that owning a racehorse was all new to Charlie: she'd mentioned it several times.

"I think a good starting place would be to look at his pedigree and find out where he came from, who bred him," Ryan said. His mind was already turning. He loved a good research project.

"I think he needs some treats," Skylar said. She ran to the feed room and grabbed some peppermints.

Charlie opened the door to the stall. She didn't know this horse, and she didn't want Skylar just barging in and spooking him. Charlie needn't have worried though. He didn't move a muscle, except that his ears flickered, like he had been listening to the conversation.

Charlie spoke quietly to him.

"Hey, boy. Hope you like your stall. I know you are probably nervous in a new place." He turned his head toward her as she walked toward him. Charlie stopped short as she looked into his eyes. The sadness reflected there was palpable and familiar. She'd felt it, and she knew her kids had felt it. She wanted so badly to know what this horse had been through, so she could help him feel better. Maybe his life had been filled with different barns, different stalls and he just thought this was the next barn at the next racetrack, where he would be demanded to run.

"Skylar, come here." Charlie pulled her close. Skylar's hand was full of peppermints. Charlie grabbed one, placed it flat in her hand, and held her breath.

"Come on, Storm, come get a treat," Skylar said.

Storm blew heavily out of his nostrils. Charlie was sure after being at the racetrack with trainers, grooms, and jockeys, he found it odd to be in a stall with a mom and her daughter, holding out a treat.

Storm stretched his head toward her hand, without moving his feet, like he was afraid to come any closer. Charlie took a step towards him. He withdrew and backed away but she continued to hold out her hand.

In the end, curiosity won over as he took a deep breath in. He could smell the peppermint.

Storm stretched out his head towards the smell. With a little tilt of his head he could just get his mouth to Charlie's hand, and he quickly nibbled the mint and retreated.

"Mom, he likes them!" Skylar squealed.

"Let's give him some space, Skylar," Charlie said to her as they backed out of the stall.

****

Charlie, Ryan, and Skylar left the barn, a sense of excitement and rebirth surrounding them. Their lives had been stagnant for the last eighteen months. Charlie woke up, packed lunches, got the kids to school then went to work: the kids did homework after school, Ryan had sports, they ate dinner, and then everyone went to bed. Their routine hadn't changed after Peter passed, but they were now three instead of four.

The new horse brought change, something different, something for the three of them to get excited about. Honestly, Charlie had been feeling a little left behind lately. She felt as though the kids had their friends and sports, and she cheered them on along the way, but she hadn't had anything to be excited about in a long time. She could see that her children were still hurting, but they were doing a better job of trying than Charlie felt she was capable of. Well, not anymore.

"Mom, can you grab his papers when we get to the house? I'd like to start researching him," said Ryan. He would know all the websites to Google which would give them as much detail as possible on the grey horse.

"Now, Ryan, I don't want you sacrificing your school work on this. School comes first." Charlie felt she had to have some semblance of responsibility in the situation she'd so recklessly caused.

"Whatever, Mom. I know that." Ryan rolled his eyes and picked up his pace so that he was no longer walking with Charlie and Skylar. Charlie breathed deeply.

"Will you turn him out with Sarge and Hershey, Mom?" Skylar asked.

"Not to start with, Skylar. Let's see how he warms up. Do you think you can be in charge of giving him daily peppermints?" Charlie asked.

"Absolutely! He will just love Hershey. Hershey can show him the ropes," Skylar said excitedly. "Hershey can teach him how to have fun when we go riding. You know, like when we go trail riding and play our riding games? Remember you and Sarge trying to race us in the ring, when we pretended we were at our own racetrack?"

"Yeah, I do. That was fun, wasn't it? I think I would like for Storm to get to know us a bit first. Remember he is a racehorse, sweet pea, he isn't used to being outside in a large turnout, or even being ridden outside of a racetrack," Charlie commented back.

"Well, maybe that is why he is so sad," Skylar said innocently, trying to fathom not having the freedom of riding across the fields and hills they called home.

"Mom, can we still race him?" Ryan cut in from ahead of them. Charlie pondered that question for a moment. She hadn't thought past claiming this creature. What was she possibly going to do with a two-year-old racehorse? He obviously didn't care to run, as he demonstrated the night before.

"He didn't run much last night, Ryan. Racing just may not be his calling. It's our job to find out what he can excel at. He might like to run, or jump, or just be a pleasure horse," said Charlie.

"You always talked about your passion for racehorses, Mom," Skylar said, her excitement catching. "Maybe Storm just didn't like racing for his old owner. I don't think we should give up on him yet."

"Didn't you always talk to Dad about how you wanted to go to the Kentucky Derby? Now you have your very own racehorse." Ryan smiled, getting caught up in the conversation. Ryan was right, of course. Going to the Kentucky Derby had been on Charlie's bucket list. All those dreams and lists seemed so long ago.

"Yes, I dreamed of that, but I gave it up," she somberly said, as reality gave her a kick in the rear. Most of her goals had been dreamt up with Peter. Now she had no one to dream with, plan goals with, share her future with. All of the responsibilities of raising children were sitting squarely on her shoulders, and that meant that she had to put her goals away and work harder for her children. She sighed heavily.

Ryan hesitantly put his arm around his mother's shoulder.

"Mom, don't go there. This is exciting. You can rely on us, Skylar and me. We can help with the horse. We can take on more chores around the farm. We want you to be happy. Remember what Grandma always says."

"And what is that, my son?" She smiled up at him. *When did he get taller than me?* she wondered.

"If you don't have a dream, you can't have a dream come true!" Ryan and Skylar said in unison.

The Phone Call

Charlie walked up the stairs and into her bedroom. She had a couple minutes to herself, so she sat on her bed and allowed a few tears to roll down her face. What was she doing? What was she thinking? She couldn't do this. She couldn't train a racehorse; especially one that hides in the back of his stall, and hates running. The small amount of courage that had filled her while she was in the barn had gone and she was feeling very alone.

And then there were the kids to think of. Of course, they loved the idea of Storm now, but would they love it when all of their spare time was taken up by races and training? Ryan was just learning how to drive, he was getting his life back, and Charlie was asking him to sacrifice normalcy, yet again. Skylar…well Charlie wasn't actually too worried about her. Nine-year-olds don't really have much of a social life, and Skylar's revolved around the horses anyway.

Charlie dragged herself from bed, like she had on so many other days, knowing she needed to be strong for her kids. She decided that she would do whatever she could to keep her children happy, and if that meant figuring out how to race Storm, well…miracles happen. She picked up the envelope with all the registration papers for Genuine Storm, off her dresser. As she turned to walk downstairs, she noticed the business card that had been under the envelope.

Charlie picked it up and held it by its corners. She needed to call and thank Doug for helping get Storm to her farm. She recalled the feeling of his hand in hers, the blue warmth of his eyes, and the ease of conversation that she hadn't had with anyone except her girlfriends, in a long time.

Maybe it wouldn't hurt to give him a quick call...

Charlie pulled her cell phone out of her back pocket. Doug Walker. That was the name on the card. It had been so exciting watching the horses race. Last night, Charlie got away from all the solemn thoughts, away from worrying about her kids and the future.

The card said Shamrock Hill Farm. It was in Maryland, from the address. Dropping the horse off at Charlie's farm was a bit out of his driver's way. It had been nice of him to offer that. Now she really needed to thank him. Charlie was smiling by the time she dialed the fifth number, and when the line started ringing, she couldn't wipe the silly grin off her face. She felt so stupid: all she had to say was, "Thank you for the ride," and then she was done. What was there to smile about?

"Doug Walker," the deep voice said. Charlie hesitated and almost hung up the phone.

"Hello?" he questioned.

Charlie took a deep breath, "Hi, thank you for the ride," she said, quickly. There was silence on the other end of the line and Charlie realized that she had neglected to give all the important, first phone call information. "Uh...this is Charlie. Charlie Jenkins. You know, the damsel in distress from last night? The crazy woman who claimed a horse with an aversion to running." *The one that grabbed your arm during that one horse race...*she thought.

"Charlie, right! I am so glad you called. Good old Cappie left you my card, I see. How's the new horse adjusting?" Doug asked. Charlie found herself intently listening to the sound of his voice.

"Ah, he's fine. Still hiding in the back of his stall." She tried to sound professional, but her grin had only grown when he sounded so happy to hear from her, and she was having trouble making her words sound normal. She coughed and went over to the mirror to give herself a stern look.

"Listen, the purpose of my call was to thank you for helping me last night and to find out how much I could pay you for the trailering?" Doug didn't say anything for a few seconds.

"Did you hear me? Do I have a bad connection?" Charlie asked. "This dumb phone is always-"

"No, no. No worries on the trailering. Cappie was glad to have the company for a bit." She could hear the smile come across the phone and she wondered if he could tell that she'd been smiling when she called.

"Yeah, I am quite sure Cappie just loved my nonstop chatter. Poor guy," Charlie said, genuinely sorry for whatever she'd put him through. Doug laughed.

"So really, how's the horse?" He asked again.

"Well, my kids were excited to find a new horse in the barn this morning. I spent the last few hours talking about how their mom had a few glasses of wine and made a spontaneous decision to buy a racehorse. And not just any racehorse, but one that doesn't want to race, let alone come out of his stall," Charlie said.

Doug chuckled on the other end of the phone. Sweat broke out on the hand that was holding the phone as Charlie grasped it tighter. She pointed to herself in the mirror and gave herself a "get a grip" look. It was not a pleasure call, it was business.

"You are not the first one to jump into the racing industry on a whim," Doug said.

"A whim? I don't know the first thing about an actual racehorse. Well, I mean racing a horse. Don't get me wrong, I love horses, particularly Thoroughbreds, but I am a hunt seat rider. You know, walk, trot, canter, followed by a couple courses of jumps. I spend my time at horseshow grounds, not racetracks," Charlie stammered.

"Charlie, a horse is a horse," Doug said. "They all need someone to care for them, feed them, brush them, love them. It didn't look like the one you got has had a lot of tender love and care. It doesn't matter if they jump, race, or hang out in a field, they all love attention and having a job to do."

He paused, "Listen, here's what I recommend, spend a few weeks getting to know your guy. Let him be a horse - turn him out in a field, let him play with some friends; feed him well, brush him, just show him you care about him. See if he comes around. Then, give me a call and I can help you figure out if he has what it takes to be a racehorse. How old is he?"

"Two," she replied.

"Well, he's still young and hopefully no long term damage has been done. I wouldn't ride him in a show, since he's used to the racetrack and not getting all braided up and the like, for an equestrian event." Once again, she could hear his smile come across the phone.

She smiled back at the phone and then scolded her reflection in the mirror before saying, "I'll take your advice, thank you. Old Sarge probably wouldn't like me riding another horse anyway. Do you think he is safe to be around my kids? I know racehorses can be high strung and temperamental."

"Like I said, ma'am, horses love attention. If a horse is high-strung and temperamental, it's probably because its owner is high-strung and temperamental. What's your show horse like?" He inquired.

"Oh, Sarge. I just love him. I've had him for years. He's a retired Thoroughbred. He even won a race when he was three. Just one, though, and I guess his owners figured he wasn't going to make it on the track. Someone else rescued him from the track and trained him to be a show hunter. Now he and I go to shows with my daughter and her pony, Hershey." Charlie realized that she'd started rambling again.

"Why do you think people use the word *rescue* when it comes to Thoroughbreds on the track?" He asked. "Not all racehorses hate their job, and not all of them are ill-treated. Do you know that there are

Thoroughbred owners that have programs in place to re-home their horses once their racing days are over, if they are not destined to go into their breeding program?" he continued.

"I…didn't know that." Doug spoke passionately about the racing industry, and Charlie found herself wondering what other things he was passionate about: what other areas of his life did he take that controlling, firmness? Her reflection started blushing.

"Well, I will get off my soap box. I am pleased to welcome a new owner to the horse racing industry! My offer still stands. Will you give me a call in a few weeks and let me know how the horse is doing?" He asked.

"Yes, of course. I can use all the help I can get," Charlie answered, a little too quickly.

"Great. Gotta run. Good luck." The phone went dead.

The Blog

At a family meeting that evening, after the barn chores had been done and the horses fed, Charlie, Ryan, and Skylar sat down to discuss their new family member. They talked about Storm's feeding program, turning him out with Sarge and Hershey, grooming him. Most of his immediate care, Charlie would handle since she wasn't comfortable with Skylar and Ryan being in the stall with a two-year-old colt.

Charlie had given Storm's registration papers to Ryan and he had already spent the day in front of his laptop, going from website to website and taking notes on the history of the horse, trying to find out his previous owners.

It was a Sunday, and the kids would go back to school the next day. Charlie took out a calendar and circled September 24, the day Storm came into their lives. Doug had said a few weeks, so to be safe, she marked off four weeks – the get-to-know-you period. She would give Doug a call towards the end of October and give him an update on the horse.

Her hands turned ice-cold as she thought about calling him. She hadn't ever dealt with this before; she'd met Peter in college and they dated and fell in love and got married and had kids. It was all comfortable and easy. This was different, and Charlie had to admit that she liked it.

She pushed the thoughts aside. She had a horse to attend to and work to catch up on. Charlie sat down at her computer.

The View From Behind the Starting Gate

I have a racehorse in the barn. What am I supposed to do with a racehorse? Well, I am going to find out. I am going to use this blog to update you, the readers, on my progress. Have you ever wanted to try something new? Were you afraid? Did you fail to make a change because you thought it would be too hard?

Believe me, I am facing all of those things right now. I am nervous, scared, and excited. It is time for a change and I believe this horse was brought into my life to help me. Together we can learn about this industry that is called, "the sport of kings" - probably because it takes a king's bank account to fund it. I am not wealthy. I wasn't born into a horse racing family. I am a mom, a widow, and a writer.

Charlie sat back from the computer screen before continuing. She was, indeed, crazy.

My day job is editor of the local news website, Leesburg Weekly. My team of freelancers sends me daily articles to consider for post. The rules are that the article needs to be linked to Leesburg in some capacity, local sports teams, restaurants, area of interest, etc. If there is breaking news, I need to post the story as soon as possible, so I'm rarely without my iPad.

My kids are all for the racehorse thing. They think it's a fun, spontaneous thing their mom did. Hopefully this spontaneous thing doesn't cause too many problems for us. We're getting back on our feet, and I don't want to wreck anything. My hope is that this blog generates some new interest in horse racing. I was at a track not long ago, and it was almost painful to look around and see all the empty seats.

Whether or not I succeed, I hope to be able to follow the path ahead of me with a bit of humor and a lot of luck.

I hope you will follow along with me on this journey.

New Routines

The next morning started their lives with, "The Storm." Charlie didn't want to let him out with either of the other horses yet. Their normal routine had Skylar and Charlie going out to the barn early in the mornings before school to feed the horses.

They went out earlier than normal during Storm's first week with them, to work with him. Skylar had her pockets filled with peppermints and Charlie brought out the brushes. Each morning, they brought Storm out of his stall and while Charlie brushed him, Skylar stood in front of him and fed him peppermints, while chatting with him about what she would be doing with her day.

The first few days, Storm hung in the back of his stall. Charlie would go in and put his halter on and lead him out into the aisle and put him on the cross ties.

Sarge had his head out his door, inspecting the new comer. Hershey also was curious and would blow through his nostrils at Storm. Being the elder statesman of the group, Hershey didn't have a lot of patience for youngsters.

Storm would stand quietly, but shirk away from the brushes when

Charlie ran them over his body. It was like he couldn't stand to be touched. He lifted his hooves dutifully, but dropped them heavily when Charlie was done picking the dirt out of them.

They did all that twice: in the morning and then in the afternoon when Skylar got home from school. Then Skylar would tell Storm exactly what had happened during her school day. Storm's ears would flick back and forth between listening to Skylar and following Charlie while she brushed him.

After they were done grooming him, they put Storm back in his stall and focused on Sarge and Hershey. Ryan had after-school sports, so they would practice their riding before he got home.

Occasionally, Charlie would see Storm looking over at them getting the horses ready, like he was interested, but didn't know how to engage. He wouldn't even approach and put his head over the stall door.

Skylar and Charlie headed out to the ring a few days after Storm's arrival.

"Mom, do you think you will ever ride Storm?" Skylar asked.

"Oh, I don't think so Skylar. He's a racehorse," she replied. A part of her jumped at the thought. Charlie had always dreamed of sitting on a racehorse and breaking out of the starting gate: feeling the anticipation while waiting for the gate to open, seeing the long stretch of racetrack ahead of her, absorbing the power of the horse as it gathered itself to spring out of the gate and then race down the track. She was one step closer to that dream becoming a reality now: the idea gave her butterflies.

"Mom, did you hear that?" Skylar brought her back to reality.

"What?" she asked.

"The whinny. Did you hear it?" Skylar said excitedly.

Charlie sat quietly on Sarge's back. Then she heard it. A soft nicker. Not a loud, impatient, or excitable sound. Just a quiet nicker, made out of curiosity. She turned to Skylar,

"Sounds like Storm is finding out he misses his friends."

The View From Behind the Starting Gate

So, here's a little blurb about the new horse. His name is Genuine Storm: a derivation of his dad, Genuine Reward, and his mom, Storm Minstrel. The name is doubly fitting, because he is deep grey, the color of a storm cloud. Grey horses are born almost black, and lighten as they get older, to the point where they are almost white.

He is a colt, which is a male horse, and is two years old. His birth certificate or registration papers say he was born on February 18, 2012. Every Thoroughbred turns a year older on January 1st of each year, no matter when their birthdate is. This means that this coming January 1, 2015, Storm will be three years old.

A horse's height is measured in hands. Storm is 16.2 hands. Let me give you some perspective. A hand translates to 4 inches. Hold up your hand (I know you already did). Press your fingers together. Hold your hand horizontally out in front of you. From the top side of your pinkie to the bottom side of your index fingers is approximately four inches. A hand's width.

So, that means Storm is a total of 66 inches, or 5 feet, 6 inches. The standard measure is to the top of the horse's withers, or generally where the mane ends on their necks.

If you are 5'6" tall, and you stood next to Storm, your eyes would be about level with the top of his back. Horses can seem much taller, however, as they carry their heads higher than their backs. In some cases, depending on the angle of a horse's neck, you can walk upright under their head!

So now you are all on board with what Storm looks like. He is beginning to perk up a bit and show interest in his surroundings. He's a big fan of the peppermints my daughter gives him, and he likes to be brushed. At first, he didn't seem to like all the attention, but I have a feeling it was just because he wasn't used to it. Now, he's a regular ham! Yesterday, after I was done brushing him, he knocked the brush off the ledge I'd set it on and when I picked it up he wiggled around, like he was so proud of himself for duping me into brushing him again.

This next week I will be introducing him to the other horses in the barn. I think we'll turn him out for a little bit and see how he likes it. Stay tuned!

Happy Hour

"Have you called that sexy owner from the track yet?" Jillian asked. Charlie smirked, but her stomach turned, just thinking about the call she was going to make the next day.

Jillian, Kate, and Charlie sat in the shade of the barn, overlooking the paddock. It was one of their rituals; Friday afternoon, the work week was done, and they could just relax with a glass of wine, and have some girl chat.

"Look at him out there. What a beauty," Jillian remarked.

Storm was certainly a handsome creature to look at. He stood in the field, his head held high, surveying his surroundings. He nickered and began a slow trot around the field, tail flowing behind him. He had come a long way in the last four weeks.

Initially, Storm didn't have any interest in the fact that Sarge and Hershey went outside during the day while he stayed in his stall. Charlie kept him in for his own safety as well as her other horses, until he got more acclimated.

In between working, meeting deadlines for the *Weekly*, and driving the kids around, Charlie worked with Storm. Her short term goal was to have him be interested in life again. While she was at it, she found that she was also finding new reasons to be alive again.

So much of the past year had been a fog, dealing with her pain of losing Peter, while trying to be strong for her kids.

"You seem a bit happier these days," Kate commented.

"It's amazing what having a new project can do." Charlie smiled. "Sarge is great, but he knows everything already and doesn't really need me. Storm needs me to help him."

Each day, Skylar and Charlie had continued their routine of going to the barn and grooming Storm. After a week, they walked into the barn and stopped short. It was the first time that Storm had his head over the stall door, like he was waiting for them. They approached his stall, and his nostrils quivered in anticipation for his morning grooming session. They couldn't stop smiling the whole time they worked.

Once Storm realized that nothing bad would happen if he put his head out of his stall, he wouldn't put it back in. It didn't matter if there was hay available or the grain had just been poured. It was like he didn't want to miss a thing. Storm would grab a bite of hay and then return to the open door and chew, all the while taking in the activity around him. He might be watching Skylar and Charlie tack up for their afternoon ride, or the barn cats rolling in the sun. He would lower his muzzle for a sloppy kiss from Critter, their mixed breed dog.

Occasionally something would frighten him, and Storm would race to his stall corner and hang his head. It was like he was waiting for his punishment. It took him a while to realize none was coming. Charlie would watch him during those times and wonder what had happened to his beautiful soul.

Ryan brought Charlie out of her reverie when he walked up with his iPad.

"Hey, handsome!" Jillian called out.

Kate got up and gave him a big hug, followed by Jillian. Charlie's friends loved her kids. Since they hadn't had any of their own, they adopted Ryan and Skylar along the way. Kate and her husband tried to have kids for years and it just never happened. They finally got fed up with the doctors and the artificial insemination, and were pursuing adoption as an option.

Jillian, on the other hand, was not interested in getting married and having kids. She loved her independence too much. Jillian was never lonely for a date. Several guys along the way had proposed but she turned them down every time. She was confident and knew her limits.

"You ready?" Charlie asked Ryan. He had spent the last four weeks doing research on Storm. Charlie had tried to find out a few things, but he refused to tell her anything. He wanted the whole picture first. It was just like Ryan to leave no stone unturned. He had such a talent at the computer and sleuthing the internet.

He tried to hide it behind his moody teenage attitudes, but Charlie thought it was safe to say that Ryan loved Storm as much as she and Skylar did. Though he didn't ride, she'd catch him coming in from his practice and heading into the barn for a quick hello to all the horses. Once she didn't realize he had been dropped from his carpool, and she found him standing at Storm's stall door just scratching behind the horse's ears and softly talking to him. Storm just stood there, with his ears flopped to the side, enjoying his evening rub. Charlie backed away, she hadn't wanted to disturb their moment together.

She imagined Ryan had a bit of a closer tie to Storm as he had been living his life through research. Now they were all going to get updated on what he'd found.

The Research

The adults all settled in with freshly poured glasses of wine.

"Skylar!" Charlie called out.

Skylar looked over from her position under the big oak tree in the field with Hershey and Sarge. She loved going out there with her book in hand and would sit for hours with the horses grazing at her feet. Skylar stood up, gave Hershey a quick hug around her neck, patted Sarge on the forehead and started running towards the house.

Suddenly the ground shook from the far side of the adjacent paddock, as Storm came tearing along the fence line. All conversations stopped and everyone just stared. Storm stretched low, covering the distance between him and Skylar in a few seconds.

Charlie's jaw dropped. She wasn't nervous for Skylar, she wasn't in the same paddock. She was speechless, watching Storm race to catch up with her. Skylar turned at the sound of Storms' approach. The other two horses had joined in the fun, racing down their side of the fence.

Skylar came to a stop and stood at the fence line. Storm tossed his head high and half reared, proud of himself for catching up with Skylar. This was not the horse Charlie had seen at the racetrack.

Storm thrust his nose over the fence, looking for the peppermints Skylar always kept in her pocket. After handing him one of the treats, Skylar kissed him on his nose and walked out of the gate towards everyone. She stopped and looked at them. She must have thought they looked like zombies, staring at her and Storm.

"He caught me today," she smiled.

"What do you mean by today?" Charlie tentatively asked.

"Well, Storm and I have been playing tag. When I come out here to read, he looks so lonely in his field by himself with no one to play with. He's just a baby you know," Skylar said with authority. "So, I started going into his field to play with him." Charlie raised her eyebrows as visions of Skylar getting trampled ran through her brain.

"He didn't really know how to play. Not like Hershey does, you know mom, when I can run and Hershey will follow?" Charlie nodded.

"So I taught him!" she exclaimed. Looking back at Storm, she blew him a kiss. "Good job, Storm! Next time, I run after you." Storm snorted and once again tossed his head as he pawed at the fence, his eyes never leaving Skylar, like he was in total agreement with a nine-year-old girl.

Charlie looked over at Ryan, and then at Kate and Jillian. A smile lit on everyone's face. They all broke into laughter.

"Come on, Ryan. Tell us what you found out about our mysterious guy here." Kate piped in, waving her arm towards Storm. Ryan grabbed a water bucket and turned it upside down and sat on it. He flipped open his iPad.

"Well, first off, I found out that Storm was born only a couple of hours from here in a town outside of Charlottesville," Ryan started off. "A place called Gordonsville. The owner of the place died suddenly, and all of his horses were sold off at auction.

"The background on our Storm here, related to his breeding, is this," Ryan continued. "His dad is Genuine Reward, and his mom Storm Minstrel. I wasn't sure initially why the breeder picked Genuine Reward, since he didn't have any success on the track. Then I started researching the extended bloodlines on both sides of his pedigree and I found out more."

Charlie looked over at Storm. He was still standing at the fence line looking at them. It didn't surprise her. Like when he was in his stall and didn't want to miss a thing, he stood and took everything in with his big brown eyes. She could see his nostrils moving as he took in all the smells around him. Skylar, Ryan, and Charlie were familiar. Kate and Jillian, not as much. They had been by a few times since Storm had arrived at the farm, but they had spent those times in the house.

It was one of the first Fridays in a while that was a perfect fall day. The temperature was a cool 75 degrees, the leaves were starting to change. Fall was in the air - crisp sweater weather after a blazing summer of over 90 degrees, the smell of a far off, wood burning stove, the long shadows coming through the trees from the sun sitting lower on the horizon.

Maybe his sire was the reason Storm didn't have success at the track and the fact that he was in a low level claiming race. If his daddy didn't want to run, that could be why he didn't have the desire to run either. At least, that is what Charlie saw at the track four weeks ago. Since then, Storm had turned into a different horse: the way he ran and caught up with Skylar, he looked like he was having fun.

Ryan continued,

"There are very successful horses in his bloodlines. Like you know, Genuine Risk is his grand-dam, which is the mom of his sire. Everyone knows her - the second filly to ever win the Kentucky Derby.

"Storm Cat is Storm Minstrel's sire. He only raced a few times until he was retired due to an injury. However, Storm Cat's offspring are big money winners and his stud fee was $500,000 at its peak! He's got the great Secretariat in his bloodlines. Did you know that when they autopsied Secretariat, they found out that his heart was twice the size of a normal horse's heart?" Ryan's face showed excitement as he went on with his story.

"Now all of those names are known Thoroughbreds and have pretty awesome accomplishments, but what I find even cooler are the unsung heroes in Storm's bloodlines. I had to dig pretty deep, but I found some neat information. Rahy, Genuine Reward's sire, was a small horse, by Thoroughbred standards; but he could come down the stretch like a bullet and outrun much larger rivals.

"Gallant Man would have won the Derby in 1930 if his jockey didn't misjudge the finish line and start pulling him up. He lost by a nose. He came back to win the Belmont. Glorious Song, one of Storm's great grandmas, is in the Canadian Horse Racing Hall of Fame. She won several older female horse awards and raced against the boys in several races, including finishing second to Spectacular Bid, the 1979 Kentucky Derby winner. She won over one million dollars in earnings throughout her career.

"Pleasant Colony, one of Storm's great grand-sires, won the 1981 Kentucky Derby and Preakness and was third in the Belmont. He is also the great grand-sire of The Green Monkey, a colt that sold at auction for a world-record sixteen million dollars!" Ryan paused to let that number sink in.

"Who buys a horse for sixteen million?" Jillian squealed.

"Someone with more money than God," Charlie said.

Ryan continued with his research,

"Blushing Groom is also one of Storm's grandsires, he had a very successful racing career in Europe. His offspring are known for their stamina and ability to win at longer distances. The Minstrel is another horse in his bloodlines that ran successfully in Europe: winner of the Epsom Derby in Britain and the Irish Derby in Ireland. Both these races run at one and a half miles, which is longer than most races." He looked over at Charlie, excited about that piece of information.

Many horses these days are bred for the shorter distances of races in the United States. The Derby, at one and a quarter miles, is the first time the horses running in the race will be asked to run that far. Then you have the Preakness at a mile and three-sixteenths, ending with the Belmont at a mile and a half - the Triple Crown. No horse has won all three races since 1978 when Affirmed did it.

"I could go on about all the other horses in Storm's pedigree. One last bit of information, Northern Dancer shows up twice in his pedigree on his mom's side. Northern Dancer won the Derby and Preakness, and finished third in the Belmont, just like Pleasant Colony. When he was retired, his offspring were so successful that he wound up commanding a stud fee of one million dollars!"

Once again everyone raised their eyebrows at the money that gets thrown around in the racing of Thoroughbreds. What was Charlie thinking, trying to compete with people that had that kind of money? Could they race their grey thundercloud, with only pocket change compared to the wealthiest people in the industry?

They sat, mesmerized by Ryan's long recital of Storm's family tree. They were all Thoroughbred junkies, certainly aware of Secretariat and Genuine Risk. But the stories he unfolded about the other horses were equally interesting. These great creatures each had a story to tell, and much of the general public didn't care: horses that ran and won, or didn't win, but still possessed the heart and desire of a champion. Big or small, many races or none at all, huge races or small, within them ran decades of Thoroughbred blood passed from generation to generation.

"So back to Storm's upbringing. Like I mentioned, his breeder, Mr. George Shilling, died and all the horses went off to auction. Many of Mr. Shilling's horses were purchased for hundreds of thousands of dollars. For instance, a yearling by the name of Royal Duke sold for $870,000," Ryan exclaimed.

"How much did Storm sell for?" Skylar asked.

"Only $10,000. I guess people weren't too keen on his pedigree, especially on the sire's side. That, coupled with the fact that Genuine Risk, his grandma, only had two offspring in her seventeen years of breeding. People moved on and they forgot how Genuine Risk fought to beat the boys, I guess. These days, it's all about pedigree and not so much about the heart and courage that a horse needs to win a race. No horse is going to win unless he, or she," he added sheepishly, "has the will to win. Right,

Aunt Kate?" Ryan asked.

Kate drew her attention from Storm over to Ryan. Charlie knew she was taking all this in. Out of all of them, Kate was the most involved in the racing side of horses. As a freelancer for *Blood-Horse Magazine*, she had insights none of the rest of them had.

"Well, honey, things have changed so much over the years. Technology is such that people can trace everything about a horse, and try and breed two horses together that capitalize on the results of the past. Sometimes it's not about the wins and losses. I wish that breeders would look to the intangibles of the horse: the drive, the courage, the heart of the animal. Look at Storm Cat. He was retired as a two-year-old due to an injury after the Breeders' Cup Juvenile, and folks were devastated. I am sure they thought he missed out on a great racing career, but it turns out that he was even more successful as a sire, and he bred many winners after he was retired to stud. Someone saw the heart and soul of this horse and knew he would be a great sire."

"But if Storm had all these famous horses in his pedigree, beyond his mom and dad, why didn't everyone want Storm?" Skylar asked. Kate patiently replied,

"I don't know. People look at a lot of things. Maybe they liked his bloodlines okay but he didn't have good conformation as a baby. Do you know what that means, Skylar?"

"Like his back was too short or his legs were too long?" Skylar replied.

Charlie was proud of her. She had learned so much in the past year. Not just the riding part, but the other things about horses, how they were built, why some horses were good jumpers and some were not. So much of a horse's success was based in its conformation: how a horse's bones, muscles and ligaments fit together.

"Right, some baby horses can be like the story, *The Ugly Duckling*," Kate remarked. Skylar opened her mouth to speak again, but Ryan cut her off.

"Can I finish, please?" Ryan chimed in, impatient to share his research. Skylar rolled her eyes at him. Ryan ignored his sister and continued,

"What I did find out was that Storm acted up in the auction ring right in front of the whole crowd. I came across a small blurb about it in the summary of the sale the day after. The guy holding him in the ring couldn't keep him under control, and one writer said, 'the odd yearling bred by Mr. Shilling was all back legs and downhill to his head,' so you were right about the conformation thing," Ryan said.

Storm certainly had become the swan, at least in Charlie's perspective. Yes, his hind end was still quite large, but isn't that what propelled a horse? Ryan continued,

"In the end, Storm was bought by a trainer whose name was Dale Blackston. I did a little research on him, too. It turns out he's been in a lot of trouble in the past for mistreating horses and using illegal devices to help win races. He was caught again recently, and a newspaper article I read about it said that his clients were leaving in droves and Blackston was selling the horses to bail himself out of trouble and pay for his legal fees."

"That's awful!" Skylar cried.

"I guess that's why he was in such a low stakes claiming race," Jillian said. They all looked back over at Storm. His ears were still turned toward them, but his head was lowered: yes, he'd come a long way since the night Charlie brought him home, but there was still a long road ahead of him. Would he ever be able to forget?

The Next Step

Charlie got up early and grabbed a cup of coffee. It was a mystery to her, how people could possibly survive without having a cup of coffee first thing in the morning. She loved the smell of it brewing, looking at the rich brown color as she poured it into her cup, and that first taste was heaven. She wasn't always one of those people that can't function without coffee in the morning, but after her kids were born and she was more sleep deprived than ever, she needed the extra help to get going. She never looked back.

It was earlier than she usually got up, but Charlie wanted to savor a few minutes by herself with Storm before the kids got up. It was finally the day. The day she would make the call that might change everything. She knew she was being melodramatic, but she had a strange feeling that Storm was brought into their lives for a reason.

Charlie put on her barn coat, because the fall chill was heavy in the air, especially at 5:30 in the morning. The frost on the grass crunched under her feet as she walked to the barn. She swung open the door, and was met with several pairs of blinking eyes. The horses weren't used to anyone being out there that early in the morning.

Sarge nickered and stretched his tilted head towards Charlie as he liked to do. She scratched him behind his ears, a place he couldn't reach himself, and he gave a big sigh. Hershey was nodding his head up and down in the stall next to them, pawing at his door, looking for the attention that was usually showered upon him by Skylar.

"Big day today, fellas," Charlie spoke to them. They all turned their heads to the big grey head looking curiously at them from across the aisle.

He waited patiently, knowing he would get Charlie's attention, but that he would be last in line. Sarge and Hershey had been there before him and he respected that. It was apparent that he had learned to appreciate the small things: the peppermints from Skylar, the head scratching from Charlie, and the quiet conversations with Ryan.

Storm did have his two-year-old tantrums, but they were few and far between; sometimes he pranced a bit too freshly and reared up while walking to the paddock in his excitement, or anxiously threw his head around while waiting for his turn. One time he threw his head in such a way, he glanced a blow off Charlie's shoulder. It was black and blue for a week. It wasn't his fault, but just like with a new puppy, rules had to be established. Since horses are herd-bound animals, there is always a hierarchy, and Charlie needed to make sure that Storm knew she was the herd leader, and that the kids followed. At over a thousand pounds, horses that don't understand their boundaries are a liability and a danger. Storm was learning his place. He was doing well, but he still had some work to do.

Charlie walked over to him and rubbed his cheek, looking into his eyes. The placid brown gazed back with full trust: earned in such a short time. Animals are so understanding. Even after horrible treatment from others, Storm didn't hold a grudge and gave his trust willingly.

Charlie could remember an incident with Critter, right after Peter's death; she was in a dark place and had a short temper because she was having to learn how to deal with life again. Critter wound up being in the wrong place at the wrong time, underfoot, and Charlie stumbled over her. Charlie had reached back and slapped her across her muzzle, in shear anger. Critter had yelped and scurried away to her bed, while Charlie dropped to the floor, crying out in pain for what she'd done. She couldn't help herself.

After bawling into her hands for several minutes, she looked up to find Critter sitting quietly in front of her, looking up at Charlie with forgiveness. Critter had walked towards Charlie and buried her head in her owner's hands, telling her it was okay, and that she loved her unconditionally. Storm pushed at Charlie with his head.

"Looking for breakfast, big guy?" Charlie laughed. She followed her normal routine, feeding the horses, appreciating the quiet morning in their presence. After she turned them out into their fields, she went back into the house to get breakfast ready for the kids.

When she got back inside, Ryan and Skylar were already at the table, cereal bowls picked clean.

"I was going to make you guys a big breakfast this morning," said Charlie.

"No worries, Mom. We got our own," Ryan said.

"When are you going to call him?" Skylar asked, bouncing in her seat. Charlie sat down next to her and across from Ryan.

"Are you sure you want me to?" asked Charlie. They were all quiet for a few seconds. They knew what Storm could do; they had seen him running in the fields for the past few weeks. He was fast: but he was having such a good time with them, and he was so happy. Sending him back to the racetrack might make him sad again. Storm wasn't the only one who might revert to old habits if Charlie made this call.

His personality was part of their little herd now, and training to race would take him away from them. They had all smiled a lot more since his arrival, joked more, and felt the mood of the last two years slowly lift. They were afraid that Storm's departure would mean things would go back to the way they were. The last thing Charlie wanted was to fall back into the rut that had plagued her for so long.

"Make the call, Mom," Ryan said. She could see a bit of pain run across Ryan's face when he said it. He would be giving up his confidant.

"Mom, he is so fast!" Skylar piped in. "We need to show him off to everybody!"

"What if he only runs fast here, Skylar, and when he goes back to the track, he doesn't want to run?" Charlie asked her.

"Oh, he'll run Mom. He knows we will be there to cheer him on. I have talked to him about all the big races he will win and how we will meet him after every race in the winner's circle and give him big kisses. And peppermints," she said matter-of-factly. Ryan smirked. Charlie grabbed each of their hands.

"Well then, I guess it is up to us to help him get on the road to win all those races."

After Charlie dropped Ryan to hockey practice and Skylar to a friend's birthday party, she sat and updated the news for the *Leesburg Weekly*. A win by the football team, the new restaurant opening on Main Street, the upcoming Halloween parade at the community center: she was procrastinating. She was afraid: afraid to pick up the phone and call Doug. Once she did, she would be setting things in motion and there was no telling how it would all turn out.

It was exhilarating and frightening at the same time. Her days were planned out to the minute. It was the same before Peter died, and it had taken her a while, but now she was back to being in control. Well, minus the unplanned horse in her barn. She didn't like uncertainty, but she was beginning to realize that sometimes a leap of faith is required.

Charlie picked up her cell phone and dialed Doug's number. It started ringing. She took a deep breath and steeled herself for the conversation. A trill of panic went through her, *What was my opening line?*

"Hello?" He picked up after two rings. Not nearly enough time for her to think about what she was supposed to say.

"Yes…is Doug there? I mean, is this Doug? I'm calling about my horse."

"This is Doug. Charlie, is that you?" There was a hint of laughter in his question. She was so flustered that she barely noticed the excited tone his question took on: like he'd been waiting for her call.

"Oh, yes. I always forget that part, don't I? Yes, it's me. Is this a bad time?"

"Not at all! I was actually starting to think you'd decided against using my help. It's been a while. How is everything going with your horse?"

"Well, Storm is great. It took some time to get him to come out of his shell, but my kids love him and he's been a really good addition to our farmily. I mean to our farm and our family. Those are hard words to say with only one cup of coffee in your system." She was hitting her forehead with her palm, hoping to knock the rest of her stupidity away, at least for the remainder of the conversation.

"I'm glad he's getting on so well. Are you thinking about racing him at all?"

"He's been running around the paddocks here and he seems like he enjoys it and he's pretty quick. I wouldn't say no to getting a professional opinion though…"

"And here I thought we were cultivating more of a friendship." She thought she could have been imagining the flirty tone, but she blushed all the same.

"Really? That's good, because I've always found professionals to be kind of self-serving, and I need someone to give it to me straight. You think you're up for the job?"

****

Charlie, Ryan, and Skylar pulled into a driveway lined with big oak trees: gleaming white fences ran the length of each side. Herds of horses lifted their heads to watch the truck and horse trailer pass by.

They were all silent in the truck, their eyes open wide, taking in the beautiful farm coming into view in front of them.

"Wow, Mom. This is amazing!" Skylar exclaimed. Before them were numerous barns, and more pastures filled with horses. Off to the left was a training racetrack circled by more gleaming white fencing, to the right were several small homes, probably for the staff.

They pulled around the circular driveway in front of the building labeled as the office.

"Stay here." Charlie got out of the truck. Her heart was beating a mile a minute. She steadied herself against the truck and took a deep breath.

It had been several days since she had made the call to Doug. She was sure he thought she was nuts after that last phone call. She couldn't blame him. She had no idea what was wrong with her. She'd met the man literally for fifteen minutes and now she couldn't hold a normal conversation with him. She felt like she was being such a school girl.

She'd made it through the remainder of the phone conversation with him, without fumbling over any more words. He'd said he was at his farm for a few weeks, but his schedule was pretty busy: could they bring Storm to the farm the following Monday? Monday was generally a quiet day on the farm and he would have some time to take a look at him. Charlie agreed before she knew what she was saying and then ended up having to reschedule a few other appointments because of her hastiness.

The kids were playing hooky from school. There was no way they were going to let Charlie take Storm without them. They were in this together. Charlie went over to the office door and walked inside.

Once again, her eyes grew wide. All around her were pictures of beautiful racehorses, some in mid-flight during a race, some in the winners' circle. The far wall was covered in shelves and filled floor to ceiling with trophies. Charlie walked over to the nearest picture. She spotted Doug quickly, holding the bridle of the winner, just like he did at the race at Charles Town. Standing next to him were several other people beaming with joy at having their horse just win a race. She traced her fingers over the name of the horse printed under the picture: "Her Majesty." She definitely lived up to the name: a stunningly beautiful black mare with a white star on her forehead.

"Want to meet her?" A voice inquired from behind Charlie. She spun around. Doug was leaning against the door jam on the opposite side of the room. He made it look so effortless, standing against that wall like he was doing it a favor. Charlie may not have known much about the racing industry, but she knew if more men that looked like Doug offered to, "evaluate her horse," she'd have drunkenly purchased a racehorse years ago. *A lot of women would*, she thought. *Maybe the sport of kings wouldn't be fading out of popularity if they had some billboards made up with Doug on them.*

"Ah, she's beautiful. And yes, of course, I would love to meet her," Charlie stammered. She was blushing, she could feel it. She tried to hide her face under the pretense of looking in her purse for a piece of gum. Of course, that backfired when she started thinking about how it would be a good thing if her breath was minty fresh, just in case…She dropped her bag on the floor and bent to pick it up and then stood stock still, avoiding eye contact. Doug strode across the room, hand extended,

"Pleased to meet you again in person, Charlie." She shook his outstretched hand, still trying to avoid his eyes.

"Thank you again for taking the time to look at Storm. He has become very special to us, we can't wait to hear what you think." Doug raised his eyebrows.

"Are your kids here? I'd love to meet them," he asked.

"Are you kidding me? They wouldn't miss this for the world. Each of us has spent a lot of time with Storm, making him feel important. He is a changed horse, that much is certain."

Doug smiled. She could tell a part of him thought of her as a child with a pony.

"Remember when I told you at the track that you need to look into a horse's eyes? To see if he had a story to tell, if he could overcome adversity?" Doug asked.

"Yes, that's what got me into this crazy situation," she said.

"What do you see in Storm's eyes?" he asked.

"A fighter," she responded without thinking twice.

"Well, let's see this fighter of yours." He put his arm around her back and steered her out the door. She almost choked on her gum.

Ryan and Skylar had gotten out of the truck and were watching the horses train on the track. They turned as Doug and Charlie came out of the office. Doug still had his arm at Charlie's waist and Ryan eyed him suspiciously.

"Doug, these are my kids, Ryan and Skylar. Kids, Mr. Walker," Charlie said. Skylar quickly came over.

"Oh hi, Mr. Doug! Are these all your horses? Do they all win? What are their names?" Skylar would have continued to ask questions if Ryan didn't cut her off.

"Hi." He put out his hand. Ryan gained a few inches as he brought himself to full height: the man of the family. He was being protective of his mother. Charlie had seen him frown slightly when he saw Doug's arm leading her out of the office. She could still feel the warmth of Doug's touch, but she wasn't there to make her son uncomfortable. She moved out of reach of Doug.

"I hear you all have done a great job with Storm," Doug said.

"Oh yes, Mr. Doug. We love Storm. He didn't want to come today but we encouraged him to get on the trailer with a lot of peppermints. Well, those plus Sarge." Skylar smiled.

"Sarge?" Doug asked.

"Mom's horse. We thought Storm would travel better with a companion," Ryan commented.

"That's true, Ryan. As I am sure you know, horses are herd animals and like to be part of a group. You were smart in bringing along Sarge," Doug said. Ryan looked like he had grown a few more inches, taking in the compliment from this man that was not his father.

"Come on, kids. Let's get them off the trailer," Charlie said opening the side doors. Storm immediately threw out his head and let out a loud whinny. Several of the horses in the fields answered him.

"Well, he certainly looks a lot different than when I saw him over a month ago," Doug commented, remembering the horse hiding in the back of his stall, not caring to lift his head. Ryan and Charlie took down the ramp, while Skylar fed Storm and Sarge peppermints nonstop.

"Should we leave Sarge in the trailer?" Charlie asked Doug.

"You can take him off. I don't like to see horses stand in the trailer for long periods of time. We have a stall we can put him in for the time being, and Storm will be more comfortable with a friend," Doug said. He made a call on his cell phone.

A few minutes later, a couple of stable helpers approached the trailer. Ryan slowly backed Storm off the trailer so as not to make him wait too long. Sarge was used to the trailer, so he wouldn't mind being second.

"Jenny will take him for you," Doug said. Jenny stepped forward. Ryan held Storm, deciding if he wanted to relinquish him to this petite, young girl.

"She's stronger than she looks," Doug laughed. Jenny smiled widely at Ryan as she grabbed Storm's lead rope. Charlie spotted a red blush come over Ryan's face. Charlie smiled too.

She backed Sarge off the trailer and gave him a big hug, thanking him for his help. Charlie was sure he was wondering what was going on. Sarge lifted his head and surveyed his surroundings. His eyes alighted on the training track as the horses galloped around. He stood very still with his head held high, nostrils working hard, taking in the smells. Charlie wondered if he was thinking about his old racing days.

Sarge wasn't a big success on the track, but he had won one race. She had a picture of him in the winners' circle, so many years ago. He dropped his head and pushed at her chest. His sign for letting her know he was ready.

Charlie caught Doug watching her with her horse. He had that smoldering look in his eyes that she had seen the night she met him. She ran her hand down Sarge's neck to stop it from shaking, and smiled. Doug walked over and gave Sarge a pat on his neck, not far from her hand.

"I see you have a strong bond with this fella," Doug said.

"He's been with me through thick and thin. I'm not sure I would have made it through some of the bad times without him," Charlie reflected.

"I totally understand," Doug said.

"I can take him from you," a young man said who appeared next to them.

"Thanks, Brandon. You can put him in stall eleven in the yearling barn," Doug instructed.

"Now what?" Charlie asked.

"We go see what you've got in that big, grey horse!" Doug exclaimed. "Come on, let me show you around while Storm settles in for a bit. We don't want to rush him right out onto the track, it may undo what you have accomplished this past month. He can settle in next to Sarge, eat some hay, and we'll tack him up in a couple of hours. You guys must be hungry too, I know it was a long drive up here, and it's lunchtime."

Farm Tour

They spent the next hour touring the grounds of Shamrock Hill Farm. Doug drove them around in a four person, bright, white golf cart with the farm's logo on the side - a green shamrock within a gold horseshoe.

From the broodmare barns to the training barns, the training track and the staff quarters, all was immaculate, and each person they met was polite and friendly. Finally, they pulled up to the last barn.

"Well, this is the last stop on the tour," Doug said. Throughout the drive around the farm, Doug pointed out the various horses and appeased Skylar by telling her each one's name. How he could remember them all, especially in a herd of ten bay yearlings that looked exactly alike, Charlie had no idea.

They all got out of the cart and waited for Doug to finish a phone call he had just received.

"This place is A-MAZ-ING," Skylar whispered to Charlie, as she wrapped her arms around her mother's waist.

"It certainly is." Charlie smiled back at her. Ryan stood off to the side, deep in thought.

"Penny for your thoughts?" Charlie asked him. He looked over at her.

"Dad would have loved this." Charlie walked over to him.

"Oh, I am not so sure, dear. Your dad loved the outdoors, yes, but he loved boats and snow. A far cry from this place."

"He would have loved to watch you, loving this." He swept his arm over the rolling hills filled with horses. "I haven't seen you smile this much in a long time. You've spent the last year worrying about Skylar and me. It's nice to see you excited about something. You've done nothing but ask Mr. Walker a gazillion questions since we got here," He smirked at her. Charlie raised her eyebrows at him. It seemed he'd warmed up to Doug, and forgotten all about that initial incident. Doug walked over after his call finished up.

"Shall we go in?" he asked. He had a peculiar look on his face. Something about that phone call had enlightened him, and judging from the way he kept smiling at her, Charlie could only guess that Storm had something to do with it.

"What is this barn, Mr. Doug?" Skylar asked. She was oblivious to the whole thing.

"Well, Skylar, this is where we keep our very special horses. Don't get me wrong, we think all our horses are special, but sometimes there are those that need some extra tender love and care. This is our retirement and rehab barn," Doug said.

"There are times when our horses get injured, and we keep this barn quieter than the others to help them recuperate. We also keep our retired horses here: those that won't continue on in our breeding program. We have a special staff assigned to these horses and they help them transition from a racehorse to something else, perhaps a show horse."

"Like Sarge?" Skylar asked.

"Yep, just like Sarge. Racing Thoroughbreds are used to a different life than a show horse, so we take the time to, 'let them down,' as we say in the business. They don't need to be in racing shape, so their diet changes. Since they are only used to trotting and galloping on the track, we use the ring out back to teach them how to walk, trot, and canter calmly. We do all we can here over a period of six months to acclimate them to a different life. Then we let folks know they are available for sale, for a minimal price. On our website is a page of all our prior racers and their new careers. It is exciting to follow them after they leave us," Doug finished.

He walked down the center aisle of the barn, petting each of the heads he passed. He stopped by a specific stall and Charlie walked up next to him. A jet black head rested over her stall door, nuzzling Doug's hand.

"Does she look familiar?" he asked. Charlie shook her head and then stopped, her memory flashed back to the picture in his office.

"Her Majesty?" she asked.

"Maggie, as we call her." He stroked her long nose.

"She's beautiful. Why is she in this barn?" Charlie asked.

"Her racing days are over. She is going to be my prized broodmare. Right now she is recuperating from a bout of colic she had last week. It was pretty bad; her intestines were pretty turned around, but the docs worked their magic and we stayed up with her for 24 straight hours and didn't have to do surgery. I decided after that episode she was ready for retirement. She has had a great racing career; she actually won the Breeders' Cup Distaff last November. It's a race for the best female horses in the country at the end of the year. That's the picture you saw in the office – all of us in the winner's circle that day."

Charlie ran her hand down Maggie's nose,

"That's amazing. She will be a great momma for you, I am sure."

"We hope so. You never can tell. One of the reasons I like to breed and race my own, is that I keep track of my own family trees and I know the nuances of all my horses. It's not just me looking at pedigrees on paper and matching horses together. I know their personalities."

After greeting a few of the other horses and being introduced to Doug's team of workers in the barn, he led the way over to the staff kitchen for some lunch. Skylar protested weakly, but when Doug reminded her about checking on Storm after, she couldn't get to the cafeteria fast enough.

Old Friend

Charlie was still wondering about that phone call while they ate. Doug was talking easily with Ryan and Skylar about what he was going to do with Storm after lunch. Charlie had to get onto Skylar about eating too fast which she did sometimes when she got too excited.

"But I'm ready to go see Storm run!" she exclaimed.

"You won't get to see him run at all if you choke on your food and we have to leave. Slow down, please." She complied, but only after Doug told her that he had a special surprise before they went to see Storm.

"What kind of surprise?" asked Ryan. Jenny, the cute worker from before, was sitting at a table behind them. Charlie could tell that Ryan was trying to act nonchalant in case she was watching him. Charlie quickly put some food in her mouth to keep herself from laughing at him, and listened to Doug's answer.

"Well, I got a phone call earlier- actually, never mind that explanation, here he comes!" Doug said, standing up. He walked towards the door and greeted a young man who was wearing a work uniform: one of his employees.

"Mom, who is that?" Skylar asked, now so excited that she couldn't eat anything. Her fork was loaded with food and halfway to her mouth, but it wasn't going any further. Charlie gently guided Skylar's hand back toward the plate as the two men approached and took seats at the table.

"Charlie, Skylar, Ryan, I'd like you to meet an employee of mine, Ben Driscoll. Ben, this is the family that owns Genuine Storm." Ben reached out and shook everyone's hand. Skylar looked delighted at being offered such a grown-up greeting. Doug continued,

"Ben here used to work for a man named Mr. Shilling, who-"

"Owned and operated the farm where Storm was born! You knew Storm as a baby?" Ryan blurted out, forgetting all about the pretty girl at the next table. Incidentally, his sudden outburst is what finally got her attention, and Charlie saw her smile at the way he passionately posed his question.

"Yeah, I did. I worked with him up until he was sold, about a year ago. It was such a shame, what happened. I tried to get that guy, Blackston, to hire me on as Storm's groom, so that I could make sure he was okay, but he wouldn't take me on. I even tried to visit Storm a few times, but they wouldn't let me on the property."

"He probably didn't want you to see how mean he really was," Skylar said, clenching her tiny fists. Doug smiled at her.

"I think you're exactly right, Skylar. Blackston and I used to work with some of the same horses, way back in the day. He was always so sure that he could make them run faster if he used a whip or some other painful device. It wasn't long before he started using illegal methods, and he was fired from the farm where we worked. I thought for sure he was done, but before I knew it, he had his own place. It still baffles me, how many people think pain is the way to go when training a horse."

"So, what happened? Did you ever get to see him, Mr. Driscoll?" Ryan asked. "We read about how Blackston is under investigation now, and all that. Did you get to see Storm before all that happened?"

"I did, but only from afar."

"What happened?" Skylar asked. She was so engrossed in the

conversation that she'd put her elbow in her lunch. Charlie grabbed a napkin and started cleaning her up, without her even noticing.

"Well finally, not too long after I started working here, I went to Blackston's farm to check on Storm. I'd scraped together enough money that I thought I could afford to buy him, it wasn't a huge amount, but I thought Blackston might go for it. I knew Blackston's reputation and I wasn't keen to let Storm stay with him any longer than I had to. I knew they'd tried racing him and he wasn't bringing them any money, so I made an offer. They laughed in my face. Blackston tried to get me to pay several thousand dollars more than a failed racehorse is worth." At this point he stopped and held up a hand to stifle the protests coming from Ryan and Skylar.

"Don't get me wrong, I knew that Storm could run, but whatever that guy was doing to him before races was not working. For all he knew, he'd bought the worst racehorse in the country: but he wouldn't sell at my price, and I didn't have the money to offer more. As I was leaving, I caught a glimpse of Storm working out on the track: they were hitting him and yelling and I'm sure the bit in his mouth was far from legal. He was trying so hard, but he looked like he was in so much pain. I saw him rear up and take off down the track, trying to run away from the pain. The jockey couldn't control him and he veered hard and went right up against the inside rail of the track."

There was a collective intake of breath. Even Skylar knew that running into the rail of a racetrack, for a horse, was bound to be one of the most painful things that can happen. Charlie had noticed a white patch of hair on Storm's shoulder that looked like it was covering some kind of scar: it must be where the rail had burned the hair off of him. Poor Storm.

"After that I couldn't watch. I didn't know what to do. I called around to see if any racing authorities would help me, but there was nothing we could do unless we saw Blackston using illegal instruments on the horses. I finally got someone to agree to do a drug test on the horses that were running in races out in Charles Town. Blackston had a few horses entered that day, and they all tested positive: it wasn't his first offence. Once again he is up to his eyeballs in fines and legal trouble, though he always seems to get himself out of it. I'm sure Blackston will be back on some track again, trying to beat the system… and his horses. "

"Good! That awful man hurt Storm and I hope he never sets foot on another track and no one ever sells him another horse!" Skylar said. Ryan nodded in agreement, though he knew the prospect was less than likely.

"So, didn't you still want Storm after Blackston got into trouble?" Skylar asked.

"Of course I did. The problem was I couldn't find Storm once Blackston started getting rid of his horses. I guess they sent him to Charles Town and entered him in that claiming race where you bought him. I never thought I'd see him again: you can imagine my surprise as I walked through the barn today and there he was, grey as ever, ears turned forward, like he's trying to pick up a radio signal or something. I called Doug right away."

"You really did all that, just for Storm?" Skylar asked. It was clear Ben had become some kind of superhero horse rescuer in her eyes. Charlie wasn't immune to the story either, though, and she had the strongest urge to hug the man, to thank him for saving the horse that had saved her family. She resisted, in part because Doug was looking at her, and she didn't know how he would react to her hugging another man.

"I did it for Storm, yes, but I also did it for Mr. Shilling. He was a great boss, and an amazing man. He loved horses and he loved racing. Storm was the last horse he bred before his accident, and I couldn't let his prized colt get beaten down by a man who has no respect for what it means to be a racehorse. I've heard Doug talk a little about you guys and I'm really glad Storm ended up with you. I think you're exactly what he needs. And…" he looked over at Doug, who smiled and nodded that he should continue,

"And if you'll have me, I'd love to be a part of Storm's racing team, if you decide to race him."

"Absolutely!" Skylar yelled, before Charlie could say anything. Ben smiled, but he looked over at Charlie for confirmation.

"We would love to have your help and expertise, Ben. We are more than happy to have all the help we can get, especially from someone who's done so much to help our horse already."

"Thank you. And I promise I'm not looking for anything else. Storm is your horse now, and I think Mr. Shilling would be proud of that." Ben smiled. Doug patted him on the back and looked over at Charlie. The favors he was doing them were really starting to pile up. Could it be possible that he was really that nice? They'd been all over his farm and hadn't come across a single disgruntled employee, or one who's name and background he didn't know. This guy was kind of blowing Charlie's mind. He'd asked for a friendship. She could give him that, at the very least…

Ryan had claimed Ben's attention, and they were talking while Skylar was asking excitedly if it was time yet to go see Storm.

"If your mom is ready, I think we can head over to the track now," Doug said.

"Ready when you are." She didn't know if she was talking about going to see Storm, or more than that: her hands were a bit clammy as she had been thinking about things other than horses. She quickly looked at his face, and smiled, a blush creeping to her cheeks. Doug, who had been watching her watch her children, seemed to catch the something extra she'd put in her words, and he smiled.

"Let's go."

The Tryout

Ryan, Skylar, and Charlie stood anxiously at the rail. They had stopped by Storm's stall to wish him good luck. Skylar gave him a handful of peppermints. They were pleasantly surprised to find out that peppermints were an old favorite of his, from back on the farm with Mr. Shilling. Skylar was particularly happy that they had brought back a part of his past without even knowing it.

Charlie didn't think anyone else noticed, because they were all wrapped up in the excitement of meeting Ben, but she could tell that Storm had retreated a bit from the horse he had become at their barn. Maybe he was picking up on the fact that he was back at a racing establishment. She was getting worried: both for him and for the excitement that they all felt in having him step on the track. Charlie had no idea what he would do when Storm stepped onto the dirt oval for the first time since his last race.

It was clear that Storm remembered Ben. He whinnied and nickered with excitement when Ben called out to him, and there was no stopping him from making a beeline straight for Ben, when his stall door opened. The hesitation about the track hadn't left him, but his muscles relaxed a bit, and Charlie could tell he was willing to go along with them, if only for the sake of his old friend.

Jenny was going to ride him. As petite as she was, she was also Doug's top exercise rider. Charlie liked the fact that Storm's rider would be a female. She seemed to have a calming demeanor and hopefully wouldn't push him.

Charlie, Ryan, and Skylar stood aside as they tacked up Storm with a small jockey saddle and bridle. Ryan watched Jenny closely. He also observed the entire process, his factual mind taking in all the steps. But was he watching Jenny for other reasons? Charlie made a mental note to ask Doug more about this girl.

"Why don't you all go stand by the rail. We will bring Storm out and gallop him a bit so Jenny can get to know him," Doug said.

They were glued to the rail watching Jenny gallop Storm around the track. The horse was beautiful. He had a great tempo in his stride and didn't seem concerned about the other goings on around him. Since it was late afternoon, there were not a lot of other horses on the track.

Doug walked up next to Charlie. Goose bumps immediately rose on her arms.

"Jenny is a pretty good rider," Charlie said, attempting to direct his focus anywhere but at herself. It didn't work, he looked right at her when he spoke.

"She ought to be; I taught her myself," he said. Charlie looked at him, confused.

"You hired someone who didn't even know how to ride?" she asked.

"Not exactly. She's my niece. When I bought the farm, I built a house for my sister's family on the far side of the property. Jenny has been helping out around here since she could walk."

"Oh, that's nice. I thought she looked a little too young to be an actual employee."

"Yeah, she's still in high school, but her mom homeschools her, and Jenny gets to come over to the stables when she's done each day and help out. She's actually gotten to be a pretty critical part of the farm, I don't know how I'd get everything done without her."

"Well Storm seems to like her too," Charlie said. Her eyes had drifted over to where her horse was, and her mind followed.

"How does he look?" he asked.

"How does he look to you?" she asked, afraid to look over at him. Charlie wanted this time to be about Storm, she couldn't keep getting caught up in the crush she was beginning to develop on this man. She needed his feedback on her horse.

"Well, he has put on some weight since I saw him at the track and that's great. He needs to be muscled up to be fit for racing. So far, he shows no aversion to the track, nor is he spooky. Those are positive signs from a two-year-old." Doug raised his arm. Jenny moved forward in her irons and started pumping at Storm to move faster.

Nothing happened.

Storm seemed perfectly content to just continue to gallop. One, two, three, four. No change in his rhythm. After they passed, one of Doug's horses in training ventured toward them and Doug waved him over.

"Let her out a bit and breeze up past that grey horse out there," he instructed. The jockey and horse did what Doug told them. They took off and came up on Storm from behind.

Storm's ears flickered at the approaching horse and he recoiled, shrinking into a smaller version of himself. He actually slowed down. Jenny continued to try and push him on, pumping her arms at him. No response. Charlie could feel the frown on her face and when she looked over at Ryan and Skylar, she saw that their faces matched her own.

"He doesn't look like he has any interest in racing. Even with another horse, he doesn't seem to be competitive," Doug commented.

"You don't know our horse," Ryan said flatly. He continued to gaze out at Storm and Jenny. She had slowed him to a trot and had turned around. She came back to where everyone was standing.

"I'm sorry," she said. "I couldn't get him to work any faster. He was great at the warm up, totally responded to my cues, but when I asked him to move out, he had no interest." Storm stood grandly in front of the rail. He tossed his head a couple of times, looking right at Charlie.

"He is a beauty, for sure," Doug said. "Maybe you should retire him and go to the breeding barn? Have you looked at his pedigree?"

"Fully," Ryan spoke up. "He has a great family tree, a racing family tree. He can run!"

"Ryan, you can't force a horse to love to run. Sometimes they just don't," Doug replied.

"His pedigree isn't the problem, and neither is his willingness. This isn't the Storm I knew. They did more damage than I thought." Ben had his fists clenched on the rail. "We have to-" He didn't get to finish his sentence. All of a sudden, Storm raised his head high and took a deep breath through his nostrils. They quivered in anticipation. Something was going through his mind. Charlie looked around.

"Where is Skylar?" she asked. Everyone looked around for the smallest member of their party.

"She was here a minute ago when we were watching Storm," Ryan said. Then Charlie spotted her. She was way down the backside of the track. She waved over at the group. That's when Charlie heard her. Loud and clear.

"Here, Storm! You're it! Come get me!" she yelled. "Come on Stormy. TAG, YOU'RE IT!" Storm pranced in place, his ears going a mile a minute, honing in on where Skylar's voice was coming from. He locked on.

Jenny had gotten tight in the saddle while Storm had been prancing around: thankfully or she wouldn't have been prepared for the quick spin Storm took to take off down the track to "find" Skylar.

Like back at the farm, Storm flattened out, gaining speed with each stride. Charlie's paddocks weren't large, so though they had seen Storm run, they had never seen him in full flight. What a sight to behold. Low to the ground, his stride ate up the track. Jenny was a blur on his back.

Storm's ears flicked back and forth as he searched out Skylar for their game of tag. Skylar was in the middle of the track, herself prancing up and down, waiting for her playmate to arrive. Storm's stride shortened as he got close, and he pulled up just short of Skylar, and nudged her shoulder with his nose. Prancing once again and tossing his head. Charlie looked over at Doug.

"Well?" She asked as she looked at his shocked expression.

"We have got to figure out how to get this horse to the races!" Charlie laughed and glanced over at Ben. He had a smile on his face now, too: hope replacing the despair that been there just moments ago.

They both turned and looked down the track at Skylar giving Storm a huge hug around his neck and inserting a peppermint in his mouth. Charlie belatedly realized that her nine-year-old was standing in the middle of a track with strange horses all around. As calmly as she could, she beckoned Skylar over to her.

"Honey, you have got to be more careful," she said when Skylar was safe at her side.

"Oh, Mom, I think you worry too much." Charlie wasn't convinced, but Skylar was okay now, and after a few deep breaths, Charlie was able to join in the conversation about how amazing their horse was.

The Plan

It was obvious that Storm had the speed to win races, but getting him to want to run was going to be a challenge. His tryout at Doug's farm had been over two weeks ago.

After Jenny walked Storm back to the rail, with Skylar at his side, it was decided that Storm would go back with Charlie and the kids for a few weeks. That way Storm would hopefully know that they were not abandoning him. Similar to dropping an animal at a kennel, it's best if the animal knows its family will be back to pick him up. It's a good idea to have the animal stay just a few hours, then just for one night, all in an effort to work up to, say, a week-long trip. Each time the animal gets picked up, it reinforces that the kennel is not a bad place, and more importantly, that his family will return.

Charlie wanted Storm to know that when he returned to Shamrock Hill Farm for training, they would not be abandoning him. He had only been with them four weeks at their farm, and she knew just leaving him at a new place would make him retreat to his old somber self very quickly, no matter who was around him. It would be in his mind: another non-caring owner.

After they put Storm back in his stall at Shamrock Hill, Jenny asked Ryan and Skylar if they wanted to help her around the barn. They both jumped at the chance. Charlie knew the kids had different motives. She imagined Skylar wanted to see the other horses, and Ryan just wanted to follow Jenny around. Doug and Charlie went to his office to chat about the logistics of racing Storm.

"Well, you certainly have surprised me, Charlie," Doug started off. "I've bred and raised some speedy horses, but I can pretty much say, even without a stopwatch, that Storm's little run out there was the fastest quarter mile I have seen in a long time." Charlie couldn't stop smiling. She put her hand in front of her mouth to hide her goofy grin.

"Don't hide behind your hand," Doug softly said. He reached up and slowly moved her hand away from her mouth. His eyes locked on her lips. Charlie sucked in her breath with a hiccup. His thumb slowly ran its way along her bottom lip. Without even realizing it, her tongue wetted her own lips: her mouth craving the kiss that she hoped would soon follow. It had been such a long time…

Charlie moved away quickly, briefly locking eyes with Doug. She wasn't ready. What if she'd forgotten how? What if she messed it up?

"We knew Storm was fast, but we hadn't ever seen him go that fast," Charlie stammered, returning to the topic at hand. Doug's sexy smirk had returned to his mouth.

"Well, Mrs. Jenkins. It's seems we have a conundrum. You have a very fast horse, as far as I have seen, but he doesn't care to use his talent to win races. It's not like we can plant Skylar in the middle of the racetrack and ask all the horses to play tag.

"There are also other things to consider. Who are you going to have train him? Who will be his jockey? It takes a lot of time and money to train a racehorse. Are you prepared to invest in this horse? It takes dedication, determination, and a lot of luck to win horse races, and everyone is involved: the owner, the trainer, the rider, the groom. Everyone spends all this time and money and the chance of you winning even one race is quite low."

Charlie slowly walked around and looked at all his pictures and trophies. Doug was right, of course. What was she thinking? Her mind drifted to the last four weeks and how happy their little group had become. How Ryan had come alive researching Storm's background, and his private chats with Storm: Skylar's chit-chat and gossip and peppermints, her reading in the field, and teaching a lost horse to love to run: her own early morning grooming sessions, finding a reason to get out of bed in the morning; all three of them finding closeness again in the common love of a horse. Storm helped blow away the somber cloud that Peter's death had left over each of them.

It would be easy to just bring Storm home and let him live out his life with Sarge and Hershey, hanging in the field: but was that just taking them back to the same routine they had adopted after Peter's death?

Training Storm would bring change and take them away from the plateau where they had just barely been getting through each day, looking for a reason to get to the next.

Storm was their new reason. He was a Thoroughbred, born and bred to race. They had taken a horse that didn't have a reason to live either, and helped him to love life again. They were all in this together: the kids, Storm, and Charlie. They all needed this new adventure, a new path in life. Charlie talked quietly,

"Eighteen months ago, my husband died of cancer. The cancer not only took his life, but it also took the life out of the rest of us. The kids and I, we have each been dealing with the loss in different ways, and I was doing the worst with it. Four weeks ago, I did something spontaneous, something I would never have done until I looked into the eyes of this animal crying out for help. Someone mentioned to me that you can look into the soul of an animal through their eyes." Charlie briefly looked over at Doug, recalling their time at the side of the track. He silently waited for her to continue.

"It turns out I needed that help. And not only that, but my kids needed it. Storm has brought our family happiness, laughter, and fun. What we have provided to him, love and support, he has returned to us. We won't abandon him. I know he has the will to win and race. It is deep in his eyes. I have seen it. What Ryan said is right, Storm has the bloodlines to race and to win. We just need to help him find his way back: like he has helped us," she finished.

Doug was quiet for a few minutes, just watching her. Charlie looked back at him determinedly. She didn't want him to think she would back away from the challenge by looking away.

"I can pay for his training, Doug. I don't know a thing about all this racing stuff, but I know you. Will you help us?" she asked.

The Money

"Doug, welcome to the Stormy Express! That's a horrible name. I'll think of something better," said Charlie. Her little speech had driven the rest of the doubt from her own mind, and apparently Doug's as well.

"I'd like to help you," Doug said.

"Help me what? Come up with a name? Honestly, I was gonna outsource that job to Ryan and Skylar."

"No, I'd like to help you pay for Storm's training."

She stopped everything. She wasn't even breathing. "Charlie?"

"I'm sorry, didn't you just get through telling me how expensive that is?"

"That's exactly why I want to help."

"Doug, I appreciate the offer, but I can't take that kind of money from you. I felt bad about eating lunch here, because I felt like I was taking advantage of your hospitality! There's no way I can justify this."

"You can consider it an investment, if that helps."

"You are an extremely generous man, but I think I've already asked more favors from you than I can possibly pay back."

"I wouldn't say that," Doug said with a slight smirk.

"I will pay for Storm and his training," Charlie reiterated.

Doug nodded. Charlie moved in to kiss his cheek, but he moved his head and their lips met. It was very brief, and very tentative, but it woke her up.

"Sorry, I shouldn't have done that. What?" He took a step back. Charlie had started laughing.

"Nothing, it's just that I'd started to wonder if I would remember how to do that."

"I think you have an excellent memory," Doug said. He grabbed her hand to pull her closer, but she resisted.

"I…I can't do this with you right now. I mean, I like you, and I liked that," he smiled and she blushed, "but I don't actually know you, and I have kids, and I just…" all of her words had gotten lost as she drew her gaze to his lips, and the gentle way he squeezed her hand.

"You need time. I get it. For now, we'll keep it professional." He let go of her hand and held his out. Charlie smiled and shook his hand. They stayed that way for a bit longer than necessary: holding hands, professionally.

Charlie was in a daze the whole way home. She barely heard the kids talking excitedly about everything that happened. There was so much to think about. As soon as she got home and got the kids settled in bed and the horses taken care of, she made a list:

1) find a way to pay for Storm

2) figure out what to do about Doug

She thought it would be a much longer list, but after she wrote the second thing, she couldn't think of anything else that needed her immediate attention. As the second task seemed far too daunting for her at the moment, she decided to focus on the first thing she'd written.

How to pay for training a racehorse? The kids, bless them, had offered up their allowance. Ryan volunteered to get a job and put his hockey playing on hold. None of that was acceptable. Charlie would figure something out. She knew she wouldn't use Peter's life insurance proceeds. That was safely invested for their daily life needs and the kids' futures and colleges. Her income from the *Leesburg Weekly* covered the small extras and the horses.

She did not have extra cash hanging around to support a racehorse. Doug said the average cost for a racehorse in training is $40,000 annually. That didn't include the race fees, which could be pretty significant depending on what races they ended up choosing for Storm.

One night a few days after they had all visited Doug's farm, Charlie was tossing and turning, trying to sleep: she suddenly sat upright. Doug had told her to think of it as an investment…

Her mind started working to piece together this idea. She'd read something about a show rider raising money to purchase a show horse with something called, "crowd-funding." He had set up a website and asked people to donate to his purchase. The people who gave money didn't have the liability of owning a horse and paying the expenses, but got to experience the fun and enjoyment: they received autographed pictures, videos and email updates on the horse and its showing career. They *invested* in the horse.

Could she get enough people interested in Storm and his return to racing? Could she make this work? She could write a feel-good story. They could do a website, a Facebook page, and a Twitter account, all to update the fans on Storm's progress. Ryan could keep it updated. He was a whiz with the internet. Charlie lay back down, finally able to close her eyes. At least she had a plan to focus on in the morning.

The View From Behind the Starting Gate

Crowd-funding. Have you heard of it? It's being used in all areas of our economy these days, from non-profits to rock bands. It's the concept of getting a lot of people to contribute money for a greater cause. I am wondering if you all would be interested. You see, the cost of racing a Thoroughbred is quite a lot. More than I can drum up: at least until he starts winning some money. My kids offered their allowance, my friends and family offered to help, but that feels too much like charity. Then I thought of all of you following Storm's progress. Would you be interested in helping him reach his potential? We can't promise anything, winning wise, but we want to give him the best chance we can, and for that, we need you.

Have you ever wanted to say you own a racehorse? Some horses these days are owned by syndicates made up of people with a financial interest in the horse. They are required to contribute each month to cover the expenses of keeping the horse. These expenses can vary and get quite expensive, from food and bedding, to trainer and jockey fees.

What I am thinking is that if I raise a fixed amount that will take Storm through his ramp up phase as we get him back to the track: in return, we will give you updates and exclusive access to watch him train and cheer him on. You won't own him, but you will be a part of his exclusive, VIP fan club. Think of it like a membership fee. There would be no further obligation. My hope is that he will start earning his own keep once we get him back into the races. I know it's a pipe dream: the odds are slim, but if you are willing to try to help us overcome them, then read on.

I don't believe in levels of exclusivity. If you believe in Storm, any amount you give would be going to his cause. I only ask that you commit a minimum of $50.

Would you give $50 to be able to say you helped a horse with a lot of potential, win a race? How about if that horse continued to win? Would you enjoy inside access to watch him?

I believe in Storm. Do you?

✷✷✷✷✷✷✷✷✷✷✷✷✷✷✷

There, she'd done it. She'd put it out there.

She spent the day worrying about it. What would people do? Would they think she was a shyster? A thief who was going to take their money and run? Her hands were shaking. She felt crazy. She had $10,000 she could commit to start training Storm at Doug's farm. She was going to borrow it against her 401k from her days of working long ago. Doug and Charlie agreed that he would give her a discount on the training until Storm proved that he could be entered in a race, and wanted to run; that was all the financial help she would accept from him. If Storm did want to run, more staff needed to come on board, such as a groom, hot walker, etc. and the cost of staying onsite at the track. For the time-being, his training would take place at Shamrock Hill Farm, under the watchful eye of Doug and his team of experts. Charlie would meet them all, and hear Doug's game plan, when she took Storm back to the farm to begin his formal training.

Charlie looked at next weekend on her calendar. She only had seven days left to enjoy her quiet time with Storm. To make sure he knew how much he was loved. To ensure him that even though he wasn't on their farm, he was in good hands. Since the kids were still in school, they couldn't be onsite every day, but Charlie had committed to traveling to the farm several times a week by herself, and then with the kids on the weekends, depending on Ryan's hockey game schedule. Luckily, Skylar's horse show season was winding down and she didn't have much on the calendar. Charlie was pretty sure both kids would push aside their weekend activities to spend some time at Shamrock Hill with Storm, but they still needed to keep their own commitments.

Seven days. Only seven days until Charlie needed to jump into the deep end of the pool. She hoped to God she wouldn't drown.

Training Begins

Charlie decided to take Sarge along to stay with Storm when he went into training. Even though she couldn't be there every day, Storm would have a familiar face. They drove again down the beautiful long driveway and pulled up to the barn where the horses would be staying for the next two weeks. It was mid-November and Doug wanted to get Storm's training underway quickly. Since he would be three years old on January 1 along with all Thoroughbreds, he was behind in his training.

"Mom, do you think Storm is going to be happy here? Why did Hershey have to stay behind? He would be a good friend to Storm," Skylar said.

"He certainly would, Skylar, but I can only afford to bring one horse, and Sarge spent years in this type of environment. He will be able to ride out on the track with Storm and keep him calm." *Or hopefully encourage him to run faster,* thought Charlie.

Doug and Charlie had talked briefly about the first few weeks of training. He was still mulling over Storm's aversion to running. They had decided it would be best to start him off galloping with Sarge to build up his muscles and endurance. It was important for him to enjoy his time on the track. Doug wanted to see how Storm did with the starting gate as well.

Over the four weeks he would be at the farm, Storm would continue to enjoy time outside in the paddocks and hopefully put on some more weight as well. The racing campaign of a three-year-old Thoroughbred takes its toll on each horse differently.

Doug had been incredulous when Charlie told him of her intention of racing Storm in the Kentucky Derby. She remembered that phone call with a smile.

"You want to race him in what?!" he exclaimed over the phone. He had seen Storm's race to Skylar and knew he had some speed, but he had no real idea what kind of animal he was taking in.

"The Kentucky Derby," Charlie said slowly, knowing he thought she was nuts. "Ryan, Skylar, and I have decided together that we want to race in the Derby." Doug sighed loudly. He knew that when she mentioned her kids as part of the decision, it was final.

Charlie and the kids had spent an evening discussing the Derby over dinner while Storm was still enjoying himself at their farm. Ryan had done his research, of course.

Over the last few years there have been over 23,000 Thoroughbreds born that could ultimately have the chance to run in the Kentucky Derby. Of those, over half don't ever make it to the racetrack due to various circumstances, such as lack of talent or injury. The chance of running in the Derby was daunting. Storm was behind in his training and didn't seem to like racing. They were way behind the curve.

"Mom, what if Storm took a traditional approach to racing?" Ryan asked through a mouth full of food. Charlie wasn't a huge fan of the way he shoveled everything down these days, but if he was talking to her, she wasn't about to nag at him.

"What are you proposing?" she asked.

"Well, back in the 50s, 60s, and 70s, horses raced a lot. Not like nowadays, where they race infrequently.

"Secretariat raced twice in April leading up to the Triple Crown races.

He ran in five races over the ten week period, winning all of them except for the Wood Memorial in which he finished third. Nowadays, horses race once every four to six weeks or longer, some don't even race as a two year old, some horses entered into the Derby have only raced once or twice before the big race. Affirmed raced twice a month in March and April, winning all four races and then went on to win not just the Derby, but the Preakness and the Belmont. "

"What does that have to do with Storm?" Skylar asked. She had a tendency to get frustrated when she didn't understand things like this, but it always sounded like she was being rude. Ryan glared over at her, and continued speaking to Charlie.

"The Derby is limited to twenty horses. In the last few years, they changed the way those twenty horses are chosen. Now there is a point system, involving certain races. The horses with the most points earn their way into the starting gate on Derby day. It's called the "Road to the Kentucky Derby." This year there are thirty-five races that began in September. Nineteen of the races are named prep races and the points that can be earned are minimal - ten for first, four for second, two for third, and one point for fourth place.

"The Championship Series, the remaining sixteen races, begins in late February. The series consists of two legs. The first leg, eight races run from mid-February to mid-March, give fifty points for first, twenty for second, ten for third and five points for fourth. The second leg, the eight races run from the end of March until mid-April, awards the most points of them all: one hundred points for first place, forty for second, twenty for third, and ten points for fourth.

"I bet Storm could get all the points!" Skylar piped in. Ryan glared over at her again. He was on a roll and his excitement shone in his eyes. Charlie intervened before a fight started.

"This is important stuff for us to know Skylar, especially if we want to try and get Storm into the Derby. We can't just sign him up. He has to qualify. Why don't we just listen to the rest of what Ryan has to say, and if you have any more questions, I'll try to answer them after he's done?" Skylar deflated a little, and nodded her head.

Ryan, un-phased by his sister's despair, continued, "So you see, if a horse hasn't run much at all and wins one of these last races, he would be pretty much guaranteed a spot in the Derby depending on the other competitors," Ryan said. "If a candidate raced a lot in the prep races, his points would be nowhere near those earned in the later races. There is one last race, called the wild card, that has a ten-four-two-one point system, for someone that needs a few last points to qualify.

"The races are held all over the country at different tracks, from Florida to New York to California. In the first year the point system was implemented, the top qualifier had just 150 points and the twentieth qualifier had twenty points." Ryan looked over at Charlie. She was deep in thought.

"By the time Storm is ready to race, the Championship Series will already have started, which isn't too bad, since the prep race points aren't that much. I think that we should race Storm as much as we can, as long as he stays healthy. He needs to remember what it's like to race. He's never won a race, we know that. He needs to win a race and get that feeling of accomplishment. Like when I scored my first goal in hockey, remember, Mom?" Charlie nodded.

Ryan hadn't taken much to sports, but he had decided to play hockey because that was what all his friends were doing. He loved being a part of the group. Peter would get up early and drive him to practice. Ryan never complained. He would do the drills and work hard, but he didn't have a mean bone in his body, so he had a hard time with the crashing and checking necessary to get the puck away from the other team. Ryan would always skate his hardest and defend his goal, but he never scored. He always cheered on his teammates.

One game, the coach was short on players, so he told Ryan he was putting him on the front line. Ryan was nervous but knew his team was relying on him. In the final minutes, the score was tied. Ryan was on the side of the net, and all of a sudden the puck came right at him. A defender was also chasing the puck. Ryan dropped his shoulder and skated as fast as he could for the puck, the defender bounced off Ryan's shoulder: at the same time, he took a swing at the puck. Into the goal it went. The fans were delirious. The team jumped all over Ryan for his game winner. Charlie could remember his smile as he turned to look at Peter and her in the crowd: it could have lit up the entire rink. From that point on, Ryan knew he could play hockey with the best of them and wasn't afraid to go after the puck when necessary. The feeling of getting that goal overcame all his reservations. Charlie saw him putting that puck under his pillow for a month after that game.

Charlie wondered if a horse would know the difference between winning and losing. She knew Doug thought so. He believed in a horse's soul, their heart and courage, but did Charlie have the courage it would take to travel down the path ahead of her? A horse race here and there was one thing, but the Kentucky Derby?

Ryan continued, "All of his races don't need to be in the series, as we certainly can't travel all over the country with Storm." Charlie could tell he was trying to placate her. Skylar, however, was having none of it.

"But why not? Wouldn't we want all of his fans to see him? Isn't that what you said, Mom, when you asked people to help contribute to his racing? We could take him from track to track and announce his arrival and have a party in his honor, with his fans."

Charlie's mind was spinning. The cost of racing this horse was going up exponentially, but if he could win some races here and there, Storm could contribute to his own success. They would definitely need to get him to win.

"Another thing, Mom: don't you want Storm to get used to travel, since he will need to go from Kentucky to Maryland for the Preakness and then to New York for the Belmont?" Skylar said innocently. Charlie raised her eyebrows at her daughter.

"You certainly have high expectations for our big grey fella." Her heart skipped a beat at the largeness of it all.

"Mom, he's the real deal. Jenny said she had never felt the power Storm exhibited on the track last week when he took off. She had to hold on tight or he would have just blown her right off his back." Ryan looked down at the table, trying to hide his blush at mentioning the petite exercise rider. He continued, looking over at Skylar,

"The other thing about racing more than every four to six weeks, is that the Preakness is only two weeks after the Derby and the Belmont is three week after that. Storm will need to have the routine as well as the endurance to be able to make it through that schedule, just like Secretariat." He was making his point.

"What about Storm's health?" Charlie asked. "There has got to be a reason why trainers today don't race their horses more than once every four to six weeks."

"Probably because trainers have different philosophies, I guess. I am sure there are a certain number of days necessary for a horses' body to recover a big workout: probably short for short races and longer for longer races. It may be based on the time clocked during the race or how hard it was to get to the wire. Was the track fast or muddy? Lots of variables, but I think we can ask Mr. Doug about it, and I can keep track of all the stats on Storm's workouts, his races and all that. I think once he starts, he will be hard to stop, especially after he wins a couple of races." Ryan smiled. He had it all planned out.

"Okay, smarty pants. Let's see what you got," said Charlie. "Skylar, it's time for you to head to bed. Ryan and I will let you know what we come up with. You need to make sure you always have peppermints." Ryan started taking out the rest of his papers while Charlie tucked Skylar into bed.

"Mom, do you think Storm will miss us?" she asked. "I want to go stay at Mr. Doug's farm with him. What if he forgets to play tag with Storm?" Skylar yawned as she brushed her teeth.

Imagining Doug, a grown man, playing hide and seek with a horse, made her smile. She quickly had to put that out of her mind though, as the thoughts progressed to him playing hide and seek with her. Finding her, maybe in an empty stall…

"Goodnight, sweet pea. I love you." Charlie gently closed her door.

✱✱✱✱✱✱✱✱✱✱✱✱✱

Ryan and Charlie spent the next two hours looking over his research and all the race options on the Road to the Kentucky Derby Championship Series. They had no idea what they were doing, no experience in the art of horse racing, but they had a love for their horse and lots of historical data. Throw in some common sense and a bit of luck, and Charlie thought maybe they would get somewhere. Once again, her mind drifted to Doug. He said to trust your gut. Storm would help show them the way.

They had decided to travel some, but not across the country, so that took out the racetracks in California, New Mexico, Texas, and Arizona, where some of the major races would be run. They also wouldn't encounter some of the major horse players vying for the points. Just as well, if they made it, they would see them soon enough.

Based upon initial conversations with Doug, they knew that their road would start in Maryland at Laurel Racetrack. Doug wanted to get him used to being back on the track in good spirits and with a positive experience. After a race or two there, they would start their path. They had wanted to take Storm to Pimlico, but live racing didn't start there until after March 1, so they needed to build their timeline before deciding.

Ryan pulled out his schedule of races in the Championship Series. They crossed off the west coast tracks and the races in February. They figured they would stay only on the east coast to reduce the travel. If they were going to race Storm a bit more often than the norm, they didn't want him to have to deal with extended travel as well. Knowing they were late to the party, they needed to add Keeneland to the list for any last minute points they might need. If Storm did well and qualified early, they could rest him the few weeks leading up to the first weekend in May, when the Derby would run. Their chart started to look like this:

Kentucky Derby Championship Series

Date	Race	Racetrack	Distance	1st	2nd	3rd	4th
Feb. 21	Fountain of Youth	Gulfstream Park (FL)	1 1/16 Miles	50	20	10	5
Feb. 21	Risen Star	Fair Grounds (LA)	1 1/16 Miles	50	20	10	5
March 7	Gotham	Aqueduct (NY)	1 1/16 Miles	50	20	10	5
March 7	Tampa Bay Derby	Tampa Bay Downs (FL)	1 1/16 Miles	50	20	10	5
March 7	San Felipe	Santa Anita (CA)	1 1/16 Miles	50	20	10	5
March 14	Rebel	Oaklawn Park (AR)	1 1/16 Miles	50	20	10	5
March 21	Spiral	Turfway Park (KY)	1 1/8 Miles	50	20	10	5
March 22	Sunland Derby	Sunland Park (NM)	1 1/8 Miles	50	20	10	5
March 28	Florida Derby	Gulfstream Park (FL)	1 1/8 Miles	100	40	20	10
March 28	Louisiana Derby	Fair Grounds (LA)	1 1/8 Miles	100	40	20	10
March 28	UAE Derby	Meydan Racecourse (India)	1 3/16 Miles	100	40	20	10
April 4	Wood Memorial	Aqueduct (NY)	1 1/8 Miles	100	40	20	10
April 4	Santa Anita Derby	Santa Anita (CA)	1 1/8 Miles	100	40	20	10
April 11	Arkansas Derby	Oaklawn Park (AR)	1 1/8 Miles	100	40	20	10
April 11	Blue Grass	Keeneland (KY)	1 1/8 Miles	100	40	20	10
April 18	Lexington (wild card)	Keeneland (KY)	1 1/16 Miles	10	4	2	1

Ryan looked up from his computer and sat back in his chair.

"Mom?" he asked, getting Charlie's attention. She had been researching the nuances of each of the races they were targeting on her iPad. She wanted to ensure it was the best selection.

"Yes, dear?" she replied.

"Well, it's November 15. The deadline for nominating Storm for the Triple Crown races is January 17 for $600. After that, we have until March 23 to file a late nomination for him, but it will cost $6,000."

Charlie pondered Ryan's comment. They wouldn't know if Storm was going to race at the Derby for a few months. Doug said it would take four to eight weeks to get him into racing shape.

"Well, I would rather lose the $600 than need to come up with the $6,000, wouldn't you?" She asked Ryan.

"Sure thing, Mom." Ryan smiled back at her. She made a reminder on her cell phone to send a check in mid-January to nominate their horse for the Kentucky Derby, Preakness, and Belmont – The Triple Crown of horse racing.

The Jockey

The sun was not up yet, but Charlie was standing and freezing in the early morning hour, standing next to the rail. She used to think getting up at 5 am for a horseshow was early, but now it was her favorite time of the morning: especially when she was at the track.

A racetrack in the early morning hours is beautiful: the grooms are the first to arrive to feed their charges. Horses hang their heads over their half doors, eager for their first meal of the day. Morning workouts begin around 6 am and the horses run with the sunrise. Several horses at a time are led onto the track for different levels of workout, maybe just walking or light jog. Others are sent out for a fast workout, called a "breeze." Generally, no more than two run alongside each other, for safety sake. Similar to any other athlete, a racehorse is on a strict workout schedule, and any change can mean the difference between a win and a loss.

This is also when younger horses are schooled in the starting gate and walked along the perimeter to look at the grandstand and other distractions of a racetrack. Many racetracks offer, "Breakfast at the Track," to encourage people to come and watch the horses workout. Not only does the early meal offer people the chance to see horses up close during their morning workouts, but the horses begin to learn to see people in the grandstand cheering them on, which will happen on race day.

Shamrock Hill Farm had a small training group at Laurel Racetrack that had arrived a few days ago. It was the first stop for Storm, in terms of determining if he had what it took to continue the path Ryan and Charlie had laid out for him.

Charlie couldn't imagine that Doug had ever had any other clients like her family. She smiled to herself. She couldn't decide if he was always so accommodating, or if maybe he had given her a little bit of special treatment. She liked to think he had kept things professional, but that could have just been wishful thinking. Usually their "business meetings" got cut short because she would forget important information due to the ridiculous butterflies she got in her stomach whenever she talked to him.

Charlie felt him approach behind her. She stood up a bit straighter.

"You ready?" he asked as he leaned on the rail next to her. She nodded. Still a bit too cold to chat: she was afraid her teeth would chatter. January in Maryland isn't warm. The day was expected to have a high of 40 degrees, but the morning started out at a brisk 25 degrees.

Ryan and Skylar had begged to watch Storm's first real track workout, but there was only so much school they could miss. They would be missing more than enough in the months to come. Charlie was suddenly very glad they weren't there. It had been a while since that first kiss in the office, and she didn't know if it was the beauty of the sunrise that made her feel romantic, or the fact that she hadn't had her coffee, but she was suddenly very aware of the way Doug's eyes lingered on her face and she moved closer to him.

"It's cold," said Charlie. He looked surprised at first, but put his arm around her all the same. She relaxed into him, and they stayed that way for several minutes: quietly watching the sun seep onto the track and the horses get ready for their day.

"I hope he's ready," Charlie sighed.

"Worried?" Doug teased.

"I just want him to be comfortable on his first trip back to a real track. Last time he was on one, he was in a sorry state of mind," she said.

Doug smiled, "He'll be fine. He's had great workouts at the farm, building muscle and more importantly, endurance. I'm eager to introduce him to Hunter."

Hunter Wilson was Doug's trainer. Hunter was down at Gulfstream Racetrack with a whole string of Shamrock Hill Farm horses in training. The group would not be back up in the area for a while. Today, Doug was running the show.

Charlie recalled their conversation the previous week at the farm.

"Why aren't you down in Florida with the rest of your racing horses?" She asked him, while watching Storm over the pasture rail. The winter sun was glistening off his dark grey coat, showing off his dapples. Occasionally, Storm would lift his head to look over at her, chewing his mouthful of grass. Like a school girl in love with her first pony, Charlie waved and blew him a kiss.

"Are you trying to get rid of me?" Doug asked, feigning a hurt tone. Charlie laughed.

"No, I'm just wondering why you chose to stay here with the misfits, is all. The horses with Hunter are bound to have better races than the ones you've got here."

Doug calmly rolled a piece of grass between his fingers. They were spending more and more time together as Storm's training progressed. Twice a week, Charlie would drop the kids off at school and then drive out to Shamrock Hill to keep a watchful eye on Storm. On the weekends, Charlie and the kids would get the chores done, attend Ryan's hockey games, and then head to the farm, which was always crawling with people as other owners visited their horses, and Doug was busy catering to their questions.

It was the weekdays, when the farm was quiet after the morning work and the workouts were done, that Charlie could just lean on the fence for hours and watch her horse. It didn't matter the weather, she was too attached. The new love of her life had four legs, and she loved every second she could spend with him.

It was also during those visits that Doug had started to show up around the barn more often, making sure his schedule coincided with Charlie's time at the farm. He would join her at the fence line. It was unnerving at first. Sometimes he would walk over, say hello, and then abruptly leave. Other times he would be on his cell phone. He'd walk by, wave and smile, and continue on.

More recently, he had started to linger longer at the fence with her. Today he'd already stayed longer than any other day. He continued to roll the piece of dead grass.

"I trust Hunter with my racing team, therefore, I don't feel like I need to be onsite every second. They do better without me," he smiled. Charlie was drawn deep into his blue eyes. The world pulled away and there she was with a handsome man, leaning against a rail, with horses surrounding them. Her breathing ran shallow. He watched her closely.

"My passion is trying to find out what makes a horse tick. They all have different personalities. You need to spend time with them, really get to know their likes and dislikes. I truly believe a horse will run its heart out, for the right reasons. You just need to find out what those reasons are." Charlie was mesmerized.

"I like to stay back here at the farm, working with the babies and the yearlings, as well as my project horses. I also need to run a business. I can't be waving and kissing at my horses all day." He laughed at her. Charlie lashed out at his shoulder for teasing her. He was quick. In an instant her hand was in his and he was holding it against his chest. His other arm pulled her to his chest.

"You are certainly an interesting woman, Charlie," he said softly. She didn't know what to do. The whole business relationship thing wasn't really working out for her, and it didn't seem like it was working for him either. She had instigated this particular instance, but was she really ready for more? She still hadn't talked to her kids, but what was she supposed to say? She didn't know what she wanted or expected, so how could she talk to them about it?

Peter flashed through her mind and she pulled her hand away quickly before he could entwine his fingers with hers, and stepped away. She stared over at Storm calmly chomping grass, taking long breaths to still her heart. Doug continued to lean against the fence and watch her closely. He didn't look hurt or offended that she'd taken her hand from him: somehow that made her feel worse about it. Here was this amazing guy who knew her situation and wasn't pressuring her one iota, and yet she was incapable of making up her mind about him.

That wasn't true; she knew how she felt about him. She just didn't know how to deal with how she felt about him. Stuck between a dead husband, whom she'd loved with all her heart, and a handsome, kind, horse-loving business owner: what was a girl to do?

"I've got to go, but next time maybe you can tell me a little about your husband," he said softly. He closed his hand over Charlie's on the fence, squeezed it, and walked off in the direction of the office. Her hand continued to tingle for a long time after he was gone.

****

Storm marched onto the track. A new rider was in the irons, named Travis. A real jockey. Jenny had been doing all the exercise rides at the farm, but now this was business.

Charlie had met Travis the day before. He seemed alright. Yes, ma'am and no, ma'am. He was one of Doug's top riders and could stick on the back of any of his project horses. Ben seemed to think Travis was a good choice, and Charlie respected that. Ben had been helping out a lot with Storm since that first day they'd met him. Doug had been kind enough to allow him to resume his old position as Storm's groom, which seemed to be equally pleasing to both Ben and Storm.

Though there hadn't been much change in his willingness to actually race, more of the playful nature he'd displayed sporadically, had come to the surface, and now Storm had progressed to chasing Charlie or Doug or

Ben down any time he saw them, in the hopes of getting a treat. They always complied, because it was so good to see him so carefree and happy, but for all the running he did in the field, they couldn't figure out how to get him to want to race. Charlie sighed and turned to watch Storm on the track.

She could see the breath coming from both the horse and rider in the pale morning light. Travis jogged Storm towards them.

"Keep it easy, Travis. Just try to get him used to being back at the track. Gallop him a mile and then see if he will breeze for you, three furloughs in fifty. Nice and easy," Doug instructed.

"Yes sir. Ma'am," He nodded his head at Charlie. She tried to smile. She was so nervous she could barely stand it. Off to the right, a commotion was going on. An unruly horse was trying to unseat its rider.

"Head off the opposite way for a light jog to avoid that craziness," Doug told Travis. As Storm jogged off, Charlie and Doug turned their attention to the commotion. There was quite a crowd gathering to try and calm the horse.

It was a beast of an animal: big and black, at least a hand bigger than Storm. He wanted none of the track or the rider on his back, who sat quietly. Charlie could see the jockey's mouth moving, talking, trying to calm the raging beast. No one could get close enough to get a hand on its bridle.

Charlie gasped suddenly, as the horse went straight up, pawing the air. He took a couple steps backwards and looked like he would tumble over on his back. The rider adjusted just slightly, the balance of weight bringing the horse back down to all fours. At no time did the rider yell or scream. He just sat quietly waiting for the horse to work through his show. Occasionally his hand would rub along the side of his neck with a calming touch.

Finally, after a few minutes, but what felt like forever, the big, black stallion stood still, his sides heaving. His temper tantrum was over. Like a calm parent, the rider on his back had not risen up to meet his anger, but sat quietly and waited for him to work through it.

Charlie noticed him giving the horse a quick pat, but he was still all business. The horse's trainer approached. The black eyes showed their whites at him, but the big horse stood still, ears turned back, listening to the murmurs of his rider. They had a short conversation. The rider jumped off, the lesson was over for today. A groom came forward and took the horse. As they walked past Doug and Charlie, the rider took off his helmet.

A long, blond ponytail fell down her back. A female jockey. Charlie was impressed and watched her closely. She was intently talking to the trainer, giving her thoughts on the horse and what needed to be done. He was listening closely.

"Who is she?" Charlie asked Doug. Her eyes stayed on the jockey's back as she walked back to the stables in the backstretch.

"Elizabeth Garrett: goes by Lilly. Works wonders with problem horses. She was a good jockey and was making quite a name for herself on the big stages - Churchill Downs, Keeneland, Aqueduct. Then one day she just up and hung up her riding silks: wouldn't take anymore rides. Rumor had it she lost her nerve, but as you can see, that is far from true. She spends her days at the lesser known tracks, helping trainers with horses that no one else can do anything with. She's kind of like our local racetrack horse whisperer," Doug said.

Charlie turned her attention back to Storm, galloping on the far side of the track. Travis settled down in his saddle, and moved his hands to step up the pace. Storm flicked his ears, but continued at his comfortable gallop.

Storm loved running with his ears forward, taking in all the sounds ahead of him. *At least he looks happy*, Charlie thought to herself. He was indeed very different than the downtrodden horse from last fall, with head hung low and ears laid back. Travis spent the next quarter mile continuing to try and get Storm to move on and increase his pace.

Nothing happened.

Travis made his way back to Doug and Charlie after going through the three quarters of a mile.

"Couldn't get him to move on, boss," Travis said, sweat running down his face. Doug had an intent look on his face, trying to figure out what to do next.

"I want her," Charlie said.

"Who?" Doug asked.

"Elizabeth Garrett," she replied. "I want Lilly to work with Storm."

"Didn't you hear me? She doesn't ride in races anymore," he said. "The rider I have lined up for Storm will do a great job with him. Plus Storm doesn't have a huge problem. He's not a bully, like that big black horse we just saw. He's got a great demeanor, anyone can ride him. We just need to get him to want to go fast."

"I guess..." Charlie replied, deep in thought.

****

A short while after Storm was done with his introductory gallop, Charlie headed to the track kitchen to grab a cup of coffee. As she waited in line, she noticed Lilly sitting by herself, reading the morning paper. Charlie filled her cup and headed over to the jockey's table.

"Mind if I sit down?" she asked. Lilly raised her eyes from her paper, an inquisitive look on her face.

"Not at all."

Charlie held out her hand.

"I'm Charlie. Charlie Jenkins." Lilly shook Charlie's outstretched hand with firmness, yet her hand was soft at the same time.

"Lilly," she replied. Charlie knew she had to say something about Storm. Doug would have her head, but her gut was guiding her actions right now, and she knew this was the right thing for her horse.

"I saw you out on the track this morning with that big black stallion. He was certainly a handful," Charlie commented.

"He's just scared," she said. "Too many owners, trainers, jockeys: too many agendas and instructions. Sometimes you just need to go back to the basics."

"Well, it was great to watch you work with him," said Charlie, unsure of how to take the conversation where she wanted it to go.

"What can I do for you, Ms. Jenkins?" Lilly asked.

"Charlie, please." She decided the direct approach was best, and she cut to the chase. "I want you to ride my horse." Lilly raised her blond eyebrows. Her face was very readable and Charlie knew she was wondering who the heck she had let sit down at her table.

"You see, I am new to all the racing stuff. I have a wonderful horse that I know can run, with the right rider," Charlie firmly said.

"What is wrong with him?" she asked.

"What makes you think there is something wrong with him?" Charlie asked back.

"Ms. Jenkins...Charlie," she corrected herself, "I usually don't get asked to ride a racehorse unless there is a problem. I don't ride the good ones, ma'am. I work with the difficult ones." She continued to stare at Charlie, her question about what was wrong with Storm still hanging in the air between them.

"We haven't been able to figure out how to get him to love running like a Thoroughbred should. He has the speed, we have seen it. He has great bloodlines, we researched it all. He just had some bad experiences, we don't know the extent of them, and he doesn't get in the game when he is up against other horses." Lilly continued to look at Charlie, her hands folded over her paper.

"He has the heart of a champion, I know it. I just need to figure out how to ignite his desire. I watched you with that black horse. You have the patience. You can help me. You can help him," Charlie concluded, holding her breath. Lilly sat back in her chair, assessing Charlie's comments. Her black helmet glistened on the chair next to her, while her long slender fingers drummed the table.

"Charlie, I don't-"

"Listen, I'm desperate. My kids and I are kind of counting on this, and I'm willing to try anything. I know you don't ride anymore, Doug told me that, but he also told me you're the local horse whisperer, and I think my horse could use someone like you," Charlie said. She was laying it all on the line. Lilly was quiet for a second.

"Doug?" she asked.

"Doug Walker," Charlie said. "He's helping me out with my horse,"

Lilly smiled.

"Doug's a good guy. He's been through a lot, but he gets it," she paused. "I'll meet you out at his barn on the backstretch at 5 am tomorrow." She grabbed her helmet and put it on her head, tucking in a few stray blond strands. Lilly held out her hand and said,

"You know, Charlie, most owners don't hang around the racetrack. And actually this is the first time I have ever met one of the owners of a horse I was going to ride. Most times I am approached by the trainer as a last resort."

"Well, I'm sticking around," said Charlie. "I want to make sure Storm has the best team around him." Lilly raised her eyebrows again, a curious look crossing her face.

"That's refreshing," she said as she turned around and walked out the door. Charlie held in her squeal of excitement until Lily had gone, but only barely. Lilly was on board: this was a win. She was well on her way to having a dream team, and her horse was one step closer to racing in the Kentucky Derby. This was good for Charlie: Storm not racing was ridiculously hard on the controlling part of her personality. She wanted him to run. She wanted him to race. She gave him everything she thought he needed, but he wouldn't go for it. She couldn't control Storm. Well, giving him the best rider she could control, and she had just done that.

Charlie briefly wondered what Doug would say: nothing she couldn't flirt her way out of, probably, which was also a win. She was having a pretty good day. Then she stopped.

What did Lilly mean, "he's been through a lot?" Charlie had never once heard Doug mention any kind of hardship, in all the time she'd known him. Not that she expected people to just come right out and tell her their problems, or anything: but he'd kissed her, and she thought he liked her…

She was suddenly feeling very foolish. She had no idea who this man was. He knew her. He knew the hardest thing she'd ever gone through. Out of necessity, he'd met her children: she'd let him into her world and she'd been so focused on him fitting, that she hadn't thought about his world at all. After she'd opened up about Peter, she didn't think there would be other difficult things for them to discuss, but that was just her being wrapped up in herself.

Charlie couldn't stop thinking about it. As she walked out of the cafeteria, she saw Doug talking to a few of his workers. He had an easy smile on his face, and he seemed to be perfectly content. Charlie turned away and headed for the barn: she needed to clear her head.

Painful Memories

When Charlie checked in on Storm, she found him happily munching his hay. He walked over and put his muzzle in her hand, looking for peppermints. She pulled one out of her pocket.

"Hey, fella, we are going to work through this issue you have. You and me. Well, and a few others. I don't know what's holding you back, but I know you have it in you to be a great racehorse." She rubbed his neck.

Storm pushed his head against her, his ears lopping to the side in a state of relaxation. When he didn't find any more treats, he returned to his hay. His grey coat glistened from all the grooming, the good diet, and his daily gallops. His muscles rippled underneath. He was still the color of a dark thundercloud.

Charlie sat in the chair outside his stall and pulled out her laptop.

The View From Behind the Starting Gate
Did you know grey horses are not born grey? Yep, they are born with a different base color, commonly bay, chestnut, or black. As the colt gets older, white hairs start to replace the base color and his coat starts to lighten. During the stages of the greying process, a horse may become dappled. A

dappled grey has dark rings with lighter hairs on the outside of the rings over the majority of the horses' body. It's quite a beautiful pattern.

Once a horse completely changes over its base coat, it will either be pure white, or flea-bitten. Flea-bitten. Doesn't that sound awful? I guess it's because the horse's white coat is interspersed with small speckles or, "freckles" throughout. I personally would prefer using the term dot-to-dot, as it reminds me of those coloring books that you draw a picture by connecting the dots. I wonder what different scenes you could draw on a dot-to-dot horse coat. Alas, I digress.

Back to Storm, that's why you're still reading, right? He is richly-dappled grey, as you can see from his pictures. I am sure he was born black, and there is a star in the center of his forehead. You can't make out the star very clearly anymore, as his color has started to lighten. The head, ears and legs start to whiten first. His coat glistens and the dapples appear to shimmer when he is out in the sun.

I love his coloring right now, though I know he will continue to get whiter. I hope he retains his dappling for a long time and then goes all white. I am not sure I can handle referring to my guy as a, "flea-bitten grey." Maybe I would change his name to Spot.

Charlie hit send, leaned back in the chair, and closed her eyes. The early mornings were starting to catch up with her and she faded into an easy nap, listening to her horse eat his hay.

✳✳✳✳✳✳✳✳✳✳✳✳✳✳✳

She could feel him staring at her. She didn't open her eyes and continued to keep her breathing even. It felt good to feel his eye appraising her without him knowing. Charlie's heart beat loudly in her chest, she could feel the thumping as it quickened under his stare. Her skin tingled. She couldn't keep it up any longer, and she slowly opened her eyes.

Doug was only a few feet away, leaning on the adjacent stall door. As she looked into his eyes, her breathing stopped short. His look was smoldering. They held each other's gaze for several long seconds. He closed the distance between them in two steps and knelt down in front of her.

"You were sleeping so peacefully," he said huskily. He put his hand on her knee. "How about we head out for some dinner?" he asked, breaking the spell.

"Uh, sure. I'm famished. Should we ask Travis to come along?" she asked.

"No, just the two of us. Can you handle that?" he smirked.

"Anything you can dish out." She tried to make it sound light, but there was a tremor in her voice that she was sure he must have heard, though he didn't let on.

"Well, then. Let me make a few phone calls and then we can head out." He pulled Charlie out of the chair and dropped her hand slowly. "I'll be back in 15 minutes." And off he went down the shed row. Charlie sighed and ran her hand through her hair. She felt hay. She did her best to remove it all as she scolded herself for taking a cat-nap in the barn.

****

Doug took her to Antonio's, a wonderful Italian restaurant down Route One from the racetrack. It was the first time they had shared a meal, just the two of them. Usually Charlie was too busy driving back and forth to the farm from her house and managing the kids' schedules and visiting Storm. She hardly had time to grab a pop-tart as she ran out the door, let alone go out for a nice dinner.

She was determined to make the evening all about Doug. She had called Ryan and told him that she would be late. He knew how to make some of the basics, so she wasn't worried about the kids going hungry, and Kate and Jillian were only a few minutes away if anything happened. Charlie let herself relax and followed Doug through the restaurant to their table.

Doug seemed to know everyone as they walked back to their table. He waved and shook hands with folks, and asked questions about their horses or their families.

"You know everyone," Charlie commented when they finally sat down.

"Comes with the territory," he replied. "When you have been in the business as long as I have, it becomes a very small world." The waitress approached.

"Can I take your drink order?"

"We will take a bottle of your Sebastiani Cabernet," Doug said without even looking at the menu. The waitress walked off.

Charlie sat across from Doug, staring at her hands, not sure what to make of the quiet little dinner with just the two of them. Was it a date? Surely not, as he was her trainer and she was the horse owner. Are there rules about dating the trainer of a horse you own?

"Are you going to stare at your lap all night?" Doug chided. Charlie looked up and smiled. His eyes turned dark.

"Watch out when you give me your best smile, Charlie, I might have to kiss it off your face." Charlie gasped at his boldness. So, it was a date after all. She was suddenly quite glad she'd double checked that all the hay was out of her hair.

The sommelier arrived with the bottle of wine. Perfect timing. After he poured the wine and departed, Doug sat back. The perfect picture of relaxation. spinning his glass of wine between his fingers.

"What are the kids up to?" he asked. Charlie took a long sip of her wine and let it linger in her mouth. He had made a great selection.

"Nothing much. School is getting harder for Ryan, but he's so determined to keep doing his sports, and I can tell it's starting to take a toll. Skylar doesn't seem to have many friends, but when I ask her about it, she just says she's got the horses and she doesn't need anyone else. I'm a little worried that I've involved them in this too much: made it too much a part of their lives and taken away time from things other normal kids do."

"Can I make an observation?" Doug asked. Charlie nodded for him to continue, while she took another long sip of wine. "Your kids seem pretty open with you, I think if they hated working with the horses, they'd tell you. That's not to say you don't have a right to worry, you're a mother, mothers worry, but I have yet to have a conversation with either Ryan or Skylar that didn't leave me feeling like they were excited to be a part of what you're trying to do with your horse." Charlie smiled and nodded.

"Yeah, I guess they would tell me. Good observation." She held up her glass and he smiled and clinked it with his own.

"I try my best. How do you like the wine?"

"It's fantastic."

"This is the wine I drank the second time I ever had a horse win a race." Doug said.

"Not the first time?"

"No, the first time one of my horses won, I had a cheap bottle of red. It tasted horrible, it made my lips dry, and I don't think I even finished one glass of it." He stared at his glass on the table, "Although it was horrible, I consider that wine the best I've ever had. I bought another bottle of it, and I'm saving it for another extremely special occasion."

"Why's that?"

"To remind me that the good and the bad go hand in hand sometimes: to remind me where I started, and what it all means. To get a sense of uniformity in an otherwise uncertain career and life." His last comment made her think of the conversation with Lilly that morning. If there was ever a time to broach the subject, it was now. Charlie reached across the table and took his hand in hers.

"I did something today." His eyes were questioning, "I ran into Lilly Garrett in the lunch room and I asked her if she would ride Storm."

"Charlie-" He half rose in his seat, and his hand tensed under hers.

"She said she would come evaluate him, but only after I'd mentioned your name." He leaned back. "She said she would do it, because you're a good guy who's been through a lot, and you get it. What does that mean, Doug?"

"You shouldn't have gone and talked to Lilly."

"Not the response I was looking for," Charlie said, bringing her hand back over to her side of the table. He drummed his fingers and looked at her several times like he wanted to say something, but he couldn't. Charlie downed the rest of her wine and poured another glass. She was determined to hash everything out before the night ended. She was there with him, and there were no kids and no workers and no horses; she couldn't imagine leaving without knowing where she stood with him.

"Here's the deal Doug: I like you. I like that you run a business and that all your employees seem like they love their jobs and that you know your horses by name even though they all look alike. I like that my kids like you, and I like that you are a good guy that, 'gets it.' What I don't like is the fact that even after the kiss in the barn and the putting your arm around me and the fact that this is a date, you don't want to share your personal life with me. I realized today that I know more about your horses than I do about you!"

Charlie sat there and glared at him across the table. She didn't know why she felt so angry all of a sudden. Frustrated was more the word. She was being quite direct, but that was the control-freak in her, coming out. She needed to know how this relationship was going to play out; was it going to be anything more than professional? Could she handle anything more than just friendship? Not if he wasn't more forthcoming than this, that's for sure.

Doug's sexy smirk was back. He reached across the table and grabbed at her hand.

Charlie didn't know how they got to the bathroom, but the next thing she knew, that's where they were. He'd turned the lock and then pushed her up against the wall without missing a beat. She didn't even know if it was the men's room or the women's room. All she knew was his hands on her body and his lips on hers.

A knock on the door brought them to their senses. He left the room first to go and ask that the food they'd ordered be made to go. He told them that Charlie didn't feel well, which wasn't necessarily a lie.

Charlie looked at herself in the mirror. Her hair was a bit messy, and her outfit needed straightening. It had been years since she'd made out with anyone in a public place. Her mind drifted back to an episode with Peter at a frat party. Tears welled in her eyes and she wiped them away. She couldn't let Doug think she regretted what just happened, that wasn't why she was crying. She fixed herself up as best as she could, but made sure she still looked a little pukey, for the benefit of the wait staff, and then she headed out.

Doug was casually talking to the hostess, holding their dinners in a "to go" bag.

"I'm so sorry you don't feel well, ma'am," said the hostess, as Charlie walked up.

"Thank you," Charlie replied. Doug stood behind the hostess with the look of a church boy on his face. "What?" he mouthed over to her, breaking into a smile. He grabbed her hand and they walked out to the car.

The ride back to Doug's farm was awkward. Neither of them knew what to say. Where do you go from there, anyway? Charlie had the bag of food on her lap and she stared out the window, watching the trees zoom past. Doug drove his car calmly with one hand on the steering wheel and the other drumming on the console.

"My dad was a gambler and an alcoholic. When he was drunk, or lost a lot of money at the track and casino, he would come home and take it out on me, my mom, my older sister, and my younger brother. He had a mean temper, drunk or not. One night he came home and went into the garage to work on his car. He called Jake, my little brother, and I into the garage. He was dead quiet, which we knew meant he was about to lose it." Doug told his story with a faraway look in his eyes. Charlie listened.

"'You boys been messin' with my tools?' He spat it at us, like he was disgusted at even having to speak to us. We told him no, we knew better than that. Jake was just five and I was ten years old. We stood still, just wishing the abuse away.

"'I don't believe you. I left my tools up on this table and now they're scattered all over the place!' He picked up one of his wrenches.

"'No, sir.' I told him, 'I promise we did not touch any of the tools.' My hands were shaking next to my sides, but I tried to move in front of Jake, to make myself the main target. The stench of beer and cigarettes circled around us.

"'You're a filthy liar, boy, and now I'm gonna teach you not to touch my tools again!' He didn't yell, he was perfectly calm. And then he lost it. The wrench came flying at us, followed by screwdrivers, tape measures, whatever he could get his hands on; everything was fair game."

Doug was quiet for a few seconds. Charlie sat still in the passenger seat. She held her breath for the little boy within him that was reliving this moment. She gripped his hand tightly, where it lay between them on the console.

"When it was over, I was huddled on the ground with my hands covering my head. Dad had marched into the house with a new beer in hand. I hadn't been hit too badly; I knew I would have a bruise or two, but it wasn't the worst I'd gotten from that man. I got up and walked over to where Jake was lying face first on the garage floor. I called his name, but he didn't move. I thought he was just too scared. I shook him, and rolled him over...

"One of the hammers my father had thrown had hit Jake in the head and...I guess it hit him just right and he was small enough that...it killed him." A tear rolled down Doug's cheek. "I couldn't protect him, my little brother. I should have stood in front of him. He didn't know what was coming and didn't drop to the ground quick enough."

Charlie didn't know what to say, but she also knew there are times when nothing should be said. She just quietly held his hand as he continued to drive.

"They came and took my father away. He went to jail, the details are fuzzy from way back then, but I remember knowing he couldn't hurt the rest of us anymore."

He didn't look away from the road once while he spoke, but Charlie was so captivated that she couldn't look anywhere but at him. His eyes shone, but his voice was steady.

"We moved to New Jersey and lived with my mom's family for a while, until she could get a job. We finally moved into a small apartment on the outskirts of Monmouth Racetrack, not the best part of town, but it was home and it was ours. My sister went off to college, and I spent my days wandering the streets, playing hooky from school. I went through a bad phase: I blamed myself for Jake's death. My mom knew she couldn't force me to go to school, so instead she said I needed to help contribute to the family and go get a job.

"There were several horse farms in the vicinity, and I finally convinced one of them to hire me as a stall cleaner. I stayed for a while and did a lot of odd jobs and learned the ropes of the inner operations of running a professional horse farm. I was hooked, I knew that that was what I wanted to do, but I also knew that I needed to have money to have a big operation. Working at the farm was the catalyst that got me to want to go to college and find a job that would allow me to support breeding and running racehorses.

"So I went back and graduated from high school, I went to college and got a business degree. Timing is everything, and I lucked out starting my company when the Internet was taking off. It took me several years, but the hard work paid off. I wanted to get out of New Jersey and I ended up finding the land that Shamrock Hill now sits on, and the rest is history."

"Your sister lives on the farm, right?" Charlie asked.

"Yes. My sister and her husband Steve, and their kids, Sam and Jenny. Steve has always had a mind for business and when I came to him with my idea of starting a farm, he supported me all the way: he's part owner of Shamrock Hill."

"What about your mom?"

"I couldn't convince my mom to move out of New Jersey, she wanted to stay close to her sisters. It's only a three hour drive to her house, so I am okay with that. I try to go up there as often as I can, and so does my sister."

He put the truck in park and Charlie looked around, confused. She had been so engrossed in his story that she hadn't realized they were pulling up to his farm. She looked down at her lap, at the food that was still warm through the bag.

"Jenny really looks up to Lilly. She rode a few problem horses for me several years ago and Jenny stuck to her side like glue. Lilly would go visit with my sister, when she was at Shamrock. That's the only way I can think that she would know anything about what I just told you. I've never spoken about it to anyone else," Doug said. Charlie was taken aback.

"I like you too, Charlie. I don't want you to feel like I'm hiding things from you, but it's not something I want to talk about, so I didn't know how to tell you, and I didn't want to bring it up until I was sure…that this was something."

"I understand." Charlie looked up at him. His eyes were bright in the dimly lit car. She put a hand on his face. "Thank you for telling me."

"You're welcome." Doug sighed, put his hand on Charlie's, and moved it so that he could kiss her palm. Then he got out of the car. Charlie sat, confused. It was too dark to see outside the car, so she couldn't tell what Doug was doing. She reached over to her door handle, and just as she was about to pull it, the door opened.

"Can we still have dinner together?" Doug asked, offering his hand to help her out of the truck. Charlie smiled and stepped out next to her date.

"Lead the way." They walked inside together. Charlie had never been to Doug's house before. It was up on a slight hill overlooking the expanse of his property. It was a modest house, with a great view of the surrounding countryside. The house was secondary to the expansive patio and outside kitchen. You could tell Doug liked to spend as much time outside as possible. The inside was sparse but immaculate. Not exactly a bachelor pad, but it was clear no women lived there.

"If I'd known you were coming over I would have cleaned, or lit a candle or something," Doug said, throwing a blanket on the couch into a basket.

"You're joking, right? This place is spotless!" He took the dinner from her hands and started getting out plates and silverware. "Hey, do you mind if I step outside and call my kids real fast? Just to let them know I'll be a bit later…"

"No problem." He smiled and Charlie saw a hint of the same look he'd had in his eye before they wound up in that bathroom. She needed to make that call. The cool night air was refreshing. She pulled out her phone and dialed, but it wasn't her kids that she called.

"So, was it a date?" Kate must have been waiting by her phone because she picked up after one ring.

"Well, we hooked up in the bathroom of the restaurant and now we're back at his place, so you tell me." Charlie had to hold the phone about a foot away from her ear so Kate's scream wouldn't burst her eardrum.

"Are you kidding me?"

"No, I'm not. I don't know what happened, I'll tell you all about it tomorrow, I was calling to see if you could go to my house until I get there. I don't know when I'll be home. If the kids are still up just tell them I had car trouble or something."

"I'm on it. Charlie, I'm so excited about this. How do you feel? Are you okay? " Charlie could hear the concern in Kate's voice.

"Charlie, your dinner is ready." Doug was standing at the door behind her.

"I have to go. Thank you, I love you. Bye." Charlie hung up without hearing Kate's response, and followed Doug back into the house. They sat down at the small island in his kitchen and ate. As they ate, they talked nonstop. After Doug shared about his past, it was like a wall had been torn down. When they finished their food, he poured more wine and they sat and talked for hours. The topics ranged from silly to serious and finally to Peter:

"Six months. That's all we had with him after they diagnosed the lung cancer. Crazy thing is that Peter never smoked. He had been coughing for a while and just kept thinking it was a winter cold that wouldn't go away. Peter had been run down from a project he was working on with his company. Little did we know that fatigue is a symptom. When I could finally get him to go to the doctor, he was already in Stage III. The cancer had already spread to the lymph nodes." Charlie paused and took a long sip of wine. Tears rolled slowly down her face. Doug reached across the table and held her hand in his.

"The experts said Peter had about fifteen months to get things in order. He was past the stage where surgery was an option, so we immediately started the chemotherapy and radiation treatments. They didn't work," Charlie said angrily, the tears flowing more quickly. "And the doctors were wrong! Peter died six months later – not fifteen months. We weren't ready, the kids and I. We thought we had more time. More time to say I love you, more time to hug, more time to talk. Peter was stronger than all of us. He took on cancer like he did everything in his life. Head on. He spent what little time he had getting everything ready for us: his life insurance was all in place, the buy-sell agreement with his partners at the firm. For weeks after he died, the kids and I would find little notes hidden around the house with his handwritten words, his hopes and dreams for all of us, how much he loved us.

"The kids have been so strong. I wasn't in a good place for many months. Every time I found a note, I broke down and would lay on my bed in the fetal position, wishing my life away. I would ask God, 'why Peter, why did he get taken from me so early? We had so many things we wanted to do together.' Ryan and Skylar would get themselves off to school, do the chores, take care of the horses. Finally, Kate was the one who came and shook me senseless, telling me how selfish I was being, that I had two beautiful kids who just lost their dad and were losing their mom. Life isn't fair, but I needed to get my act together for them. So I did. I worked my way back to reality. It was a slow process, but I made sure that when I was with the kids, I put on my happy face and started getting back to life.

"As the days passed, the pain of losing Peter lessened. Days turned into months and life finally returned to some version of normalcy for the three of us. Hockey games, horseshows, my job, I kept myself very busy to help hide the pain. My friends, Kate and Jillian, are part of my family, and they helped us through the darkest time of our lives. So one day, after they figured enough time had passed, they took it upon themselves to get me back into the social scene: which brings us to girl's night out at the track." Her tears had dried as she talked through the last eighteen months. She just sat quietly, holding Doug's hand.

"I haven't dated anyone or sat at a nice dinner with a man since Peter died," Charlie finished. Doug scooted his chair closer to hers so that he could put his arm around her, and she leaned her head on his shoulder. They sat that way for a long time.

It wasn't what she thought she would notice in a moment like that, but Charlie couldn't stop looking at Doug's fingernails. Every time she'd shaken his hand, she always felt hands that she assumed would look as perfect as they felt: and in all the time she'd spent with him, she never noticed how beaten up they actually were.

Several of his nails were chipped down to the point where it looked like they'd bled, and his thumb nail was so bruised, it took her a minute to realize it wasn't painted.

Charlie always saw him around the farm talking on his cell phone or giving orders, or filling out paperwork, she'd never pictured him actually *working* on a farm. Now that the evidence was staring her in the face, she didn't know why. He certainly had the body for it, that's for sure. That's one thing she'd noticed a long time ago. She'd just assumed he did other workouts, like jogging or something, or he was one of those wealthy men that bought those health supplements from infomercials. Now that she thought about it, Doug didn't seem like the infomercial type. He did seem like the type to help his employees any chance he got, whether that meant manual labor, or, yes, filling out paperwork.

"What did you do to your thumb?" She asked him. She didn't know what she was expecting, exactly: something to do with a rogue horse and one of those cool golf carts he gets to drive around all day, maybe.

"Oh, I wasn't looking where I was leaning and it got shut in a door." Well Doug, way to kill the fantasy.

"And what about this finger? What happened to the nail?"

"I was helping shoe a horse and I hit it my finger with the hammer. The nail fell off a few days later, but it got infected and it was so mangled, only half the nail grew back." She laughed away the few tears that were still in her eyes. It was nice to have someone listen to her story who didn't know Peter. Doug cared about what happened, but he cared about it because of her, not because he missed Peter too. He wanted to comfort Charlie, that was all.

"It's a good thing I asked after dinner." Charlie said, laughing. Doug smiled and Charlie saw his eyes drift to the clock above the oven.

"Are your kids okay with you staying out this late?" he asked. Charlie could tell he didn't actually want her to go, but as always, he was being respectful and giving her an out. This time, however, she wasn't going to take it.

"Is that a hint? Do you want me to leave?" She moved to stand up, and he tensed briefly, before letting her go. She turned to look at him: always the gentleman.

"Just the opposite," he said. He looked serious, but hesitant.

"Doug, about what happened at the restaurant-"

"I'm sorry, I shouldn't have put you in that situation, you're-"

"Thank you." He stared at her for a moment.

"If I say, 'you're welcome' does that make me a cocky bastard? Cause this feels like a trap."

"After you left, I realized something…I still love my husband."

"Oh…okay. I'll just um-" Doug looked at Charlie with pure confusion. She put a hand on his face, to stop him from moving.

"The truth is, I think a part of me would have always held back a little until I knew that dating didn't mean that I loved Peter any less. I don't know that I could have really let myself believe that if we hadn't…gone to dinner tonight. Maybe it wasn't the right thing to do, but now I know that it can be right again." He was still sitting on his barstool, which made her slightly taller than him. Charlie leaned down and kissed him and he returned the kiss eagerly.

"In that case, you're welcome," he said, breaking away and standing up. Charlie smiled and let her hands drift over his chest.

"I called Kate to stay with the kids tonight. I have no curfew. I'm all yours, if you want me." His only reply was to pick her up and carry her to his bedroom.

The Whisperer

At 5 am sharp, Lilly walked down the barn aisle towards Doug and Charlie. Doug held his arms open.

"Hello, my dear Lilly!" he called out. Lilly looked like a waif in his big hug: she was only 4'11" and probably not a pound over 100. Charlie noticed she let him hug her, but there wasn't a hug in return. She seemed to just accept the gesture but it was clear that she wanted to get down to business. When she pulled away, she had a sad smile on her face.

"What do you have for me, Doug?" Lilly asked quietly.

"Let me introduce you to Charlie Jenkin. Oh right, you two have already met," he said with a bit of sarcasm, giving Charlie a quick wink: a reminder that he wasn't used to his owners taking such big a role in their horse's development.

"Good morning, Ms. Jenkins." Lilly held out her hand.

"Charlie," she reminded her, taking her hand. Once again Charlie was reminded of the softness within the firm grip.

"Lilly, I know you can work wonders with unruly horses. That's not this one's problem." Doug started and Charlie let him take the lead. "Storm has the personality of a saint, good appetite, follows orders. It's just that we can't get him to engage in head-to-head racing. He won't breeze, he won't go much above an easy gallop out there on the track."

"How do you know he possesses the speed to race?" Lilly asked. Doug looked over at Charlie. Her turn.

"My daughter taught him to play tag," she said confidently. Lilly looked over at Charlie, raising her eyebrows.

"Go on," Lilly said.

"Out in our fields at home and at Doug's training track, we watched Skylar call to Storm from quite a distance. The speed he demonstrated in going to catch her was staggering," Charlie said.

"I think he would have clocked a 22 for the quarter mile, Lilly," Doug chimed in. "And that's without any conditioning."

"What's his backstory?" she asked. Again, Doug turned to Charlie.

"I claimed him at Charles Town back in September," she said, not going into too many other details.

"That's where I met Charlie," Doug said. "She was in the barn after claiming Storm and didn't know what do to next. I can tell you that Storm was in a sorry state."

"He finished in the middle of the pack in his race. I noticed he didn't really look like he enjoyed himself," Charlie added.

"When I walked into his stall, the only thing I could think of was abuse. He was quite a bit underweight, he stood in the far corner of his stall, his head hung low, and basically had no interest in the goings-on around him. I told Charlie to take him home, put some weight on him, and just let him be a horse with some tender love and care," Doug concluded and Charlie picked up the story.

"So, for several weeks my kids, my fifteen year-old son and nine year-old daughter, doted on Storm: fed him, groomed him, introduced him to our other two horses. He really came around. When we first got him, he wouldn't come near his stall door, but now he is interested in everything around him. See?" Charlie pointed over Lilly's shoulder.

Lilly turned around to find a big grey head with deep brown eyes surveying their little group. Storm pushed his nose towards them, tilting his head slightly, like a dog does when it looks like he is listening to what people are saying. Storm then nodded his head, as if in total agreement with what Charlie had just communicated to Lilly. Lilly walked up to his stall.

"Tag, huh?" she said running a hand down his long nose. "Well, let's see if we can make racing a game for you." Sarge had just figured out that they were outside the stalls and didn't want Storm getting all the attention. Lilly's back was to him, and she was a bit shocked when she felt a big kiss from Sarge on her neck.

"Well, hello!" she said, slowly turning around. Charlie noticed she did not move quickly around the horses. All her movements were deliberate, nothing that would spook them.

"That's Sarge, Storm's side kick. He helps keep him calm. He's my retired Thoroughbred that I show with my daughter," Charlie explained.

"He is quite a ways from the show ring," Lilly commented.

"He loves being back at the track, I think. He thinks he's big man on campus. Probably brings back memories. He hasn't batted an eye. I think he had some good experiences when he was racing. He's been a great friend to me, and Storm," she finished quietly.

"Well, maybe you can help us out," Lilly said to Sarge, repeating her slow rub down his long nose, like she did with Storm. Lilly turned back to Doug and Charlie.

"Alright, I'll see what I can help you with. I will throw a leg up on him this morning for his work-out and see what we have to work with. I have some others to ride later this morning. Once I ride Storm, I will have a better idea of what we might be able to do to engage him, and we can meet over a late lunch. Sound okay?"

"Sounds good," Doug replied.

"If he does engage, what's your plan for him? Race him here at Laurel and then head to the live dates at Pimlico?" Lilly asked. Doug looked over at Charlie again, raising his eyebrows just a bit and giving her his smirky smile.

"We, my kids and I, would like to race him in the Derby," Charlie said calmly.

"The Derby? Like in the Kentucky Derby?" Lilly asked. Charlie could tell Lilly was someone who didn't raise her voice, but if she was, Charlie was sure her comments would have been yelled.

"Yes," Charlie said firmly. Lilly looked over at Doug. He just shrugged his shoulders.

"She's the owner," was all he said, though a big smile lit up his face. Damn, Charlie was really starting to like that man.

****

Charlie needed to get back to her farm, but she wanted to make sure she heard Lilly's report from her ride on Storm. She rode a few times around the track on him, not doing much more than a gallop. Charlie called Kate, who was still with the kids.

"How's it going?" Charlie asked her.

"Great here, the kids are excited to hear what is going on with Storm. How's he doing? Get him to run yet?" Kate asked.

"Not pushing him yet, but I found a jockey that I want to use," Charlie told her.

"Really? Not one of Doug's regular riders?" Kate inquired.

"No. Her name is Lilly Garrett. I saw her yesterday on the track working with a big old hellion. A big black horse that she calmed right down. She has a reputation of being some sort of horse whisperer. I figured since none of us can figure out how to encourage Storm to really run, that maybe she could. We are going to late lunch to get her feedback from her ride this morning and then I will head back your way," Charlie said.

"Oh, yeah, one sec, I'll just walk out there," she said. Charlie was very confused.

"What?"

"Hold on..." Charlie heard a door shut, "I had to get away from the kids. How was your night? Tell me everything. What did you do? Scratch that, I know what you did just tell me how you are doing," Kate said. She was keeping her voice low, but her tone was concerned. Charlie blushed hard.

"I would tell you all about it, but I have to go. For now, let me just say I owe you big time for staying with the kids."

"I'm dying here! You're telling me everything tonight when you get home."

"Deal." They hung up, but it took her a good five minutes to erase the smile from her face.

"Ready?" Doug found her at the end of the barn aisle.

"Yep. Let's go see what our horse whisperer has to say," Charlie quipped.

****

They ended up going to lunch at a nearby restaurant. Doug and Charlie had the novelty of ordering anything they wanted. Lilly, on the other hand, ordered a small salad. Jockeys need to make sure they watch their weight because it is closely monitored by the stewards of the racetrack. Charlie made a note to make her next blog about that very topic. She got right to the point with Lilly,

"So what do you think?" Lilly looked at her and then over at Doug.

"Direct, isn't she?" Lilly asked. Doug smiled,

"I am finding that out quickly myself," he bantered. Lilly sat with her ponytail hanging over the back of her chair. While she had been working her other horses, Charlie had made a point to do a little research on her.

Lilly was thirty-two years old. Not too old for a jockey. At the age of eighteen, she had started out her jockey apprenticeship at Pimlico Race Course and had blossomed under trainer Tom Malone. She had grown up in Baltimore, spending her days peering over the fence to see the horses race. One day, Tom took notice of the young waif and invited her to his barn of racehorses on the backside of the track.

Lilly started as a hot walker, walking horses after they had been worked. Tom noticed she had a quiet way about her, and taught her how to ride. She quickly moved her way up to Tom's main exercise rider. He was quoted many times as saying that his horses won because of the care Lilly gave them during their morning workouts. Tom urged her to get her jockey credentials, which she did at 24. They made a great team.

For four years, Lilly traveled the country getting rides at all the major racetracks. She stayed true to Tom, and was his regular rider whenever he ran a horse he wanted her to ride. She earned praise from the trainers and owners she rode for on a consistent basis. Some, however, found her style quite odd: she refused to use a whip on any of her mounts.

Charlie couldn't find any more information after that period. It was like Lilly had disappeared, until Doug pointed her out. Charlie couldn't find any information about her riding anywhere for the last four years. At the age of twenty-eight, Lilly had literally dropped off the face of the racing world.

"I do like your Storm. He has a great way of going when I galloped him. Just like the others before me, I wasn't successful in getting him to go any faster than a steady gallop. But I will say, he was not angry or annoyed when I kept asking him. He just plodded along on his merry way, ears flickering, listening to me, but not interested in moving on for me. His muscling is great and his breathing was clean. I would like for you to take him home for a few days and I will come out to the farm and observe him in a relaxed environment. Sound like a start?" asked Lilly.

"Yes, of course. Whatever you say," Charlie said. She truly loved Lilly's demeanor. She was very quick in her conversation, and business like. It would be fun to get to know more about her. What had this young, talented rider been doing, and why didn't she ride in races anymore? Charlie pondered that while they ordered lunch and made small talk while they ate.

Home Again

Charlie crawled into her bed, exhausted. It was late, 1 am. Doug and Charlie had talked for a while after Lilly left. He said he wanted to pay for Lilly's services. Charlie declined. Lilly was her idea and she would figure it out.

As soon as Charlie left the racetrack, after saying goodbye to Storm, she called Kate again. They decided to grab dinner so that Charlie could tell her all about her romantic night with Doug. Charlie called the kids and told them it was going to be a little while longer before she could get home, Ryan seemed more perturbed than usual, but Charlie decided to ask about it when she got home.

Kate's reception of Charlie's story of the night before started off worried and consoling, but became more and more excited as the details of the night unfolded.

"I don't know how it happened, but he locked the door and I just kind of melted into him," Charlie said.

"And no one tried to come in? I mean, you think of a restaurant bathroom, and it never seems to be empty for long," Kate chimed in.

"There were a few knocks, but we just ignored them for a while. Kate, it was just good. And I looked at myself after he left and I looked happy. It's okay for me to like him!" Charlie said. Kate smiled and nodded her head.

"I can't believe I'm getting to see you this happy again. You deserve it, don't get me wrong! There was just a chunk of time there when I wondered if I would ever see a real smile from you again." She took a sip from her wine glass and picked up her fork, "How do you think the kids are gonna take it?"

"I don't know. They both really like Doug, which is a good thing. And they both keep telling me that they want me to be happy. I don't know. I'm a little afraid to tell them. I shouldn't have stayed with him last night, that was a bad mom move." Charlie closed her eyes and rested her head in her hands.

"Charlie, your kids were safe and in good hands. If you really feel that bad about it, just don't do it again." Kate was very good at the non-judgmental thing. Charlie's phone buzzed on the table next to her plate. She picked it up and looked at the text on the screen. "Thinking of you," was all it said. From Doug. She smiled and wrote, "back atcha."

Not long after that, they said goodbye and Charlie headed home. Storm and Sarge had waited patiently in the trailer in the parking lot, but Charlie sped a little bit on her way back to the farm, so that she could get them out as quickly as possible.

It was late by the time Charlie got the horses all settled back in the barn and Skylar was in bed already. Ryan was on the couch when Charlie walked in.

"You should be in bed, mister," Charlie said, giving his shoulder an affectionate squeeze as she walked by him.

"Just waiting for you," he said, annoyed.

"What's up? Did you need something?"

"No, I don't need anything from you." Charlie didn't know what she'd done to deserve the attitude he was giving her. She just watched her angry child storm off. That night, she drifted into a deep sleep with conflicting thoughts of Doug's affection and her son's angry standoffishness.

****

Skylar jumped on top of Charlie, bringing back memories of that morning so many months ago, the day she had brought Storm home.

"He's back! Mom, he's back. You brought Storm home!" She bounced on the bed. Charlie looked up at Skylar from under her arm that she had positioned to keep the light out so she could get a few more minutes of sleep. Charlie smiled at her beautiful, innocent daughter.

"Yes, I brought him home for a few days," Charlie said.

"Didn't he run fast?" she asked. Charlie didn't want to dash her hopes. She pulled Skylar next to her in bed.

"Storm did just fine. He just missed you and Hershey and wanted to come home and play. Training is hard work and he told me he needed a break." Skylar turned in her mother's arms and looked at her. It was like she was looking into the eyes of a ghost. Peter's eyes shone bright, through his daughter. Charlie held Skylar tight. What was she doing, thinking she could get this horse to the Kentucky Derby, the most prestigious race in the country?

"Come on, Mom, let's get out to the barn. I'll go tell Ryan!" She jumped out of bed and was down the hall before Charlie could move.

****

Ryan was already downstairs when Skylar went to get breakfast. He was sitting at the table, working on his computer.

"Ryan, Storm's back!" She ran up behind him.

"I know!" was his exasperated reply. The typical teenager reaction to the enthusiasm of his nine-year-old sister. She stood behind him, deflated. Of course he didn't notice. Ryan truly didn't have a clue as to how much his sister idolized him. She recovered quickly.

"What are you looking at?" she asked, coming up next to him.

"Stuff," was his reply.

"Be nice to your sister," Charlie said softly but sternly, not wanting to ruin the morning. Ryan turned and looked at his mother. He glared at the dark circles under her eyes, and the hair that looked like a crow's nest, but he rephrased his reply to his sister,

"I am looking up the progress of all the horses nominated for the Derby."

"Cool. Can I see?" she asked. He turned the computer towards her and she pulled a chair close. Charlie decided that she was going to have to talk to Ryan about the attitude he was giving her. It was probably just teenage moodiness, and her lack of sleep was making it seem worse, but it was starting to get old, and he needed to know it wasn't okay.

As she made her coffee, Ryan explained the point standings of all the horses listed to be able to qualify to run in the Derby. The Road to the Kentucky Derby Prep Series had started: the first nineteen races where horses could start earning points. So the race was on, literally, to determine the top three- year-olds in the country. Would Storm make it on that list? As a two-year-old, Storm had been in a few races under that horrid trainer, Blackston. His record wasn't good: he did not finish in the money in any of them. It was really no wonder people thought Charlie was crazy, putting him in the running.

"How'd you know Storm was back?" Charlie asked Ryan, innocently. She had to be very careful about how she asked her teenager a question these days. Sometimes he got defensive and she would get no more information out of him. As close as they had all grown over the last year and half, Ryan was still a boy going through puberty.

"After you went to bed, I went out and said hello, even though it was the middle of the night," Ryan said without lifting his eyes from the screen or his fingers from the keyboard. Charlie had to take a deep breath before she responded. He was clearly mad about something, but rising to the bait now wasn't going to get her anywhere.

"Well I'm glad you got to see him, honey. I know he missed you," she said sweetly, before taking a sip of her coffee.

Charlie was sure he'd stayed out with Storm for a while. He had a lot to tell his confidant, about the weeks he had been gone. They didn't have any alone time during his visits to Shamrock Hill, so it made sense that he wanted to take advantage of it being just him and Storm in their own barn. What he talked about, Charlie swore she would never ask. It was between a boy and his horse. She knew how beneficial her relationship with Sarge was, and she wanted Ryan to have that too: someone to lean on, talk to, someone that doesn't judge.

****

They ate their breakfast out at the barn - if a large mug of coffee for Charlie and strawberry pop-tarts for the kids counted as breakfast. While Skylar busied herself with feeding bits of her pop-tart to Storm, Sarge, and Hershey, Ryan shot questions at Charlie.

"How did he do, Mom?" he asked. He was all business.

"We still couldn't get him to run faster, but I think I found someone who will be able to help us with that. We're still in the fight." Charlie said.

"What does Doug think?" Ryan's stream of questions continued. Charlie noticed a slight grimace on Ryan's face as he uttered Doug's name.

"He thinks Storm's conditioning is great," Charlie said as she watched Storm in the field, his muscles glistening in the morning sun. They had let the horses out to enjoy the sunshine. Storm was definitely enjoying his time home. He tantalized Sarge and Hershey in the field with him. He nipped at their hips, trying to get them to play and tossed his head in all his happiness to be home playing with his buds. At Shamrock Hill, he didn't go out with others. At the track there was no turnout at all: just 30 minutes of work, followed by hand walking and grazing, then twenty-three hours in the stall. Not necessarily the best routine for a horse as energetic as Storm. Charlie wondered why it had come to that for racehorses.

Years ago, their training was overwhelming. In the old days, the horse did the farm work, pulled the carriage, and then was sent off to a match race, where two farmers bet on which one of their horses could run the fastest.

Now, racehorses were a means to an end. For some, they were

treasured athletes, for others, money-making tools of the trade. The emotion had been taken out of the industry. They say don't get too close to your horse, it is not a pet, it is a business.

How can people live like that? Of course they are pets! How can you feed them, ride them, train them and not develop an attachment?

****

As Ryan and Charlie talked, a small two-door convertible pulled into the driveway. Charlie hadn't gotten to the topic of, "the rider," yet with Ryan.

"Who's that?" he asked.

"Our jockey." She smiled at him and waved to Lilly as she pulled her car up to the barn.

"A girl?" He looked over at Charlie and back to Lilly. She looked even tinier in her small car, her blond hair pulled back into a tight pony tail. Charlie smiled at Ryan again as she went to greet Lilly.

"Welcome," Charlie held out her hand.

"It is beautiful out here," Lilly said, glancing around at the small barn and surrounding paddocks.

"Thanks. My husband and I found the land several years ago and we built all of this together," Charlie told her.

"Well, I look forward to meeting the man who helped you," she said. Charlie's smile wavered. Lilly noticed.

"He passed away eighteen months ago. Well, I guess it is now almost two years," Charlie said. "His passing was sudden: it threw us for a loop for quite some time." She looked over at the kids, standing by the pasture, watching the exchange.

"I'm sorry," Lilly said compassionately, putting her hand on Charlie's arm. "I know how painful a sudden loss can be." Charlie turned her gaze back to Lilly. Her face lit up with a dazzling smile Charlie had not seen before. It was likely Lily didn't give it to too many people.

"I want to meet your kids and see Storm in his natural environment." Charlie blinked back the tears that had filled her eyes, glad to redirect her thinking. It was still hard, even after almost two years, thinking about Peter and all that they had accomplished together and all that they would never accomplish.

Charlie fought through her melancholy and smiled back at Lilly, finding a deeper bond with this woman. They walked over to Skylar and Ryan.

"Meet Lilly, Storm's new rider," Charlie said.

"Hello," Ryan said hesitantly.

"Hi!" Skylar said. "Are you going to be riding Storm in the Kentucky Derby?" Right to the point, Skylar. Charlie laughed; the apple doesn't fall far from the tree. Lilly didn't miss a beat, though Charlie knew she thought they were all certifiably crazy on the topic of the Derby.

"I am here to help Storm learn how to run fast on the track again. I will ride him, yes. But as to riding him in a race, I will leave that to the professional jockeys." Ryan glanced over at Charlie again. Right now she needed Lilly to help with Storm so that he could actually get to the races, then Charlie would address Lilly about riding him herself.

They walked over to the fence and watched Storm. The horses were at the far end of the field. Storm was still messing around, not at all interested in grazing. Sarge had had enough. Storm came around Hershey to nip at him and Sarge whirled around on him and went to nip him back. Storm was too fast, his reflexes quicker than most horses Charlie had ever seen, and moved easily out of the way, galloping to the other side of Hershey. Sarge caught everyone watching them, and knowing Charlie would protect him from his tormentor, took off at a gallop towards her.

Storm was facing the other way, his attention diverted momentarily from his friends by something blowing in the trees on the other side of the fence. He hadn't yet noticed Sarge leaving his happy herd of three. Lilly was watching him closely. Skylar was giddy.

"Do you think he remembers, Mom?"

"I don't know, sweet pea. Why don't you call him?" Charlie replied.

"Storm, Storm!" Skylar yelled to him. "Hurry, Sarge is going to beat you. Tag! You're it!" Storm wheeled around at the sound of Skylar's voice. He stood stock still for several seconds, assessing the situation, his ears, nose and eyes on full alert. He noticed Hershey still munching happily in front of him, not one to fall prey to silly games when there was grass to be eaten. He searched out Sarge who was already halfway to the fence where Skylar stood calling him. He lifted his head several inches higher and flared his nostrils, his ears flicking back and forth.

Everyone stood there in anticipation. Ryan, Skylar, and Charlie had already experienced Storm's burst of speed. Charlie glanced over at Lilly, and saw her gaze intent on Storm. Storm coiled and burst into a full gallop as if breaking from the starting gate. He swerved around Hershey and set his sights on Sarge. Sarge's ears flicked back to Storm, though his eyes searched Charlie out. She could see him pick up a bit of speed; he was not going to let the little hellion get the best of him. At twelve years old, Sarge still had some speed in him.

However, as much as Charlie loved Sarge, she knew he was no match for Storm. Storm was gaining as if Sarge was standing still. His speed was a sight to behold. It was not something Charlie could have ever explained to Lilly. She had to see it herself to believe it.

Charlie still urged her old man on, to beat the young colt. Storm would not be denied. He overtook Sarge easily, nipping over at him as he pulled up alongside, as if to say "Tag, You're it." They matched stride for stride for several seconds. Then he turned his attention to Skylar and the peppermints that awaited him, and dug in, passing Sarge. He pulled up in front of the small crowd, jogging up and down the fence line as if saying to Sarge, "What took you so long?"

Skylar held out the peppermints over the fence for Storm.

"Meanie," she said. "Toying with Sarge like that. You should let him win one day." She patted his nose. And he blew out his nostrils at her. Lilly absorbed it all, her eyes half closed, her mind working through all she had just seen.

A little while later, everyone was back in the house. They had shown

Lilly around the place and she had spent some time talking to Skylar and Ryan individually, wanting to get to know them and their relationship with Storm.

Charlie had gone into the kitchen to prepare lunch. Ryan was warming up to Lilly. Charlie could hear him talking about all his research and the plan he had devised on how to prepare Storm for the Derby. He showed her Storm's Facebook page with 250 fans. Most of who were friends and friends of friends. Lilly was very gracious, and she was now listening intently to, and following him on his computer screen, where he kept all the statistics and details of his plan.

Skylar had played the ultimate hostess, showing Lilly all the ribbons from her horse shows as well as her school projects that were scattered throughout the family room.

"Lunch is ready!" Charlie called out to them in the living room. Once everyone was seated, Skylar's chatter started again.

"Where are you from, Miss Lilly? Did you grow up with horses? How long have you been riding? Have you always been a jockey?" Charlie sat there, waiting to see if Lilly would respond. She knew some of the answers already, but wanted to hear them, straight from the horse's mouth. Unfortunately, Lilly expertly avoided directly answering Skylar's inquest.

"So I recall you said that you want to run your horse in the Kentucky Derby," Lilly directed her question to Skylar.

"Oh yes. He is the fastest horse in the world!" Skylar replied excitedly. "Mom had always talked about the Derby. We watch it every year on the TV and Mom and Dad would have a big party here at the farm. Everyone wore fancy hats. Mom said she always wanted to have her own horse in the Derby. Now her dream is going to come true!" Lilly smiled gently at Skylar and raised her eyes to Charlie's. She kept her conversation with Skylar.

"You know, your mom isn't the only one who dreams of going to the Derby," Lilly said.

"I know that! It's a very prestigious and historical race. A ton of people wanna go there!" Charlie raised her eyebrows at her daughter's vocabulary, and made a mental note to start closing the tabs on her computer after she'd looked up things like, "The Prestige and History of the Kentucky Derby."

"Well, Skylar, you're not wrong. Some of the great history of the Derby is in its fabled stories. One of my favorites is the story of Exterminator, or 'Old Bones,' as he had become known, the horse who won the Derby in 1918: a horse with all the attributes of a champion Thoroughbred - speed, courage, stamina, intelligence, and the most important, durability. Exterminator got the name Old Bones due to his bony frame, and was sometimes referred to as the, 'Galloping Hat Rack.'" Skylar burst out laughing.

"Yep, Old Bones was originally just a workout companion for a more impressive Thoroughbred in his barn, but when the more esteemed Thoroughbred was unfit to race in the Derby, the trainer convinced the owner to run Old Bones - without ever having raced as a three-year-old. He had a few races under his belt as a two-year-old, with two wins, but imagine in your first race as a three-year-old, it is the most prestigious in the country - and then you go on to win it!

"Exterminator went on to race for six more years, something unheard of these days. He won races at distances six furlongs to two and a quarter miles, on tracks that were fast, muddy, and everything in between. He had several different trainers and jockeys, it didn't matter to him, Old Bones would still stare down his competitors and with his quiet, determined way, come out on top. He became a national hero and won 50% of his 100 races, finally retiring at the age of nine. What an awesome story of resilience and will to win." Lilly stopped to take a breath.

"A Kentucky Derby story would not be complete without mentioning the famous Calumet Farm, a dynasty of breeding and racing horses, owned by the Wright family in the mid-1900s. In the history of the Derby, Calumet saddled eight winners, came in second four times and third one time; in the money thirteen out of twenty tries. Two of their horses were

Triple Crown winners, but those stories are for another day. Calumet is a fairy tale, a story of successful breeding and racing that will possibly never be equaled."

"Is it possible for a one-horse owner to win the Derby, Lilly? Like us?" Skylar asked innocently.

"Of course, it is possible, Skylar. Though it is not easy. The big operations have numbers on their side. They have many foals a year to evaluate and train to race. You have one. But if he is the one, all the other horses in the world won't be able to beat him. There can only be one winner of the Derby," Lilly said compassionately.

Though Lilly was all business when it came to riding and evaluating horses, she showed her soft side while she talked to Skylar.

"Wow," Skylar said, clearly enthralled with Lilly's passionate stories of the Derby. They all were. The time had flown by as they listened to Lilly talk about the many horses that had won the infamous race. They hadn't gotten into any conversation about Storm yet. Charlie thought that may have been her point.

"Thank you so much for your hospitality, all of you," Lilly said, standing up. "I need to get back to Laurel, I have some meetings this evening and early morning workouts tomorrow."

"But what about Storm?" Ryan asked, disappointed that she was leaving.

"I've seen all that I need to see. You have been great on all the information and background you have provided to me. Thank you," Lilly said. She looked up at Charlie standing behind Ryan, then she leaned down to Skylar. Nose to nose, and said,

"Looks to me like your mom may be able to live out her dream." Skylar threw her arms around Lilly's neck. She was startled by Skylar's quick show of affection and excitement, but she smiled at Charlie as she tentatively returned Skylar's hug.

"Let Storm relax here for tomorrow and bring him up to Doug's the day after. We will start his training then. Please bring everyone, the kids as well as Sarge and Hershey." She unwrapped Skylar from around her neck, shook Ryan's hand and gave Charlie a wave. "I look forward to working with you all."

Skylar skipped back to the fields, humming as she went. Ryan returned to his computer to follow up on many of Lilly's stories. Charlie decided it was about time for another blog post, and she went inside, poured herself a cup of coffee, and sat down at her computer.

The View From Behind the Starting Gate

We have found the perfect training rider for Storm! The kids are so excited, and I have a great feeling about this. She's exactly what we need: calm, smart, and not much bigger than Skylar. Seriously.

The life of a jockey is hard.

Every track sets weight requirements for each race, depending on the horse's age, sex, and skill level and the race's distance. Yet the predominant weight scale remains largely unchanged from the original outline set in 1858, when humans were smaller. The weights horses carry generally range from 112 to 126 pounds. That figure includes the jockey plus about seven pounds of gear.

Each state's racing commission sets its own weight standards. The minimum weight for nearly all races in many jurisdictions is 116 pounds.

Depending on specific race and track guidelines, a jockey must weigh between 108 and 118 pounds without clothing and equipment, which can add a significant number of pounds. Not only each track, but each race has its own specific weight requirements. For instance, a jockey riding in the Kentucky Derby cannot exceed 126 pounds in weight, including clothes and equipment.

To ensure the race is fair and all horses are carrying the same weight, if the jockey and his tack don't reach 126 pounds, then weights are added to the saddle pad.

There are no height limits for jockeys. However, jockeys tend to be shorter than normal to meet the weight guidelines. The average height for a jockey is between four feet ten inches and five feet six inches.

Before and after each race, the jockeys weigh in with their gear to make sure the weight has not changed and given a horse an advantage by carrying lesser weight.

Our new rider is petite, to say the least. The mother in me wanted to do nothing but feed her, but the horse owner in me couldn't be happier that she has agreed to help us out with Storm. I have absolute faith that Storm will be tearing up the tracks in no time at all.

Training to Race

Two days later found the Jenkins family on the rail yet again, at Doug's Shamrock Hill Farm. It was great to see Doug. The three days Charlie had been away felt like a month. She had come to appreciate their banter, as well as the way he looked at her, and all the other little perks of their relationship.

They all stood waiting for Lilly. She had just arrived and asked that they wait for her at the rail and she would explain her plan. She had called Charlie the night before and asked that she and Skylar be prepared to ride, so Charlie was quite curious as to what she was thinking.

Doug had sent Cappie to pick up all three horses, since Charlie only had a two-horse trailer. The two horses and pony had happily loaded and after some peppermints from Skylar, their merry band had been on their way. Ryan rode in the cab with Cappie. Skylar and Charlie followed in her SUV.

Lilly walked up to them, ready to ride. Helmet on, hair pulled back into her tight blond ponytail. She had put on a set of Doug's racing silks-kelly green with the farms logo of green shamrock within a gold horseshoe on the front and back. The helmet cover was green and gold.

"Ready to go?" Lilly asked as she approached.

"Go where?" Skylar asked.

"To help train your Storm," Lilly calmly replied. Charlie looked at her anxiously.

"What do you have in mind?" Charlie asked, getting an inkling of what she was thinking, since she had asked them to bring their riding helmets.

"Well, having observed how much Storm reacts to your presence, it is important that we transfer the love of running he exhibited in the field, to the track. We are going to do this in a series of steps. First, Storm is going to have fun with his buddies on the track. We are going to play your game of tag on the track, with Skylar and Hershey, you and Sarge," Lilly paused.

Charlie was experiencing a mixture of excitement and anxiety, realizing that she would be able to actually ride on a racetrack, but also concerned that Skylar would be in the midst of horses running a lot faster than she was accustomed to.

"Once Storm starts to realize how he can have as much fun on the track, with someone riding him, as he does in the field, we will start to introduce other horses into the mix. I hope to get to the point where he will realize he can have fun, not just with Sarge and Hershey, but with the other horses he's racing with. Storm will stop thinking of the racetrack as a place of pain and suffering, but a place where he can have fun," She concluded. "So, back to my first question: ready to get started?"

Charlie could feel the color was draining from her face as the anxiety started getting the best of her. Doug put a hand on her elbow.

"You okay?" he asked. She looked over at him. Of course, all this was normal for him: horses running as fast as they could, hooves pounding the dirt. Accidents happen and jockeys fall off. Horses trip and fall. People get hurt. Now they were talking about her daughter out there on the track. Charlie's mind buzzed with worry.

"Wait a minute, Lilly. Let me take a walk with Charlie for a few minutes," Charlie heard Doug say. Skylar was again talking a mile a minute, excited for the opportunity to be going fast on her pony, helping Storm.

Doug guided Charlie away from the group, as a stream of horrible thoughts rattled through her brain - Skylar falling off Hershey, getting trampled, her crippled lifeless form on the track. Charlie couldn't breathe. Her chest was caving in on her and it felt like fifty pounds had been placed on it.

In her darkest hours, after Peter died, she found herself daydreaming of accidents that could happen to take one of her other loved ones away from her. If Ryan was late from school, she envisioned his bus in a fiery accident. During his hockey games, she worried about him getting checked so hard by an opponent that he fell backwards and cracked his head. She worried about Skylar getting kidnapped on her way home from a friend's house.

Now she was being asked to allow her only daughter out on a race track with horses running over thirty miles per hour. Charlie closed her eyes and leaned back against the barn. Doug had been smart enough to get her out of sight of the kids, especially Ryan's concerned eyes.

"Hey. Are you in there?" Doug asked. Charlie nodded her head slightly and tried to remember the breathing techniques her therapist taught her. In, out. Slow deep breath in, let it out slowly. She opened her eyes. Doug's worried eyes searched her face.

"Ever seen an anxiety attack in progress?" Charlie asked him.

"Can't say I have," he said. "I'm really worried about you. You're as pale as a ghost."

"Don't worry, the color will come back in a few minutes. I just needed to get my thoughts under control. I started thinking the worst about Skylar going out onto the track. I used to get them more frequently right after Peter died," she said, still concentrating on her breathing. As she looked up into Doug's blue eyes, concern written all over his face, the worst of the anxiety lifted, and she smiled.

"You were that concerned?" she asked.

"Well, you practically couldn't stand up by yourself by the time I got you to lean against the barn."

"Maybe I should have fallen so you could have caught me," she said without thinking. The air turned electric between them. Three days really was a long time…

"Maybe I can get you thinking about something else?" He put his hand above her head, against the wall of the barn and leaned in. She tilted her head up to his to meet his kiss full on: all her pent up anxiety spilling into the feeling of his lips on hers. He held it for a long time and then slowly moved away, without touching her anywhere else. Her body tingled with anticipation.

"You can now think of me when you're on the track, fulfilling your life-long dream, instead of all the nasty thoughts you were just wrestling with. Come on." He grabbed her hand and walked her toward the end of the barn. Before they turned the corner and into sight of the others, he gave her hand a big squeeze and then dropped it, moving away a few more inches.

Sarge and Charlie were placed at the halfway mark on the track and Skylar was placed about a hundred feet from the finish line. Lilly had recognized Charlie's concern and didn't want Skylar galloping for too long a time at a fast pace. It wasn't even her intention to allow Storm to get close to them, but allow her to get far enough ahead for him to see her and want to run towards her and Hershey. Charlie was expected to take most of the run: but again, Lilly didn't want an all-out run, just enough to see if Storm would step it up a bit. Would he do more than his normal gallop with his friends on the track?

Lilly was in full silks, as she would be from then on, so Storm would get to understand that it was important. She wanted to mimic race day every time he stepped onto the track. She was even going to start him from the gate. Another horse, ridden by Jenny was going to be there as well to help with the simulation, but would drop back once Storm got underway. Lilly didn't want too many variables. She wanted to encourage him to focus from target to target. Targets: that would be Charlie, and then Skylar.

The gate was moved so Storm would break and go half a mile. Charlie was sitting at the quarter mile pole. Sarge was prancing a bit, though nothing she couldn't handle. She could see Storm behind the starting gate. They hadn't brought him out of the barn until after Skylar and Charlie were positioned. Ryan was with Skylar, keeping her company while everyone got into place. He was to stay with her until they loaded Storm in the gate, and he then was instructed to move to the outside of the track, near the rail. Charlie could practically hear Skylar chatting a mile a minute, and Ryan rolling his eyes, from where they were on the track. Ryan was keen to get this test underway. He was probably reminding Skylar what she needed to do.

When Storm broke out of the gate, Skylar and Hershey were to canter towards the finish line, staying in the center of the track. That way Lilly could bring Storm along either side of them depending on how he was doing, and not be too close.

Doug was at the finish line. He was keeping the time. Ben would be helping at the gate, and he would have a watch on Storm as well, so they could compare. Charlie watched as Jenny walked one of Doug's training horses toward the starting gate. Her mind wandered to the moment Doug kissed her. He was right, it did distract her from the anxiety. She could feel the goose bumps on her arms and the butterflies in her belly. He was certainly under her skin.

✳✳✳✳✳✳✳✳✳✳✳✳✳✳✳

In the starting gate, Lilly sat quietly on Storm's back, wondering if he would figure out what she wanted. Through the grills of the starting gate, she saw Charlie and Sarge and then at the turn, Skylar and Hershey. Ryan was still holding Hershey's bridle, probably to ensure he didn't wander to the inside rail and start munching the grass. Skylar would have a hard time pulling him away from the lush green grass.

She could see Charlie sitting calmly on Sarge, down the track in front of them. Thank goodness for Doug. He had calmed her panic attack. Lilly didn't know what he had said, but when they returned, Charlie was all business and ready to proceed.

They approached the starting gate. Coming from the barn, Storm had been distracted by the other horse that they were loading. He hadn't noticed the other players out on the track in this game that Lilly had devised. Now, she knew he had picked up on Sarge down the track. His ears were pricked forward and he was pushing his nose up against the grill. He was prancing more than he ever had in the starting gate. In the past, when she had him in the starting gate, he had stood calmly almost like he was bored with the whole thing. To feel his new-found energy level was encouraging. At first, his ears had been turned toward the horse to his left, but he was now fully focused on Sarge down the track, his nostrils having fully caught his and Charlie's scents.

Lilly braced herself, looked over to Cappie, who was in charge of the gate.

"Ready?" he called over to her. She nodded. The gate sprang open.

Both horses uncoiled as one. In the past, Storm had loped out of the gate, allowing the other horses to get out ahead. Not this time. There was no way Storm was allowing the other horse to get in his way to his friend. Lilly felt him reach deep into the dirt. His ears were forward, his eyes set on Sarge and Charlie, and he leaped out of the gate and into a full gallop

"Go on, Storm. Go get them. Tag, you're it." Storms ears pivoted back to Lilly, listening to her voice. "Hurry up, Storm or they'll beat you to Skylar and Hershey."

Storm reached out with his long legs, swallowing up the ground between him and Sarge. The horse to their left disappeared, as instructed, to allow Storm to focus on just Sarge ahead. Lilly crouched low over his back, absorbing the smooth rhythm of his increasing pace. He was running differently now. He indeed had the ability to race the wind when he wanted to.

They were almost upon Sarge. Lilly knew Storm had an aversion to the inside rail, so she steered him to the outside of Charlie. One issue at a time. Lilly kept a good five feet between the horses so as not to scare Charlie.

✱✱✱✱✱✱✱✱✱✱✱✱✱✱✱

When the gate clanged opened, Charlie had urged Sarge into a gallop. For a few seconds she absorbed the excitement of running fast and free on a racetrack. Her dream of racing a horse on the track coming to fruition. Then she heard Storm coming. The little hairs on her arms rose as she envisioned Storm racing down on them. Her Storm, trying to catch up. Charlie glanced to her right, knowing Lilly would bring him along that side due to Storm's fear of the inside rail. His big grey head was reaching out towards her. The enjoyment of a full out gallop got the best of her, and Charlie crouched lower over Sarge's neck.

"Come on, Sarge. Here he comes. Let's give him something to chase!" Charlie yelled in the heat of the moment. Sarge, at his age, still could remember the feeling of being at the racetrack. He rose to the level of the race and dug in, matching stride for stride with Storm as he pulled up alongside. Alas, it was only for a few brief seconds because Storm had locked in on Skylar and Hershey up ahead.

Charlie looked over at Lilly as they raced pass. Though Lilly was focused on the task at hand, a huge smile played across her face. Charlie could only be a spectator as they raced on by. She sent a prayer up to heaven to keep her little girl safe, as her grey steam engine barreled down on them.

✱✱✱✱✱✱

Lilly could barely breathe. It was one thing to see Storm's speed when he ran in the field, and to feel him race towards Sarge and Charlie. Now it was a completely different experience to feel the jolt of energy he possessed when he realized Skylar and Hershey were galloping ahead of them. He had been so locked on Sarge and Charlie that it wasn't until he pulled up next to them and started to slow a bit that he realized there was another player in this game.

Storm unleashed a fury of speed that Lilly had never felt before. He lowered his head with laser focus on Skylar. Lilly could only hope she could steer him properly around them. She now understood why Charlie had been anxious. Storm was solely focused on reaching Skylar, whose long brunette ponytail was flopping under her helmet as she cantered along on her pony.

****

"Here he comes, Ryan. Let me go!" Skylar said excitedly. Ryan and Skylar had watched Storm load into the gate and then stared in awe as he ran under Lilly's light touch, trying to catch up to their mom and Sarge. Ryan forgot he was supposed to get out of the way and let Skylar canter on her way once Storm broke out of the gate. They had both been distracted by the force of Storm barreling out of the gate, watching the training horse fall quickly behind.

Hershey knew something was up and his nose worked quickly and his ears tuned into Storm galloping on the other side of the track.

"Ryan!" Skylar yelled at him. Ryan had a hard time letting go of the bridle and allowing his sister to run into the path of the thundercloud that was bearing down on his mom, and would certainly turn his attention to his sister. Running in the field with Skylar safely on one side of the fence was one thing, having her on the back of her nervous pony, in the line of flight was another. Skylar pulled hard on Hershey's rein and Ryan's sweaty hand slipped off.

"Come on, Hershey, let's go!" She said with all the confidence of a nine-year-old girl on the back of her best friend. She had no idea how dangerous the next few seconds could be. Hershey broke into a canter and gained speed as Skylar encouraged him down the track towards the finish line.

****

Storm was breathing easily. All his conditioning was paying off as he flew to catch his friends. Lilly listened for all the details: the sound of his feet hitting the dirt, the in and out of air through his nostrils, the bobbing of his head, the position of his ears.

His ears. That was the thing Lilly noticed the most. Storm never laid them flat against his head. They were rarely facing backward. Mostly Storm had his ears forward, listening for all the sounds in front of him.

Those ears were now set on Skylar up ahead. Lilly could hear her too.

"Come on Storm, come catch me!" Skylar was yelling. Within her urgings to Storm, Lilly could catch her saying words to Hershey. The words of a courageous young girl,

"You're okay, Hershey. Storm won't hurt us. It's just like being in the big field." Soothing her nervous pony, whose ears were turned back listening to the approaching Storm. The ground between the horse and pony closed quickly. Lilly decided again to keep Storm to the outside of the track and come up on the right side of Skylar. Lilly tried to keep some distance between them, but Storm would have none of it. He wanted to tag his playmate. He drew up close to Hershey and reached out to nip at his flank. This would not be acceptable in a race, of course. Lilly kept a strong touch on the reins and talked to Storm, sternly but with compassion.

"No you don't, big guy. Not allowed to actually tag your opponents." Storm turned his ears to Lilly. Racing up next to Skylar, Storm kept his eye focused on her, leaning close over her pony's neck. He began to slow his charge, knowing he'd caught up with her. He bobbed his head a few times, thrilled with this new game. They raced under the finish line, the big grey horse with his small pony friend.

As they slowed the horses to a walk, Lilly's mind was going a mile a minute. *Now what? How to get him to go past without wanting to slow down.* She decided to think about that later. Right now, she wanted to get with Doug and Ben to find out if the outrageous time she clocked in her head was really how fast Storm had run.

Skylar was breathing hard and sweating when Lilly approached her. Slowing Hershey had been an easy task, while Storm still had to canter out his speed to a manageable level. At the first chance he had, Hershey had dropped his head and was happily munching the lush infield green grass.

"That was so fun!" Skylar exclaimed. "I want to be a jockey just like you, Lilly!" Lilly smiled at her.

"Come on, champ. Let's go see what the others have to say." Skylar pulled Hershey away from the grass and he dutifully followed Storm back to where the others were gathered. Charlie had dismounted Sarge, who was back to napping, and was standing with Doug, Ben, Ryan, Jenny, and Cappie. From their body language and the way they were talking, Lilly could tell the time in her head was spot on.

A half mile in 46 seconds. 2 seconds off the record for a half mile and a whole second faster than the most recent Kentucky Derby half mile time.

The View from Behind the Starting Gate.

A furlong. An interesting word. Eons ago the word was used as a unit of measure. It means furrow length, or the distance a team of oxen could plough without resting. Its use in medieval times was the length of one furrow in one acre of a ploughed open field. The furlong was once called an acres length. Are you with me so far? I won't bore you with the rest of the history of the furlong, which has to do with rods and feet and yards and even the Roman Stade, just know that its use as a formal unit of measure was abolished in the United Kingdom in 1985. At its high point of use, the furlong was measured to be 220 yards, or 1/8 of a mile.

What does this have to do with horse racing, you ask? Well, everything. The distances of horse races are given in furlongs. A horse is clocked in how fast it can run a furlong. A good pace is considered to be twelve seconds per furlong. So for a quarter mile, a good pace would be twenty-four seconds; the half mile in forty-eight seconds and the mile in one minute, thirty-six seconds. And for the Derby distance of one mile and a quarter, two minutes.

Which is where you get the saying that the Kentucky Derby is the most exciting two minutes in sports!

The quickest Derby run was by Secretariat in 1973 at 1.59 2/5, a race record that still stands today.

So between you and me, our horse is demonstrating he is pretty fast. We still don't know if we can transfer his speed to a race, but we are taking baby steps and Storm is responding. He is re-learning his love of running. Will he learn fast enough to make our goal of running in the Kentucky Derby?

It's been a fun ride so far, will you stick with us? Please forward this to all your friends. Get them on the bandwagon. We need all the support and positive thinking we can get!

Jockey Silks

"Have you thought about your colors?" Doug asked.

"Colors, what colors?" Charlie asked back.

They were once again standing at the fence line of the paddock, Charlie gazing at Storm, Doug gazing at Charlie. She soaked it all in.

"Your jockey colors," Doug replied. She turned to look at him in surprise.

"My colors? I thought we were using your jockey silks. Lilly's been wearing them each time she sits on Storm."

"No ma'am. You need your own. Storm runs under your name, so you need your own colors." Charlie pondered his reply, chewing on the inside of her cheek. She thought of the colors of Secretariat, the blue and white checkerboard. They were one of the most recognizable jockey silks in all of racing.

"Well, I will certainly need to consult my team of experts," Charlie smiled at him.

"Yes, of course you do." He leaned in for a kiss and she didn't stop him.

Storm glanced up, tossed his head and trotted up to them. He thrust his big head between them. Charlie pulled away and laughed.

"I don't give you enough attention, big guy?" she patted him on the nose and slipped a peppermint from her pocket for him.

****

Later that night over dinner, Charlie brought up the topic of the color of the jockey silks with Ryan and Skylar: her team of experts.

"Awesome, let's pick purple!" Skylar exclaimed.

"No way," Ryan cut in.

"So I had an idea driving back from the farm today. Why don't we let Storm's fans decide?" Charlie asked. Ryan and Skylar were quiet for a few seconds.

"What if we don't like what they pick?" Skylar asked.

"We can have veto power," Charlie smiled.

"I think that is a good idea. It will increase the connection with the fan base and they will feel even more involved with Storm. We are only at two hundred and fifty fans. Maybe this contest will help spread the word about Storm and help bring him some cash with the crowd funding campaign." Ryan was always the reasonable child.

After dinner Ryan got to work announcing the contest on Storm's Facebook page and other media sites, with a link to the crowd funding page on Indiegogo. Charlie sat down to write her blog.

A View From Behind the Starting Gate

An earlier post was about jockeys. Well, this one is about what they wear.

Jockey silks are one of the longest running traditions in horse racing. The term "jockey silks" refers to the colors of the jacket and helmet cover worn by each jockey in a horse race. Colors and designs can vary widely.

This tradition dates back to the 1700s, some say earlier: that it started during chariot races in Ancient Rome. The purpose is to be able to distinguish between horses within a race, since usually there are many horses of the same color racing against each other.

It has been brought to my attention that we need to pick out the colors of the silks that Storm's jockey will wear. Therefore, we are having a contest with all of you. If you are interested in helping to select the colors, you can visit our crowd funding page at Indiegogo and for a small donation, submit your color selection. At the end of the week, we will post the top three colors submitted, for a vote.

Once the colors are selected, a design will be created and the official silks get registered with the Jockey Club. Forever.

Please join us and participate in a piece of history.

The contest was a hit. Recommendations on jockey colors flooded Charlie's inbox and the blog's comment section. Soon their fans were arguing on the Facebook page. Every night Charlie, Ryan, and Skylar sat at dinner going through the different ideas. Storm clouds, lightning bolts, some ideas were funny, some outlandish.

The great thing that was happening was the contest was going viral. The fans were getting their friends to participate and by the end of the contest Storm had more than doubled his fan base to five hundred. Even though they only took the options that came through the crowd-funding site, Charlie and the kids enjoyed reading all the comments.

On Friday, Charlie posted the top three colors, blue, yellow, and pink. The "investors" had a week to vote. Skylar was keeping her fingers crossed that pink would make the final two.

At the end of the week, they tallied the vote. Blue and yellow were the top two, to Skylar's chagrin and now they had colors to work with to decide on a design. The design would be simple, solid blue with three yellow bands on the arms, representing the three of them. The cap would be solid yellow. Charlie's one addition was the white ribbon on each sleeve to represent lung cancer awareness, in honor of Peter.

They had their silks, now they just needed their horse to get to the races.

Race Day

It was time to put their money where their mouths were. Race day.

Three weeks had passed since Lilly implemented her plan for Storm. So far so good. Each day, Storm had gotten more comfortable and excited about running fast on the race track. After that first trial with Sarge and Hershey, Lilly had worked with Storm, gradually including more horses in his training. Sarge and Hershey were used for the first week, but with professional riders on their backs. Lilly knew Charlie couldn't stomach another round of chase with a more crowded track with horses running over thirty miles per hour.

Storm continued to improve. Although Skylar and Charlie were not on the backs of Sarge and Hershey, he still put on the power to race them down in the homestretch. When not training, Storm was in his stall with a new buddy on each side of him. Sarge and Hershey were across the aisle where he could see them, but he was getting to know his other stable-mates.

When outside, Storm was put in a pasture with two other colts that were training at the farm. Lilly's intent was to get him to transfer his friendship to these other horses as well, to include them in his game of tag.

So far, the plan had worked and Lilly was able to get Storm to want to work faster. She was smart enough to know that they couldn't force Storm to do anything he didn't want to do.

A trainer once told Charlie that it was important to find out what each individual horse was destined to become. For example, as a junior rider, Charlie had a horse that she desperately wanted to show as a hunter. The horse was a beautiful mover, but she wouldn't do the strides, and she tossed her head, fighting with Charlie the whole course. After many tries to force her to work within the hunter discipline, Charlie decided to enter her in a jumper class, where pretty didn't matter, but time did. They won the class. As they came out of the ring, Charlie's trainer said that they would never step foot in another hunter ring. They spent the next two years having a blast in the jumper world, and her horse was happier for it.

Given that Storm hadn't officially raced since the night Charlie bought him six months earlier, everyone was on edge. They'd all driven out to Laurel Racetrack to watch Storm. It was about an hour until his race and Charlie was standing outside his stall.

"Ready for your big debut?" she asked him. Doug had generously redirected the kids down the barn a bit to allow her some alone time with Storm. Her hand was shaking as she ran it down his long nose. He knew today was different, but Storm wasn't acting nervous. He stood regally in his stall, like he had known this day would come.

"He's going to win, Mr. Doug, I just know it." Charlie heard Skylar busily chattering to Doug. Charlie's thoughts turned again to that night several weeks ago. Nothing else had transpired between them. She hadn't been able to be around the barn much, since the kids were busy in school and Ryan's hockey schedule had gotten busier. Lilly and Doug had overseen Storm's last few weeks of training. When she arrived at the track and saw Doug, it was hard for her to fight the electricity between them, and it looked to her like he was holding back as well.

Doug had been more than gracious and entered two of Storm's training buddies in the same race so Storm would be more comfortable. It wasn't a big race; there were only six entries - Storm, Doug's two horses, and three others. It was a good first test for Storm.

"Mom, it's time to head to the paddock." Ryan walked up to Charlie and pulled her out of her daydreams.

"Oh, right." She stood back. Ben had come from the grooms' room with Storm's bridle and lead rope. They would walk over together and Lilly would meet them in the paddock. Charlie still knew very little about Lilly. It had taken a lot of convincing to get her to ride Storm in the race. She had initially been adamant about not riding in a race again, but she wouldn't provide any information as to why. Charlie knew how to be pretty persuasive, but Lilly wouldn't budge: at least not until the week before.

Lilly had tried several other riders on Storm, even Jenny and other females, and none of them could illicit the same blast of power that Storm would exhibit with her on his back. Yet another sign they couldn't force Storm to do anything he didn't want to do. He had developed a bond with Lilly and wasn't going to run for anybody else.

The established horse whisperer had tried everything, but she couldn't crack the issue. She acknowledged that she had to deal with the rail issue and could work around that, but she personally had to deal with the rider issue. After several days, Lilly had called and agreed to ride in Storm's first race.

They agreed to take it one race at a time, and she could remove herself as his rider whenever she wanted. Charlie knew it was asking a lot, but they were all wrestling with their own demons. They were in it together. All of them - Charlie, the kids, Doug, Lilly, even Cappie, Jenny and Ben. They had all come so far.

Ben walked Storm out of his stall and the small, nervous group made their way over to the paddock area.

"Hi team!" Lilly called out. She was trying to put on a brave face, but she was as pale as a ghost. Charlie worried that she had asked too much of her. Doug gave Lilly a big hug. Charlie saw her take a deep breath and appear to relax. Doug had that way about him. The, "it's okay, I'll take care of you," approach. Charlie, too, found it calming. Lilly walked over to Charlie and the kids.

"Good luck, Miss Lilly," Skylar said to her, giving her another hug. Followed by Ryan, then Charlie. Charlie held her hands a moment longer.

"Thank you," was all she said. Charlie squeezed her hands, and Lilly squeezed Charlie's in return.

"We will be just fine. It's a fun race. No expectations, right?" she asked.

"Right," said Charlie.

"Riders up!" came the call. Lilly put her knee in Doug's out-reached hands and she vaulted into the saddle. As always, she didn't carry a crop. No last minute instructions. Unlike the rest of the owners, trainers, and jockeys, Lilly knew exactly what to do with Storm.

Theirs was a mixed bag. No trainer per se: just a very involved owner, a horse whisperer and a knowledgeable, handsome man, plus two bossy kids. They had worked together to bring a beautiful, grey horse to a race. If nothing else, they had had a great time and had met fabulous people.

Charlie, Doug, Skylar and Ryan made their way up to the grandstand to watch the race. Ben excused himself to watch from the rail near the finish line. Everyone stared intently as Storm walked onto the track, accompanied by Sarge, ridden by Cappie, as his side pony. Doug had pulled some strings and got them to accept Sarge and Cappie on the track. It was another way to keep Storm more relaxed and it seemed to be working. Two of the horses were very familiar to him and he wasn't giving much attention to the other three. Charlie started to shiver in the cool air of February.

"You okay?" Doug asked, from his place next to her.

"Yes, just cold plus the nerves. How do you stand it with all the horses you have racing?" she asked. He looked over at her.

"I only enter and watch the ones I can handle." He smiled, "If I had entered a horse that I didn't think had a chance, I would be nervous, but since I only enter horses that have a legitimate chance to win, and put the best jockeys on them, I leave it in their hands." He put his arm around her shoulders. Mistake. Charlie immediately went from chilly to very hot. She couldn't be distracted in this moment with Storm on the track. She gently removed Doug's arm.

"As much as I would love to keep your arm around me, I cannot be distracted from my horse," Charlie said smiling. Doug returned the smile,

"Understood." He leaned down to Skylar. "Want a better view?" he asked.

"Yes!" she clamored. Doug hoisted Skylar up on his shoulders. "Yippee. Go, Storm!" Skylar yelled. Several other patrons around them smiled up at her.

"My horse is running in this race," she informed all who would listen.

"Well, good luck!" came several replies. Charlie looked around, noting once again that there were not very many people there to cheer on the horses. She didn't have time to ponder the reasons because the horses came up and entered the starting gate.

"And they're off!" yelled the announcer. Five horses broke as one. One horse broke out of the gate late: Storm. Within a few hundred yards, the horses were a good three lengths ahead of him. He looked bit discombobulated, like he was trying to figure out this new training exercise. Lilly sat quietly on his back, waiting for him to settle. They wouldn't have long, as the race was only six furlongs, or ¾ of a mile. Charlie's hands were clenched together and she only had eyes for Storm.

****

Lilly waited as Storm assessed the situation, galloping slowly. Ahead of him raced the five other horses. Two of the horses he knew, three he did not. All their smells floated back to him. He was used to the jockeys being in full silks. Nothing was really too different from their training at Doug's place, or the past week where they worked Storm in the mornings on this track. Would he engage?

She watched his ears. They were pricked straight forward listening to the horses ahead. She knew his nostrils were taking in big gulps of air.

Suddenly, he found his stride, a smooth long gait that ate up the dirt below her. The distance between them and the group ahead started to close.

"Come on, Storm. Let's show 'em what you've got!" Lilly called to him. She tucked herself low over his neck and ran her hand along it, one of the signs she had started to give him to ask him to move on. She never used a whip. Storm responded. Lilly saw that the trailers up ahead were Doug's two horses, which meant that Storm would have to go by them to get to the leaders.

"Mom, he's doing it!" Skylar clapped her hands from on top of Doug's shoulders. Charlie stood on tippy toes, every nerve in her body on edge. They all leaned in to see Storm's surge up on the pack. Would he pass Doug's horses? The ones he knew and had been training with? Would he go after the leader?

Ryan stood still next to Charlie. Her hand found his. He didn't take his eyes off the race, but squeezed her hand in return before pulling away.

"He'll do it, Mom. He's made for this." Charlie's eyes filled with tears as her son and daughter cheered on their horse. She couldn't remember the last time they had all stood together in such anticipation. She turned her attention back to the race.

****

Storm raced up and drew abreast of Doug's horses. He paused a few seconds, confused at what to do now. He had caught the horses he knew, but there were still horses up ahead. Was the game over? He flicked his ears back and forth, searching for guidance. He felt Lilly's knees squeeze him on and heard her encouraging words, "Come on, Storm, you can do this. Go run them down!"

She wanted him to keep going. He turned his ears forward. Storm reached down another gear and went on, chasing the leaders up ahead.

Lilly smiled. He did it! In her mind, the race was already won. Track was running out under their feet and she knew he couldn't catch the front runner in time. The finish line was just a few hundred feet up ahead. Lilly continued to urge Storm on down the center of the track. He raced by one more horse before racing in under the wire, finishing third.

******

Charlie let the breath she had been holding, out. She caught Doug's eye and he smiled. He saw what she had. Storm had run on, passed his horses, and gone after the ones ahead. He was learning. The game of tag didn't need to be with just the horses he knew, but other challengers. Charlie smiled brightly. One step at a time.

After the Race

The barn was quiet. It was late. Charlie had taken Ryan and Skylar back to the hotel after dinner, but she couldn't sleep. After tucking her tired girl in, she told Ryan to keep the TV volume down, and she left to go back to the backstretch of Laurel to spend some time with her horse. She craved that time alone with Storm. He had filled the void left by Peter's passing and she loved just sitting, petting, and talking to him. He was a good listener.

Charlie set the wine bottle down next to the bale of hay and with glass in hand, slid into Storm's stall and sat on the floor, leaning against the wall.

"Well, what do you think of yourself now?" she asked him. Storm leaned his head over to her in between bites of hay. She blew softly up his nostrils. He blew back.

"Ryan has mapped everything out, you know," Charlie spoke softly. Storm shook his head up and down, breaking up the hay - or maybe acknowledging her comment.

"You did a great job today. Doug said your time, one minute, fourteen seconds doesn't tell the whole story. Given you broke late, coupled with a slow down towards the end of the race when you were trying to figure out whether to go after those other horses. He said your middle quarter time was twenty-three seconds! That's awesome. The good thing is that others won't know you're coming, Storm. They will only look at the final time and that you finished third in a no name race." Storm nibbled on Charlie's jeans, looking for a peppermint. She pulled one out of her pocket and he gently took it. His black velvet nose was soft against her hand.

"A Storm is a-comin'. Soon everyone will be running for cover, you big, old goofball." She tugged at Storm's ears and rubbed his poll, the bone centered between them. The area he couldn't itch just right.

"It's the calm before the storm, right?" Charlie looked up, startled. Doug was casually leaning over Storm's half-door. "I figured I'd find you here. I texted a few times, but you didn't answer. Savoring your first race as an owner?" She smiled,

"Just having a little chat with my favorite racehorse. Well, my only racehorse." Charlie started to stand up.

"No, don't get up. I'll join you." Doug grabbed the bottle of wine, slid around Storm's nosey head and plopped himself down next to her on the ground. He moved so easily. Charlie took a long sip of wine.

"Do you mind?" he asked holding up the bottle. Charlie handed him her glass. He filled it to the brim and then took a long sip himself. Storm checked, but found no peppermints from Doug, so he wandered to the other side of the stall, hitched his hind right leg, and promptly fell asleep.

"Guess he's a bit tired from his effort today," Charlie commented.

"Don't kid yourself, he's just giving us a little privacy." Doug's sexy smirk had returned. Charlie definitely missed that. She grabbed the wine glass from him and took another long sip.

"You're not going to get all tipsy like the first night I met you, are you?" he asked.

"Liquid courage," she replied, looking over at him. He moved in close, wrapping his hand around hers on the wine glass.

"Fight you for the last sip?" There was no fight in her. She leaned in, remembering that lone kiss behind the barn, and the night they had dinner. Doug's other hand laced itself around her neck and into her hair, drawing her against him, his lips searching hers. She kissed him with all the pain and loneliness she had been holding inside her since Peter died.

Doug slowly moved and laid her down on the soft bedding in the stall. He lay next to her, leaning on his elbow.

"You are beautiful, you know," he said. "And smart, curious, demanding, over-protective, and over-involved in the training of your horse." He smiled down at her. She pulled his lips back to hers and they spent the next hour exploring each other and whispering while the big, grey thundercloud that brought them together dozed above them.

Storm's Troopers

So the Road to the Kentucky Derby began. Storm's Troopers. That is what they started to call themselves. It had been Ryan's idea; he was a *Star Wars* fanatic. The original troopers were Charlie, Ryan, Skylar, Doug, Cappie, Ben, and Jenny, as well as Sarge and Hershey.

Ryan started incorporating the use of Storm's Troopers into all his Facebook, Twitter, and Instagram postings. The fans loved it and the name took off. As Charlie continued to write her blog each week, she noticed the reply comments were getting longer and several of her followers were signing off as a, "trooper." Their following got larger.

Charlie was adamant with Doug and Lilly that they follow the plan she and Ryan had come up with to try and earn points to qualify for the Derby. They decided one more low-level race at Laurel and then they were off to Florida for the Tampa Bay Derby.

Charlie was on cloud nine. She had come to a place where she felt like everything was going her way. Things with her kids were on track, Storm was learning and improving with each race, and Doug continued to woo her. It was really the best of all worlds.

Along their personal Road to the Kentucky Derby, the fan base increased, with more and more people coming out to the races in which Storm raced. From Florida and the Tampa Bay Derby to Louisiana and the Louisiana Derby and then to Kentucky for the Blue Grass Stakes, the people they met along the way cheering on their horse was staggering. Word was starting to spread and those that couldn't make it to the race followed their progress online, posting words of encouragement along the way.

Charlie would update their progress through her blog posts and Ryan had a continual linkup to their Facebook page and other social media outlets.

The travel was tough on the family, with Charlie and the kids flying back and forth between races in order to continue some semblance of normal life: going to school and participating in their sports. Everyone's nerves were on edge.

One Friday, a few weeks into the hectic racing schedule, Kate and Jillian came over for dinner. Charlie left them with Skylar, while she went to get Ryan from hockey practice. It was one of the first weekends in a long time that they were going to be able to sit at home and have dinner together. She could tell by the way Ryan opened the car door that it was going to be a rough night. He'd been working so hard and he was so grumpy lately. She tried not to say anything to set him off.

"Dinner will be ready when we get home. I bet you're hungry," she said. Food was always a good opener.

"Yeah, I am, because you didn't pack me enough for lunch today," he spat.

"Oh, I'll pack you more next week."

"What are we having for dinner?" he asked, less hostile.

"Your Aunt Kate made Chicken Alfredo."

"Oh man, Aunt Kate is there? Are you going somewhere?"

"No, why would you say that?"

"Last time Aunt Kate came over, you went to dinner with Doug." He said the last word as if it had a bad taste. Charlie couldn't believe what she was hearing.

"I thought you liked Doug," she said, suddenly nervous.

"That doesn't mean I want you to date him."

"We're not-"

"I saw you guys kiss! Don't lie!" Ryan was yelling now, he'd turned in his seat to face her.

"When did you see that?" Charlie's mind was racing. She could feel all the positive things that she'd been feeling about her relationship with Doug slipping away.

"That first day Lilly rode Storm, back at the farm. You got all freaked out about Skylar, and Doug took you around the back of the barn, and when I went to go check on you, I saw you guys kissing."

"Okay, you weren't supposed to see that."

"I bet you weren't even really worried about Skylar, you just wanted a reason to go make out with dad's replacement." Charlie slammed on the brakes, and the car came screeching to a halt. "Ow, Mom, what the-"

"Now you listen to me: your father was the love of my life. I miss him every day. If there was any way for me to get him back, I would do it. But I can't. You and your sister are all I have left of him, so you bet your ass I was actually worried about her that day." Ryan opened his mouth to speak but Charlie cut him off, "No, you're done talking, it's my turn. I have been lonely and depressed for two years, Ryan. Doug will *never* replace your father, but he is a good man, and I like him. I wanted to tell you and Skylar about it before we started anything official."

There was a thick silence in the car for several long seconds.

"Is this why you've been so horrible to me lately? And why you stopped wanting to go watch Storm train? Because you didn't want to see me with Doug?"

"I just…felt like you were forgetting about Dad." Ryan was crying. Charlie leaned over and embraced her son, tears pouring down her own face.

"Oh, honey, I will never ever forget him. He gave me all the best things in life," Charlie assured him. After a few minutes, they had both calmed down enough to finish the drive home. When they pulled into the driveway, Charlie opened her door, but Ryan stopped her.

"Mom, wait."

"What's up?"

"I think you should make it official…with Doug. I think it would be okay." Charlie smiled at her firstborn. They got out of the car, and walked up to the house, smiling and talking. Over dinner that night, Charlie told Skylar about Doug. That conversation went a little differently:

"What?! I love him! He's the nicest, most horse-knowing person of all time! If you guys get married, would I be able to play with all of his horses?" Charlie laughed. Kate and Jillian smiled at her, and teased her, along with her kids. After all was said and done, it was exactly the night at home Charlie had wanted, surrounded by the people that meant the most to her.

Qualifier

Storm hadn't finished well in the Blue Grass Stakes. It would have pushed him over the edge and into the top twenty if he had finished first, second or third. When they got Storm back to the barn after the race, where he finished eighth, Lilly was convinced something was wrong. Charlie had the vet go over Storm with a fine toothed comb. Storm was running a fever, nothing he could attribute to anything, and he showed no other signs of sickness. Charlie was all but certain it was the aggressive racing schedule, taking its toll on Storm.

With only twenty points, they were ranked thirtieth and the possibility of getting into the Derby was practically non-existent.

They called a group meeting to discuss what they should do. The only chance was to enter Storm in the Lexington Stakes the very next Saturday and try to get a few more points. The current cutoff was twenty-six. If Storm could win it, he would get another ten points and be in the top twenty. The other horses entered into the Lexington Stakes did not have enough points to make a difference, but it would mean Storm racing in back to back races, unheard of these days; but it was their only chance.

Storm had yet to demonstrate that he would move past the front runner to win a race. His game of tag required him to get up to the leader, but once he, "tagged him" Storm would start to slow. Lilly hadn't been able to figure out a way to get him to move past the leader to win the race.

Charlie, Ryan, Doug, and Lilly sat around on the bales of hay outside of Storm's stall at Keeneland late into the night debating the pros and cons of running Storm so quickly after a race. Skylar slept soundly in the corner of the groom's stall, after a bout of crying; her concern over Storm's well-being was wreaking havoc on her small body.

"It's not unheard of," Doug commented.

Charlie and Ryan were silent. They didn't want any harm to come to their horse after all they had been through.

Lilly stood up and walked around a bit. They turned to follow her and she wandered over to Storm's stall. He poked his head over his stall guard, looking for the ever present peppermint. They had all started to carry them in their pockets. Lilly pulled one from its wrapper and gave it to him. She spent a few moments rubbing her hand along his neck. Storm nodded his head and blew out his nostrils.

She turned back to the group.

"As you mentioned, Doug, it is not unheard of. Years ago, horses would run back to back races, and be no worse for wear. Let me tell you a little about our guy's great, great, great grandfather, Native Dancer.

"Towards the end of his two-year-old racing campaign, Native Dancer raced almost every weekend in the month of August, four races, and won all of them. He dazzled the racing industry. During the time when TV programs were only in black and white, everyone was glued to their screens, waiting to see the "Grey Ghost," come around the turn and part the sea of dark horses ahead of him. It was an exciting time not just for the racing community, but the public at large. Native Dancer captured a generation who fell in love with him and horse racing. So much so that during the time, horse racing became the number one spectator sport – even over baseball.

"Leading up to the 1953 Kentucky Derby, Native Dancer raced in both the Gotham Stakes and Wood Memorial, the two weekends prior, and won both races. Running in the Kentucky Derby would be three weeks in a row."

They all sat there spellbound once again listening to one of Lilly's stories about a Kentucky Derby winner. Or so they thought. Lilly was silent.

"Well?" Ryan asked.

"He came in second," Lilly said. They all let out a collective sigh.

"But," she continued, "His jockey had him all over the track trying to get to the front and he was fouled twice during his run up, and he *still* came in second."

"Native Dancer finished off his racing career winning twenty-one of twenty-two races, many of which were run back to back," she finished.

"Now, I know Storm hasn't demonstrated anything like that, but I think he is ready to break out. He's got the conditioning and he is learning in each race he runs in. I wouldn't recommend anything if I thought it was going to be detrimental to the horse. But, my vote is that we go for it, as long as his temperature is normal each day this week. If he doesn't run well, he will get a nice long break." She smiled.

Ryan jumped up and hugged Lilly. After a few seconds, Lilly gently pushed Ryan away, uncomfortable with the human touch, but tolerating it from him. Charlie once again wondered what had happened to this intelligent, beautiful woman.

So they were all in for one last effort to qualify for the Derby.

It worked out. Although Storm still wouldn't move past the leader, he came in second and picked up another four points.

What a whirlwind. Everyone was in a bit of depression. They had finished off their Road to the Derby, ranked twenty-second in points, and only the top twenty qualified to run on Derby Day. Storm had earned twenty-four points with his third in the Tampa Bay Derby, fourth in the Louisiana Derby, and second in the Lexington Stakes.

Now they were back home, and it was time to start letting reality sink in: they'd come close, but not close enough. Charlie put a crying Skylar to bed, and tried to cheer Ryan up, before she herself fell prey to the depression seeping through their home.

That's when the phone rang.

Two of the top twenty had to withdraw. One had stepped on himself while training that morning and opened a deep gash in his front fetlock that wouldn't heal in time, and the other was scratched, as the owners felt the distance was going to be too much for their colt and wanted to save him for the Preakness. They were in. Charlie had to erase days of feeling like a failure to let that sink in. Her horse was going to the Kentucky Derby.

For several long moments Charlie held the phone and sat quietly soaking in the news, a smile slowly spreading across her face. Then she ran up the stairs, calling the kids. Both Ryan and Skylar stumbled into the hall, rubbing their eyes.

"What's wrong, Mom?" Ryan asked.

"I just got off the phone with the people who run the Derby. Some horses had to drop out and that means...Storm's in the Derby!" she exclaimed, hugging both of them.

"Wait, what?" asked Ryan.

"Really, Mom?" Skylar asked still coming out of her sleep.

"Really, honey," Charlie said. They all started screaming and hugging and jumping up and down. They were in. Just like that. Five days out. They needed to get to Kentucky from Virginia. Charlie called Doug.

"Hi!" she said when he picked up.

"Hello, Charlie," he said back. She briefly wondered if she would ever stop holding her breath when he answered the phone.

"We're in," she stated. Silence on the other end.

"Say again?" he asked.

"We are in! We are going to the Derby!" Charlie screamed into the phone, unable to control her emotions, Ryan and Skylar jumped up and down beside her. They had become quite a team. They were just as excited to tell Doug as Charlie was.

"Seriously?" Doug exclaimed.

"Yes, two horses withdrew, so the next two horses on the list get to move up in to the nineteenth and twentieth spots," Charlie said quickly. Doug was quiet on the line.

"I am so happy for you, Charlie. You have all worked so hard and I believe Storm has a good shot."

"I'm happy for all of us! If it wasn't for you, we wouldn't be where we are today," she said. "When can we leave?"

"I'll send Cappie with the trailer early tomorrow. Be ready to leave no later than 7 am." Doug was all business now, mentally working through what the next five days would look like. "I'll drive down with him and then drive with you to talk through our game plan. I am sure you will have a lot of input." A little bit of sarcasm was noted in Doug's voice. Charlie ignored it; she knew he actually loved that she was involved in every step of the way with Storm.

"We'll be ready!" she practically yelled into the phone.

Genuine Storm would be running in the Kentucky Derby.

Churchill Downs

Charlie didn't sleep after they got the call; she was too busy planning for the week. She needed to pack the kids' clothes and get someone to look after Critter and Hershey.

She took care of all the immediate needs, knowing she could inform her friends and family during the long ride to Kentucky. She did however, need to update the fans, they would want to know the horse they supported had actually made it into the Derby, and she didn't want them finding out through the local news channels.

Charlie pulled up Storm's Facebook and Twitter pages and updated his status: "Kentucky Derby Bound!" with a few explanatory sentences about moving up to number twenty due to the withdrawal of two of the other horses that had previously qualified.

As she scurried around the house gathering things for the trip, she could hear the pinging of responses on the Facebook page. They were coming in, one after the other. Doesn't anyone ever sleep anymore? Charlie walked by and peeked at the comments.

"Good luck, Storm!"

"I knew he would get in."

"I am searching for Derby tickets as I write this. We will be there to cheer him on!"

"Us too!"

"Me too!" And on and on. Storm had over 5,000 fans on his Facebook page now, and the number increased daily. Ryan had done a great job updating his status, and people were really interested in following him. It had been awesome to see more and more of his fans coming out to the qualifying races. Charlie wondered how many would make it to Derby Day.

Cappie was right on schedule. He pulled into the driveway at 6:45 am sharp.

"Hello, ma'am." He touched his cap, leaning outside the driver's side window as he maneuvered the big rig around Charlie's small driveway. Doug jumped down from the passenger side.

"Hi Doug!" Skylar yelled from the open barn door. She'd dropped the "Mr." after Charlie told her they were dating. She thought it was too formal.

"Hi, yourself." Doug smiled, not minding the informality one bit. Everyone else was smiling too: like a bunch of goofy clowns. Skylar ran up and he wrapped her in a big bear hug.

"Exciting, huh?" Ryan walked up and held out his hand to shake Doug's, Doug pulled him into a bear hug as well: their excitement palpable. Charlie's eyes swelled with tears, watching them. Ryan had grown particularly close to Doug over the last few months, and she was so relieved to see that he hadn't let his anxiety about his late father get in the way of the blossoming relationship with Doug. He had been missing a male figure in his life and Doug had taken that on without question. Charlie walked over.

"Good morning," she said, holding tightly to her warm cup of coffee.

"Ready for the show?" Doug asked.

"Yes!" they all yelled in unison.

"He's all ready to go, Doug," Skylar said. "We have been chatting with him all morning about his big day. He knows what is going on, he just does."

"I am sure he does, Skylar," Doug replied, looking over Skylar's shoulder at Charlie. "Well, let's get this show on the road! Ben left right after I told him the news last night. He couldn't sleep and said he needed to get everything ready at the Downs for Storm's arrival. We have a long trip. Ryan, do you want to ride with Cappie? Your mom and I have planning to do while we drive."

"Sure," Ryan said. He eyed Charlie suspiciously, but one shake of the head from her, and he relaxed. He may have decided to like Doug, but that didn't mean he wasn't going to look after his mom. As a teenager, he'd rationalized that it was okay for him to treat her poorly sometimes, or a lot of the time, but it certainly was not okay for anyone else to mistreat her.

"Come on, young man, help me get your horse so we can be on our way," Cappie commanded, with a hitch in his step.

"I'll grab Sarge." Charlie followed. Storm would not be going anywhere without his sidekick side pony. Sarge knew something was up as well. He seemed to stand taller: he didn't want to be outdone by the young colt across the aisle.

"Yep, you are going too, old man." She patted his nose. "You need to help him stay calm."

"Sorry, Hershey, just the Thoroughbreds," Skylar told her pony. "But we'll bring you back some roses from the ones draped over Storm's neck when he wins!" Hershey whinnied in reply. They all laughed as they led the horses out of the barn and up the ramp to start their journey.

Backside at the Downs

Charlie sipped her coffee as the steam rose from the top and into the early morning mist. She looked to her left at all the tents set up, the TV stations getting ready for their Derby coverage broadcasts.

She took in a deep breath and looked in front of her: across the infield stood the most recognizable grandstand in all of horse racing - the twin spires of Churchill Downs. Each time she looked at them, she had to pinch herself. She was having a lot of trouble believing she wasn't in a dream.

Churchill Downs had expanded over the years, with the addition of suite and seating options that looked like big Lego blocks on each side of the spires. But if you held up your hands just right, you could still just frame out the original grandstand.

It was, "Backside at the Downs", the day where fans with special access are allowed to go see their favorites take their last preparation workouts before Saturday's big race. Storm's group got there early because they were hosting a small group of people to see Storm take his turn out on the track. There were special bleachers set up to allow the observers to get a good view of their favorite as they galloped by.

Charlie had offered this backstage pass to those that had invested the most in the crowd-funding campaign when it first started. Back then, Storm didn't have any experience and this group had entrusted their money to help get Storm to the next level. They had donated much-needed cash to pay Storm's upkeep and race entry fees.

Luckily, since Storm started finishing in the money in his races, he was now paying his own way. Charlie still kept the campaign open for those who wanted to contribute. Anyone coming on board now received personalized updates and pictures as well as old horse shoes of Storm's, when they came available. However, it was the early supporters that Charlie felt her family owed their hearts and successes to.

Early on Derby day, everyone would spend some time in the infield interacting with all of Storm's fans. Not just those that supported him financially, but those that followed his progress on Facebook and Twitter and other social media sites. Their words of encouragement helped Charlie get through the days when she was not sure Storm would run for them.

Charlie felt two arms come around from behind her.

"What do you think about all this?" Doug asked in her ear. She felt the familiar tingling, and goose bumps rose on her arms. She continued to stand still, soaking everything in, including the man behind her

"Ms. Jenkins, is that you, Ms. Jenkins?" A reporter came over from the tents with a microphone in hand, and cameraman right behind him. They had found her. That would be the end of her alone time for the next three days.

She squeezed Doug's hands and removed them from around her. It was probably better to not be on camera with a goofy school girl grin on her face.

"Yes, I am Charlie Jenkins," Doug stayed close, probably ready to defend her honor.

"You think you actually have a chance in the Derby with that grey horse of yours?" His name tag said Brian, along with WAVE3, the NBC affiliate in Louisville.

"We wouldn't be here if we didn't think we had a chance, Brian," Charlie responded calmly.

"Ms. Jenkins, there have only been eight grey horses to win the Kentucky Derby in its 140 runnings, that's just 5%. It would seem that history and statistics are against you," he stated.

"It's not the color that dictates a champion, Brian, it's beneath the surface: their heart, their courage, their desire. We believe our Storm is ready to unleash his fury on Saturday," she smiled politely.

"How do you feel about being the first female owner to have a horse in the Derby in over twenty years?" he asked.

"Well, it's an equal opportunity race, isn't it?" she quipped back. Brian looked over her shoulder and cut his interview short.

"Ah, thank you, Ms. Jenkins. Mr. Riley! We are excited to see Duke work out this morning…" He called out and off he went with his entourage to talk to the owner of the favorite to win the Kentucky Derby.

"I guess I'm not that interesting of a story." Charlie smiled over at Doug, watching him look over at the group talking to Duke's owner.

"He'll be tough to beat, Charlie," he said.

"Who?" she asked.

"Duke, Royal Duke. He has been tearing up the tracks out on the west coast and is the top qualifier. I have been watching his races and he has done it all, won from in front and come from behind. Storm will have to be on the top of his game," Doug finished. Charlie linked her arm through his,

"Worried?" she smiled up at him. He turned his focus back to her and away from Duke's group,

"Not worried, I just like to know the competition and be prepared. This is your show, I am just along for the ride. And what a ride it has been." He leaned down and planted a big kiss. Charlie let it deepen while they stood with the beautiful famous spires of Churchill Downs as their backdrop.

"Come on, we have a horse to train this morning," Doug broke up the moment. "People will start to think you are more interested in kissing me than getting your horse ready to race." He jokingly said and swatted her on the backside.

Walking hand in hand, they went to go get their horse ready.

On their way to the track, they ran into Jillian and Kate, who had arrived last night to support their friend. Kate was the first to notice Charlie and Doug walking their way. She smiled at their intertwined fingers.

"Good morning, you two," Kate said, drawing Jillian's attention to her friend.

"Oh, aren't you two just precious? Well, while you have been busy being on TV, we found the cafeteria serving breakfast and drinks. Mimosa?" She held out her glass.

"I think I'll skip the alcohol this morning, thanks. That's actually what got me into this mess," Charlie joked. Everyone laughed and they all made their way to the track to watch Storm getting ready for his big race. Doug walked ahead to talk to Cappie, and when he left, Jillian put the glass in Charlie's hand.

"I know you could use a sip to calm your nerves." Charlie looked at the glass in her hand and sighed before taking a long sip out of the straw.

"I've never been this nervous in my life," she confided. Kate put an arm around her shoulder and Jillian linked arms with her, and the three of them walked the rest of the way to the track laughing and talking about the excitement of the next two days as well as the handsome man that walked in front of them.

Derby Traditions

It had been a long day at the track, taking in all the races, culminating in the running of the Kentucky Oaks – similar to the Derby, but only for fillies. Charlie drove back to their hotel with Ryan, Skylar, Kate, and Jillian. The excitement was building and it was great to watch the owners of Elegant Dawn hold up the trophy for winning the Oaks. They could only hope it would be them the next day.

"I just can't believe this is happening," Jillian commented from the back seat. "It's amazing that we were just three gals having a girls night out, only eight months ago, and now, here we are at the Kentucky Derby!"

Charlie smiled at her in the rearview mirror. Well, what she could see of her. Jillian always fully embraced traditions, and hats on Oaks Day and Derby Day was no exception. This year's pick was above and beyond. God knows what she would wear tomorrow. Charlie had had a hard time fitting the hat in the car with them: Jillian had to take it off and fit it in sideways. Her own hat was much less ostentatious. It was an old floppy brim that Peter had given to her when he first learned how much she truly loved horse racing. She wore it every year during their Derby party and since she only had one hat, it would be on her head tomorrow as well. It was also comforting to know a piece of Peter would be with her.

"I'm so glad neither of us stopped you from buying Storm that night," Kate said.

"Good friends would have," Charlie teased.

"We are your *best* friends, because we know what's *best* for you. I knew he was a champion the first time I saw Storm," Jillian said. Her hat was tall enough that it was covering her face, so she had to shout to be heard.

"You liar," Kate said, laughing. Charlie and Jillian laughed along with her, but Charlie's giddiness didn't last long. The butterflies in her stomach were just getting worse. She needed to stop and pick up some Tums or Rolaids, maybe some Ginger Ale. She already knew she wasn't going to sleep a wink that night.

"Hey, do you guys mind if we stop at the store to grab a few things?" Charlie asked. She hated to stop, Skylar was fast asleep and drooling between Kate and Jillian, and she wanted to get her little girl back to the hotel. "I will just be a few minutes." Charlie pulled into the parking lot of Kroger's, the local grocery chain.

"I need to use the bathroom," Skylar piped up. She'd started awake when the car stopped.

"Come on, sweet pea, come in to the store with me while I pick up a few things and we will find the bathroom." The store was packed with people. Charlie didn't understand: since when was Friday night a big night for grocery shopping? Suddenly, she panicked. Charlie hadn't been listening to the weather recently, was there a thunderstorm coming? Were they in tornado country? Charlie grabbed Skylar's hand,

"Let's go find the restroom." They walked up to an employee standing off to the side. "Can you point us to your bathroom?" Charlie asked.

"It's right over here. I can show you," The elderly employee said.

"Thanks a bunch, Linda," Charlie replied as she glanced at her nametag. Charlie waited outside the restroom for Skylar. She turned to Linda who was organizing grocery bags at each of the registers.

"What is going on?" she asked. Linda looked over at Charlie.

"Why, it's the roses, ma'am."

"The roses?" Charlie asked.

"Yes, ma'am, for the winner of the Kentucky Derby tomorrow. The garland that gets draped on the winner is stitched right here in our store." She smiled proudly. Skylar had just walked out of the restroom and pulled at Charlie's hand,

"Come on, Mom, let's go see the roses that will be draped around Storm!" she squealed. Linda raised her eyebrows.

"Storm, as in Genuine Storm, the long shot running tomorrow?" In Louisville, everyone knew who was running the first Saturday in May, be it the favorite or the long shot.

"The very same," Charlie replied.

"Well, I'll be. Can't say we have ever had a real life Derby horse owner in the store! Come on, let me get you a closer look at the ladies." Linda started parting the large crowd to move them through.

"Comin' though, horse owner here!" People started to stare and take pictures. Charlie put her arm around Skylar. The questions came from all around. "Which horse? Do you have a chance? We will root for you!"

Linda brought them right to the front of the crowd. It was an amazing sight. Roses everywhere, and in front of several ladies was a long strip of cloth to which they were stitching individual roses, each in their own individual water vial.

"Wow!" Skylar said.

"Wow, is right," Charlie said in return. "I need to get Kate and Jillian and Ryan in here." She pulled out her cell phone and called out to the car. In minutes, the others had made their way to where Charlie and Skylar were standing.

"So beautiful," Kate commented. "Can you give us a bit of background on what is happening?" She asked, turning to Linda who was standing off to the side.

"Of course!" Linda replied. She was obviously proud of the role Kroger played in the biggest day of Louisville's year. She told them that she had been a part of the making of the garland for years, and had worked for the florist shop that had designed the original garland.

"Roses initially made their way to the Derby in 1883, when they were given to all the ladies at a party by a fine gentleman from New York. The ladies were so taken with the flowers that the track president decided to name the rose as the official flower for the 1884 Derby. In subsequent years, the roses started to get draped over the winner of the Derby. Finally, a formal design for the garland was commissioned, and it hasn't changed much over the years." Linda looked over at Ryan.

"Now you know why the race is called the 'Run for the Roses.' There are 554 roses stitched into a background of green, they say the tradition of 554 represents the number of ladies that were given roses back on that day in 1883." Linda winked over at Jillian, Kate, and Charlie. "The garland has the Seal of the Commonwealth of Kentucky on one side, and the Twin Spires with the number of years the Derby has been run, stitched on the other. It is 122 inches long, 22 inches wide, and weighs approximately 40 pounds."

"See over there," Linda pointed over to one of the floral designers, "She is making the crown of roses on the garland with a rose for each horse running this year and a single rose that rises to the sky in the center, signifying the heart required to win the Derby."

"What a labor of love," Kate commented.

"Yes, young lady, all these women take great pride in stitching the garland. They have been here since 4pm and they will be here late into the evening putting the finishing touches on it. At 8:45 am tomorrow morning, the Garland of Roses, along with the Jockey's Bouquet, sixty matching long-stem roses wrapped in ten yards of ribbon, will be taken to Churchill Downs with a police escort. They will be on exhibit and then stored for safe keeping until they are presented to the winner of tomorrow's Kentucky Derby," Linda finished up her history lesson.

"The roses are perfectly beautiful." Jillian eyed them lovingly.

"They certainly are," Linda replied, "They are 'Freedom' roses – said to be a perfect patriotic red - named after the events of 9/11 in tribute to the victims, the families, and those serving in the armed forces."

They all stood there quietly and in amazement, watching the progress of the master designers as they continued to work on the garland. Skylar broke the silence with a large yawn. Linda smiled at her.

"You outta get some sleep, little miss. You have a big day tomorrow!" Charlie reached out and pulled Linda into a hug, which the elderly woman returned without hesitation.

"Thank you so much for showing us all this. It really means the world to us," Charlie said. Linda grabbed Charlie's hand with both of her wrinkled ones,

"God bless you, and your horse. I will be betting on him to be wearing this garland tomorrow." Charlie's eyes filled with tears and she fought not to let them roll down her cheeks. She was so overwhelmed. Could she possibly keep it all together over the next twenty-four hours?

"I will let Storm know he has a lot of local people rooting for him, and especially those that have a hand in the making of the prize at the end." Linda walked them to the exit of the store. On their way, she grabbed a bag of carrots from the produce section.

"Please give these to Storm, I am sure he would like these more than the roses."

"Oh, he knows all about the roses," Skylar said, "We've been talking to him about them for a long time." Linda gave Skylar a grandmotherly hug and waved to the small group as they made their way to the car.

Derby Song

Charlie grabbed a cup of coffee and sat quietly. *Breathe*, she kept telling herself. It was finally the day. Derby Day – May 2 – the first Saturday in May. The day they had all been working so hard to get to. Everyone was still sleeping and that was to be expected at three in the morning. Charlie, however, couldn't sleep, so she decided to get up. She had lain down with Skylar earlier in the night, to help her sleep. Her little girl was so excited. It had been a long day for her, and it would be an even longer one today.

Ryan had been busy updating Facebook with pictures from the day at the track, watching the fillies run in the Kentucky Oaks race. It had all been extremely exciting, but that was just a precursor to what Derby Day would bring. Everyone had been so encouraging: they wished Charlie and the kids good luck wherever they went. Even though Storm was one of the longest shots in the field at 35-1, people were excited that he had the opportunity to be there.

Charlie knew the infield would have a big contingent of Storm's supporters. Their fans had been posting all week about their arrival to cheer on, "their" horse. The Storm Team would spend some time with the fans early in the day to thank them for their support. Charlie still couldn't believe the fan base had grown to over 7,500 during the past week. Storm's fan base had exploded over the past few weeks as the excitement grew culminating with him qualifying to run for the roses. Charlie pulled out her iPad: time for a blog post.

The View From Behind the Starting Gate

Run for the Roses. Did you know that Dan Fogelberg wrote a song dedicated to this race? I remember playing it over and over again as a kid. My mom had gotten his album to listen to the songs, "Same Old Lang Syne" and, "Leader of the Band," which she said reminded her of her dad. On the album was the song, "Run for the Roses." As a horse-crazy kid, you can understand why I kept playing it. I recently found out it was commissioned by the ABC Network for the 106th running of the Kentucky Derby – the year Genuine Risk won, Storm's grandmother. Signs – do you believe in them?

Like when I was a kid, I have been playing the song on my iPhone over and over again. There is a line that keeps ringing in my head, "It's breeding and it's training, and it's something unknown that drives you and carries you home."

We know Storm's breeding and have done all we can with his training. It is now up to him, that unknown characteristic that makes a winner. Is it courage, heart, desire? What is deep within an athlete's soul that makes them drive to the finish line when their body is spent. I guess we will all find out later today.

It has certainly been a wild ride. I wanted to take this moment to thank you all for your support, encouragement, and faith. It has meant the world to me and my family. I look forward to celebrating with you after the race, no matter the result, as it is an honor just to be here.

Charlie hit send and took a sip of her coffee. She looked at the phone: 3:45 am. She wanted to call Doug. Her thumb hovered over his name in her phone. They had come so far together and he was such a big part of their daily lives now. Storm had brought them all together. Her hesitation boiled down to one simple question: how would this all end? After the race, what would change? Would anything? If Storm lost…

Her reverie was cut short by her phone vibrating. Doug's name showed brightly in the dim light of the room.

"Hi," she said.

"Figured you couldn't sleep. Neither could I. You okay with me calling?" Doug's deep voice carried over the line, melting some of the anxiety she was feeling.

"I am glad you did. And no, I couldn't sleep. This is so unreal. Nine months ago, who would have thought that I would be sitting in a hotel room in Louisville, Kentucky, about to watch my horse in the Kentucky Derby?" she said quietly.

"It's been a fun ride. I wouldn't have thought I would be in this situation either," Doug replied. Charlie pondered that comment.

"What do you mean? I'm sure you have tons of horses that could make it to the Derby," she said.

"That's not the situation I was referring to," Doug said slowly. Charlie's breath caught in her throat.

"What situation are you referring to?" she asked, smiling through the phone.

"Oh, just that I have fallen head over heels in love with the owner of one of the horses running in the Kentucky Derby," he said. Her smile faltered slightly. She knew what it was to have a heart broken into a million pieces. She never imagined she would find that same level of love and trust in someone again. Was she ready to love him fully?

She still held the phone tightly to her ear, unsure of how to respond to Doug's declaration of love. The silence thickened.

"I know you have been through a lot, and I am not trying to take Peter's place in your heart. I just wanted you to know," Doug said quietly.

"Thank you," was all she could say. Her tongue was heavy in her mouth, her heart beat loudly in the quiet room.

"Try to get some sleep. It will be a long day and I can't have you falling asleep in the winner's circle," Doug said, lightening up the conversation.

"Okay, boss," Charlie said. He hung up but she still kept the phone pressed to her ear, not wanting to lose the connection.

Derby Morning

Charlie heard the knock on the hotel door from where she stood in the bathroom. She couldn't move; the anxiety was overbearing. She was breathing slowly, trying to get her beating heart under control.

"Well, don't you just look like the cat's meow?" She heard Jillian say to Ryan, knowing he was dressed in a suit and tie, hair gelled just so.

"Hi, Aunt Jillian! Hi, Aunt Kate!" Skylar's voice came through the door.

"You are absolutely gorgeous," Jillian doted on her. Skylar's dress was a deep blue to match the riding silks that Lilly would be wearing that afternoon. She had a bright yellow ribbon around her waist to go with the three yellow bands around the arms of the racing silks. Her outfit was complete with a simple yellow hat to match the ribbon around her waist. Skylar was beside herself with glee over being able to show off her outfit later at the track.

"Since I want to be a jockey one day, I wanted to match with Lilly!" she said excitedly.

"Of course!" Jillian responded.

"Where is your mom?" Kate asked.

"She is in the bathroom," Ryan replied, with concern in his eyes that

Kate and Jillian picked up on. Charlie barely heard the knock at the bathroom door as she continued her breathing exercises.

"Open the door, Charlie," Kate's voice was clear. Charlie slowly reached for the door and turned the knob just so the lock would disengage and returned to her breathing.

Kate opened the door, took one look at her in the mirror and quickly closed the door behind her. Jillian stayed with the kids, keeping them distracted by talking about their outfits and the day ahead of them.

"Well, you are a sight," Kate smiled at her. Charlie was dressed in just her bra and underwear. Her dress hung on the shower rail and her hat sat on the back of the toilet.

"Shut up," Charlie replied between deep breaths.

Kate laughed, "Come on, Charlie, this is what you have been dreaming of." Charlie slid down the wall and burst into tears,

"I know!"

Kate sat down next to her, "Listen, this was bound to happen. You have been on a roller coaster and haven't slowed down. But it is all great, it's just so different from before Storm came into your life. I am so proud of you."

"I miss Peter," Charlie sobbed.

"You will always miss Peter," Kate replied, "He will always be a part of everything you do, it doesn't mean you can't experience new and exciting things."

"I feel guilty," Charlie replied.

"Well, you will have to get over that. Peter would be the first one to get on your case for not living your life to the fullest. He lived life with such enthusiasm, and he handed that down to your kids. Now, you can sit here and pout and Jillian and I will take the kids to cheer on Storm during the biggest race of his life; or you can get your act together, put your guilty thoughts aside, and meet that wonderfully handsome man at the track to watch your horse, and your dreams come true," Kate said.

"Do you think Peter would approve of Doug?" Charlie asked.

"He would love to see you happy, and Doug has helped pull you out of the gloom and doom and brought laughter back into your life," Kate said.

Kate stood up, cracked the door, "Jillian, we need you in here!"

"Is Mom okay?" Ryan asked from the other room.

"She's fine. She just needs some Jillian makeup magic to make her outfit complete," Kate replied.

"Oh boy! What do we have here?" Jillian said with a frown on her face. Charlie looked up at her with red eyes and swollen lips. She quickly shut the door,

"We will be right out!" she called to the kids.

"Okay, let's go to work!" Jillian said. It was just what Charlie needed, she burst out laughing. The hat that Jillian had on her head was a work of art. It wasn't as large as the previous day's hat, but the design to complement her outfit was a bit over the top. In a checkerboard white and black dress that barely covered her boobs and butt, Jillian's hat was all sorts of black and white twisty-twirls, going this way and that. She would have to watch it or she would poke someone's eye out.

"What?" she smirked at Charlie as she went to work on her face.

"It's just that you are classic Jillian, the one and only," Charlie said.

"I'll take that as a complement," Jillian smiled

After fifteen minutes of working Jillian's magic, and getting Charlie into her dress and making sure her hat sat just right on her head, the girls walked out of the bathroom.

"You look great, Mom," Ryan said.

Skylar ran over and gave her a hug. They were a matched pair, with Charlie's dress the mirror opposite of Skylar's, a rich yellow with blue ribbon around her waist and matching blue ribbon around the hat Peter had given her. All of them had the white cancer ribbon pinned to their outfits, coordinating with the ribbon on the jockey silks. They would be handing out ribbons to all their supporters throughout the day. Honoring Peter's life was a part their journey.

"Ready to go watch our Storm win his first race?" Charlie asked her kids and best friends.

"Yes!" They yelled in unison. They left the hotel. Soon they would find out how their Road to the Kentucky Derby would end.

The Track

Charlie's phone rang as they sat in traffic heading into the parking lot at Churchill Downs, "Hello?" Charlie said and smiled when she heard the voice on the other end.

"Hi, Mom. Yes, we are about to go into the track. Thank you. Look for us on TV. We love you," Charlie said, making the conversation as quick as possible to keep her mother from hearing the nervous tremor in her voice.

"Grandma and Poppop say hello and good luck. They are sorry they couldn't make it to watch in person," Charlie told Ryan and Skylar.

"I hope they see us on TV," Skylar said.

"I am sure they will," Charlie replied, her cell phone beeping with all the texts coming in from her friends wishing them luck. Her phone rang again.

"Hi," she said into the phone, "Yes, we are just pulling into the parking lot…Okay, we will meet you there." She hung up. "That was Doug, he is already here and said to meet him at the Turf Club."

Charlie parked the car and they made their way to the looming grandstand of Churchill Downs, the twin spires rising above them.

The number of people entering the track was astonishing. Charlie grabbed for Skylar's hand so as not to lose her in the mass of humanity. They walked through the crowd, relatively unknown, given what a long shot their horse was: past the celebrity red carpet, where the who's who were showing off their outfits and hats, past the vendors, and out to the paddock area. Above and around them were listed all the prior winners of the Kentucky Derby.

"Don't worry, Mom. Storm's name will look great up on that wall," Skylar said quietly to her.

"It sure will," Charlie said squeezing her hand. Doug called down to them from above,

"Up this way."

As their group walked up the steps to meet him, Doug handed everyone a glass off a tray next to him. Charlie looked at it closely. The glass was designed with the logo for the 141st running of the Kentucky Derby, along with a listing of all prior winners engraved on it.

"It's a beautiful glass," Charlie said to Doug.

"Yes, it is certainly a keepsake. They design a new glass each year, and have since 1938, and in it is the very well-known Mint Julep, the official drink of the Derby," Doug replied.

"I hope not in the kids glasses!" She quipped.

"Of course not," Doug laughed at her. "Root beer for the kids." He winked at Skylar and Ryan.

"We have a busy day ahead of us, so don't imbibe too much," Doug chided Charlie.

She swatted at him. "Oh please, it's not like the first time we met when I got drunk and bought a racehorse. I'm a lady, you know," she said in her most sophisticated tone.

"True. True," Doug said, smiling at her. For a moment they were lost in just staring at each other, forgetting the rest of the group around them.

"Come on, you two, we have some fans to meet!" Kate grabbed Charlie's arm.

They did have a busy day ahead of them. It was only 11 am and they had to do a meet and greet in the infield with their fans, and Charlie was scheduled for some interviews in the early afternoon. They would then make their way to the backside to see Storm. They would follow him as he made his way from his stall, along the track and into the paddock area in preparation for the greatest two minutes in sports.

Post time was set for 5:35 pm. It was going to be the longest day of their lives.

The Derby

Storm stood quivering in the small confines of the starting gate. His head held high, nostrils flared. Lilly sat perched high on his back, allowing the gate crew to crawl all over them. There wasn't much she could do for Storm, except whisper softly. She held her reins tight, hoping that her love for him would flow through them and calm him a bit. She grabbed a fist full of mane to steady herself.

Storm was still distracted by the events in the paddock and the post parade. Lilly knew why: Blackston. He had been there. Horses remember. After what they knew Storm went through with that man, there was no way he wasn't having flashbacks.

The paddock had been crowded with all the owners and their guests, along with the trainers and jockeys. Storm wasn't used to that much commotion prior to a race. The crowd outside the paddock was at least ten people deep, calling to their favorites with wishing of good luck to the jockeys. The state police were standing in different locations in and around the paddock to ensure that pandemonium did not ensue. With the biggest party of the year, no one wanted anyone to do anything stupid.

Charlie and Lilly had microphones thrust in their faces by ESPN and

NBC, as well as the horse racing cable channels and websites. Everyone wanted to get a quote in case your horse was the one that won it all.

Ben and Jenny had been busy walking Storm around the ring, showing him off to the masses, when Storm began to fret and jig a bit more than usual. One of the other horses in the Derby had just entered the paddock area, accompanied by none other than Dale Blackston. Charlie had never seen him so didn't know who he was, but Doug and Lilly had broken away from the mob of reporters and motioned Ben to bring Storm into his designated stall to tack up.

"Did you know he was going to be here?" Lilly quietly asked Doug.

"No. I was pretty sure he was still dealing with his legal issues. I guess he found another way to convince an owner he could bring home a winner. He doesn't look like he's the main trainer, though." He motioned to Lilly as Blackston hung around in the background of the trainer talking to the jockey of the horse he walked in with. He glanced their way several times, as if trying to make a connection.

"What are you all whispering about?" Charlie said as she walked up.

"Oh, just how beautiful you are at handling all those reporters," Doug calmly said, not wanted to worry Charlie about another thing, especially the presence of Dale Blackston.

They had called riders up, and Lilly had softly landed on Storm's back. Charlie had given him a good luck pat, and Skylar gave him one last peppermint treat. Doug and Ryan were close by, exuding nervous energy. Storm tossed his head, and Lilly patted his neck trying to rid him of the horrible memories.

Ben moved up close to Storm, "You have nothing to worry about, Stormy, my old friend. You are in great hands. Don't let those bad memories get the best of you."

Ben walked Storm out of the paddock and through the tunnel that runs under the grandstand. Exiting the tunnel, the huge oval appeared in front of them, with a sea of people in the infield. When he approached the track he turned Storm and Lilly over to Cappie sitting on Sarge, giving him a final pat, "Good luck, you two."

The horses were led out onto the track to the grand tune of, "My Old Kentucky Home." A quietness descended upon the crowd and as the University of Louisville marching band played, thousands of voices sang out the words as the horses paraded in front of the grandstand. Lilly wiped a tear away from her cheek.

Storm jigged nervously next to Sarge. A few times he bumped pretty hard into the big bay.

"You okay?" Cappie asked Lilly. Her face was white as a ghost. Cappie continued to hold Storm's bridle tight up against his thigh, allowing Sarge to bear the brunt of Storm's jitters.

"Yeah, something's got him riled up. He's never been this nervous in the post parade," Lilly replied. She was too nervous herself to go into everything. Riding in the Derby was not something she'd wanted to do.

Sarge knew his job. He kept his breathing even and his pace slow. Sarge knew that Storm couldn't leave his race in the post parade. The horse shouldn't exert all his energy being nervous beforehand and have nothing left when it is time to run the race.

Finally they turned. Cappie and Sarge let go of Storm and Lilly and let them go on their way to warm-up.

"You got this, Lilly," Cappie said encouragingly. He smiled as best he could, trying not to show how nervous he was for them both.

"Thanks Cappie!" Lilly called as she trotted off. Storm worked up into a gallop. Lilly took deep breathes to try and calm her nerves. The big race. There she was, up on a beautiful grey horse, with the eyes of the world watching. Six months ago, she would have never dreamed she would be back in a horse race, let alone the Kentucky Derby.

Lilly continued to work Storm through his pre-race warm-ups, trying to calm him down. He wasn't shaking as much, but his entire body was covered in so much sweat that he appeared almost black. The horses approached the starting gate. Buck Wheeler on Duke, pulled up next to Lilly.

"Glad to see you back, Lilly." He smiled over at her. Storm pranced underneath Lilly and half-reared. Lilly nodded at Buck, but kept her focus on Storm. Storm knew the other horse. Lilly knew they'd both been bred by Mr. Shilling. Storm was reaching out and trying to smell Duke, trying to place him, perhaps. Lilly worked on keeping him calm and focused on the gate.

The horses were almost all loaded. Lilly was relieved that their post position was in the second auxiliary gate. She was well aware of Storm's aversion to the rail. She had tried to train Storm out of his fear of the rail, but nothing had worked. She had learned a long time ago to accept the things she could not change. A member of the gate crew approached to guide Storm into the starting gate. Storm tossed his head and pawed the air.

"Come on boy, just like all the other races. I know there's a lot going on, but we've gotta focus. It's only the Kentucky Derby," Lilly smirked as she talked to Storm to try and calm him. Storm walked into the gate.

All was still. Each horse and jockey anticipated the ringing of the bell, the gates springing open in front of them. Their eyes looked out between the bars at the long expanse of track in front of them. The overflowing grandstand to their right and the crowded infield to their left; the wave of humanity collectively holding their breath.

Inside the gate, the gate crew stood on a small platform to the left of each horse's head keeping them in line and looking straight ahead. The starter waited for the moment when each of the horses was settled. The first ones to load had been in the longest and start to get fidgety; the last ones loaded need a second to get set after the gates behind them closed. Tails need to be free, placed over the gates behind them. Some of the horses leaned their haunches against the back gate to propel them forward, some leaned forward, anticipating the jump.

Storm and Lilly became one. A small girl on the back of a mass of muscle. She crouched low over Storm's neck, and felt Storm gather himself underneath her.

Storm's distraction clearly hadn't left him, and before Lilly could call him back, the starter hit the button, the bell rang, and the gates in front of them flew open. Those few seconds of distraction meant that Storm was left behind.

"Come on, Storm!" Lilly urged in his ear. He coiled like a snake and burst out of the gate, but by this time, he was several lengths behind the field.

****

"And they're off!" yelled the announcer. "Out of the gate, Lucky Charm takes the lead with American Pie just at his shoulder. Charming Cove is third, another length back, with Royal Duke sitting in fourth. The 141st Derby is under way!

Behind Royal Duke stretches the rest of the field. Black Knight, Natures Miracle and Legoland are tightly bunched, Toasted Head, followed by Act of Kindness on the outside, Rainbow Bandz is another length back with Anxiety Ridden and Imagine That, back another two lengths is Mocha Latte, Shooting Star and Granite Man, Buster Brown is moving along at a steady pace with Big Champ, Financial Wizard, and Candyman.

"And far behind the field is Genuine Storm. He's at least ten lengths behind the leading horse and continuing to fall behind after a bad start. It looked like he didn't want to come out of the gate."

****

"Mom, what's wrong with Storm?" Skylar asked anxiously tugging at Charlie's sleeve. Oh, poor Storm. Maybe they pushed him too much and shouldn't have raced him as much as they did. He had gotten pretty wired up in the paddock, which was so unlike him. They had watched him closely in the post parade and he had glistened with sweat. More than normal. Maybe he was sick. Charlie tried to rationalize his behavior with it being the Derby.

****

The most exciting two minutes in sports. Seconds were quickly passing. Lilly sat quietly on Storm, knowing he was wrestling with something. He had to work through it on his own and if he didn't engage in the race, there was nothing she could do about it. However, they were running out of time. Literally.

She clicked off the first quarter in her head. Twenty-four seconds. Not very fast, but not terribly slow either. With nineteen horses ahead of her, she couldn't see what was going on up ahead. She focused on calming Storm. His body was terribly tense and he hadn't smoothed out into a steady pace yet.

Given his late break, Lilly had all the room she needed to ease Storm over to the rail. She knew she couldn't get him as close as she would like, given his aversion to running against the rail, but getting as close as she could would save valuable time around the turns.

They had a long run to the first turn, running in front of the multitudes in the grandstands for the first time. That was good since it allowed Lilly time to move Storm over and provide him some time to settle before he had to switch leads going into the first turn. The crowd was screaming as they raced by the first time.

The Derby is the only race where you don't hear the ringing of the bell when the gates open, you hear the crowds roar and you know the race is on. Storm turned his ears to the crowd.

"Come on, Storm. Go get them. You can do it. It doesn't matter how far ahead they are. You can catch them," Lilly spoke quietly, talking to Storm, it seemed to sooth him. Lilly did everything she could to tell him it was going to be alright. Her hands were quiet on his mouth. Not tugging. Not forcing him to do anything he wasn't prepared to do. She knew he trusted her, so she would wait for him to decide.

Lilly saw his eyes focused on the horses in front of him, his ears pricked forward, his nose taking in big amounts of air. She wondered if he had caught Duke's scent ahead of him. Somewhere up in the herd of horses was his friend, a friend he could play with.

"Come on Storm, you can't let them get your peppermints! Run for me, big guy!" Lilly urged.

Lilly could sense when Storm locked on. His pace evened out and he took the bit from her. They had already passed the half mile pole; the ground would run out on them. Would Storm get there in time? The second quarter had been run in twenty-four and one-fifth seconds. So far the pace up ahead was pretty even.

Lilly knew the front runners would come back to them. The pace was fast enough so there would be no wire-to-wire win for whoever was in the lead. They were bunched pretty tightly ahead of them, but Storm was starting to pick up the stragglers.

Down the backstretch she kept Storm off the rail. They moved on past Candyman and Mocha Latte. Horses were changing positions pretty quickly as they were getting prepared to make their final press into the homestretch. Storm continued his assault on Granite Man and Shooting Star. Fifteen horses were still strung out in front of them.

****

"Mom, he's doing it!" Skylar yelled, squeezing Charlie's hand. "He's moving up on the rest of them!"

They could see Storm bearing down on the rest of the pack, determination written all over his body. The thundercloud had awakened. His ears pricked forward. Lilly was just a blur on his back.

****

"Lucky Charm still has the lead heading into the final turn, will he be able to pull off a wire to wire win? Morning Glory having made an early move, is running smoothly at his hip, half a length back. Duke is sitting chilly, another length back on the rail, waiting to make his move. Toasted Head and Imagine That are neck and neck in fourth and fifth. And picking up horses at the back of the pack is Genuine Storm. He's moved up to the tenth spot, fifteen lengths behind the leaders. He is really on a roll, swinging four wide around the turn, he will have a lot of ground to make up!" the announcer called out over the PA system.

****

Ryan was quiet next to Charlie watching Storm's every move. He announced Storm's time as each quarter ticked away. Twenty-four seconds for the third quarter. His first two quarters had been slow with his late start. Now he was starting to roll. Doug was behind them. Charlie could hear his cheers. He had come to love Storm as much as all of Charlie's family did. A true believer in the spirit of a horse. The champions that needed to reach into their souls to overcome adversity. Storm was living that out on the track today, running for them.

Would Storm make it in time? He was picking up horses quickly and now sat in seventh place coming out of the final turn. The long stretch run in front of him. The noise around Charlie was deafening as the horses came into full view. Everyone cheering for their favorite.

****

There he was. Duke, just ahead of them. Storm zeroed in as Duke made his move to swing around the tiring leaders.

****

The Kentucky Derby, at one mile and a quarter is the first time three-year-olds run at that distance. All the races leading up to the Derby top off at one mile and an eighth. No one truly knows how their horse will run in that last eighth of a mile. Will he tire? Will he be able to push through and get to the finish line? Will he meet the challenges of the late stretch runners who had saved up their last bursts of energy to come from behind and reach for the finish line?

****

Lilly used all her senses to help guide Storm and support him as he threaded his way through the field of horses ahead of him. Storm would need her help in that last eighth of a mile.

The Homestretch

The sound of thunder. Twenty horses. Eighty hooves pounding the dirt. There is no other sound like it. In no other race in these horses' lives will they have so much to overcome: the large field of twenty horses, each one trying to find their way; the distance, more than they had ever run; the bunching together of horse flesh, only a hand width between them as they fight for position. Jockeys looking for room on the rail or needing to swing wide and around horses; holes opening where there had been none to run through and then quickly closing. Jockeys guiding a thousand-pound horse at over thirty-five miles per hour and making split second decisions.

Sometimes the horse needs to make the decision.

Storm bore down on the leaders. The grandstand loomed again on his right. Lilly knew he was listening for the voices he cherished.

"They're out there, big guy, cheering you on. You're doing great. Come on, Storm. Run for Charlie. Run for your family." Storm lay low and lengthened his stride like he never had before, making up valuable ground.

✶✶✶✶✶✶✶✶✶✶✶✶✶✶✶

Lilly felt Storm's body lengthen out, feeling it stretch to a new vantage point. She saw the eighth mile pole pass and knew it was now or never. The last eighth mile of the Kentucky Derby is the real test to see if your horse can run the distance.

Two horses remained ahead. Just two lengths to make up. She hid close to Storm's back, trying to reduce the wind resistance. He was running hard. Giving all he had. All she could do was not interfere with his effort. They were all on the straight away so there was no saving ground. She pulled on her outside rein to swing Storm out and around. It would take up a few seconds but they would have a clear path ahead of them.

Suddenly, the outside horse ahead of them slowed and veered out. A small hole opened up between the two horses. Before Lilly could make a decision, Storm reached a new level and surged between them. He was now running up between horses, saving a few valuable seconds.

****

"Down the stretch they come!" yelled the announcer. The excitement surrounding the favorite and the long shot going head-to-head nearly overwhelmed him.

"Duke has the inside track and is a neck ahead of Genuine Storm. Storm is reaching another plateau, gaining on Duke by inches now. Can he overtake the favorite?! He is running out of track!" The announcer was jumping out of his chair in excitement.

****

Charlie's hands were numb from squeezing Skylar's and Ryan's hands. They were all straining along with Storm. Living the run down the homestretch as if they were all on his back.

"Come on Storm!" Charlie yelled.

"You can do it!" Skylar screamed.

"Go after him, Storm!" Ryan quietly urged him.

"Dig deep, fella," came from Doug behind, his hands on Charlie's shoulders.

****

Storm pulled up alongside Duke. Straining, running as one, they came barreling down the last hundred yards. Storm reached deep down and surged by Duke as they raced across the finish line. Storm swirled his ears forward, his trademark, knowing he had come out ahead.

****

Pandemonium! The stands were in an uproar. The beloved long shot had just stolen the Derby from the favorite. No matter who they bet on, the excitement of the race overtook the betting ticket in their hands. A new hero was born.

Skylar jumped up and down next to Charlie. Ryan was hugging and shaking hands with whoever he could grab. Charlie stood in her silent world, thinking of Peter and how he would have so loved to be there in that moment. She needed to let him go. Just like Storm needed to overcome his pain. He could do it. So could she. Charlie turned around to Doug beaming behind her, and wrapped her arms around his neck, giving him all the love she could transfer in that one moment.

****

Lilly slowly brought Storm down off his gallop. Both were exhausted, having strained as one during the last hundred yards. Sweat poured off both of them. Storm's ears were forward, listening to the cheers. All for him. He pranced down the track as Lilly turned him. Buck Wheeler pulled Duke up next to him.

"Great job with him, Lilly."

"Thanks, but it was all Storm. He made that last decision to come between horses. I had wanted him to go around you both," she smiled.

"He's a fighter for sure. But you were right there with him. Like I said, it's great to see you back in a race." Lilly nervously looked down.

"Thanks."

"Gotta go and weigh in." Donna Brothers was fast approaching to interview Lilly for the TV audience. "See you at the Preakness?" He asked.

"Not sure about that. I only committed to come back and ride him in this one. He seems to have worked through his issues. You know I don't stick around once they figure it out," she quickly said.

"Hope you change your mind." And off he rode. Donna rode up on them.

"How does it feel Lilly? To be the first female jockey to win the Kentucky Derby and on the long shot as well?"

"He's a great horse. I was lucky to be along for the ride," Lilly commented.

The Winner's Circle

Genuine Storm marched into the winner's circle, searching out his biggest fans. The crowd was wild with excitement over their newly crowned champion. His eyes locked on Skylar. With purposeful steps he stuck his nose right into her outstretched hand holding his reward – a peppermint.

"You see, Storm, all the peppermints you want! I knew you could do it," Skylar said wrapping her arms around her playmate, "Great job at tagging all the other horses! You won!"

Ryan patted Storm on his neck, "I knew you could do it." Tears that he wouldn't let fall, glistened in his eyes.

Charlie stood at his head, rubbed her hand up and down his nose and up between his ears where he liked it best. No words came out of her mouth. She couldn't talk or else she would dissolve into a pool of tears. Doug stood behind her, his arm around her waist, giving her the support she needed to keep her legs underneath her.

Ben kept a tight hold of Storm's bridle, "Mr. Shilling would be so proud of you. You lived up to your grandma's name today, big guy."

Several people approached, carrying the large garland of roses that they all had witnessed being made the night before.

"Here it comes, Storm! The roses, just like I've been telling you!" Skylar said loudly. The crowd around them laughed.

They draped it over his withers, in front of Lilly sitting in the saddle and handed her up the Jockey's Bouquet.

Lilly sat quietly, continuing to talk to Storm in a soft voice to keep him calm. He had run his heart out, making decisions along the way without her. He had learned his final lesson, reaching his nose in front of Duke to come out on top. She wouldn't be needed anymore.

"Did you think your horse would win, little lady?" the newsman asked Skylar.

"Of course. We have been talking about it every day since Storm came to our barn," Skylar replied innocently.

The newsman smiled, "Well, Genuine Storm certainly has a great back story. Claimed for just $2,500 and now standing here in the winner's circle of the Kentucky Derby. Are you excited to be heading to the Preakness?" he asked his question to Charlie.

Charlie turned her attention to the newsman and microphone thrust in front of her.

She hesitated before speaking, "We hadn't given much thought to what would happen after the Derby. This race had been our goal. For everyone here, my kids, my friends, the team at Shamrock Hill Farm that took us in," she squeezed Doug's hand at her waist, "Storm couldn't have done this without each of them. I particularly would like to thank our legion of fans and especially those early contributors to our efforts! You will all be receiving a rose out of this garland!" she announced.

The crowd cheered happily. Charlie glanced around her and saw many familiar faces. The fans that they had met along the way had shown up in full force to cheer on their horse. Storm was the people's horse, Charlie thought, as she looked around her, choking on her emotions again.

"The Preakness, Ms. Jenkins?" the newsman asked her again.

Charlie brought her attention back to him, "I can't make any promises today. Like in all the decisions we have made along our road here, I need to consult my team of experts." Charlie wrapped her arms around Ryan and Skylar, "Right, team?"

"Right!" They answered in unison, while Genuine Storm stood regally behind them. The setting sun glistening off his dappled grey coat. The thundercloud had indeed been unleashed.

Epilogue

The tears came fast and wouldn't stop. *Get a grip on yourself*, Lilly chided herself. She sat on the ground outside of Storm's stall, her back leaning against a bale of hay. *You just won the biggest race of your life and you are sitting her crying like a baby.*

Lilly didn't think she could do it again. It had taken a lot out of her to get on Storm's back the last few weeks, race after race. Each race took a little more out of her. He didn't need her anymore, he knew what to do now.

The others had left to go to the winner's party. Lilly had begged off, claiming how tired she was, but she really couldn't handle that group. She knew those people would be there that had started to shun her years ago, saying she would never make it. She still had her supporters, but it had been too much.

Lilly got up and leaned over the stall door. Storm was laying down in the deep straw.

"You did great today," she said to him. He looked up at her out of his drooping eyes. He was tired, she knew. The effort had been a big one. To overcome the late break and still go on to win took a special horse with a lot of heart.

She knew she needed to tell them. Charlie and Doug had been discussing Preakness options after they came back to the barn. Of course, they were moving on. Storm was the only horse that had a legitimate shot at winning the Triple Crown. Only one horse each year had that honor after winning the Kentucky Derby. They had talked strategy on how to get Storm rested up, given the hectic schedule leading up to the Derby and needing to race so many weeks to qualify.

She couldn't ride another race. Even if it was the Preakness. The pressure would be intense. She wouldn't be able to handle it.

Here had been a little bit easier given they were the underdog. Not a lot of attention was put on them. But in Baltimore, all the attention would be on Storm. And Lilly.

The media would dig up anything they could find on her. The past would come out. She wouldn't be able to handle it. What would Charlie think of her? Lilly was lost in her thoughts as memories she had pushed aside ran through her head.

"Hello, Elizabeth," a voice came from behind her. Lilly froze.

"You did a great job out there today," the voice continued. "Just like old times."

Lilly slowly forced herself to turn around. Storm got up from the back of the stall and came over to the stall door, leaning his head into her shoulder. She wrapped her arm around his neck, a lifeline to steady her.

"What are you doing here, Tom?" Lilly calmly said, keeping her voice from wavering.

"Just here to cheer on my girl," Tom replied.

"I'm not your girl anymore."

"You will always be my girl," Tom said as he approached.

Lilly grabbed at Genuine Storm tighter in the dark night. Her savior against this man she had vowed to avoid her entire life.

To be continued in...

The Eye of the Storm

The second book in the *Triple Crown Trilogy*.

Author's Note

Genuine Storm is the result of a fictional breeding between two actual Thoroughbreds: Genuine Reward, his sire, and Storm Minstrel, his dam. My research for Genuine Storm started with Genuine Risk. Genuine Risk won the Kentucky Derby during the height of my obsession with horses as a child and I can remember watching her cross the finish line on my television. I had the honor of meeting Genuine Risk the year before her passing. As for Storm Minstrel, she won the part due to her coloring. Since Genuine Reward was a chestnut in coloring, I needed a grey horse for the dam in order for Storm to turn out a grey. I came upon her name while researching the character of George Shilling and a large bloodstock disbursal at Keeneland.

The pedigree provided at the end of this book represents the actual lineage of Genuine Reward and Storm Minstrel. The stories about these ancestors told within this novel are true and reflect the depth and breadth of an industry that prides itself on its heritage.

I look forward to introducing you to more of these wonderful and courageous Thoroughbreds in *The Eye of the Storm* and *The Height of the Storm*, the second and third books in the *Triple Crown Trilogy*.

Pedigree - Genuine Storm (USA)
gr/r. C. 2012

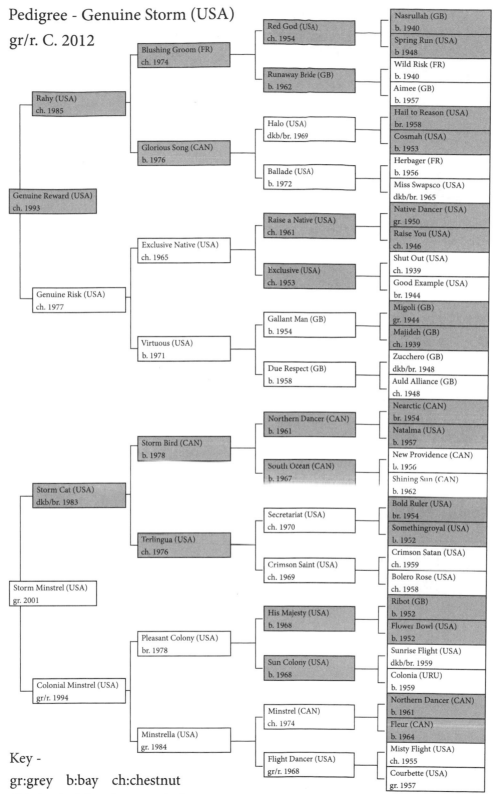

Genuine Reward (USA) ch. 1993	Rahy (USA) ch. 1985	Blushing Groom (FR) ch. 1974	Red God (USA) ch. 1954
			Nasrullah (GB) b. 1940
			Spring Run (USA) b. 1948
			Runaway Bride (GB) b. 1962
			Wild Risk (FR) b. 1940
			Aimee (GB) b. 1957
		Glorious Song (CAN) b. 1976	Halo (USA) dkb/br. 1969
			Hail to Reason (USA) br. 1958
			Cosmah (USA) b. 1953
			Ballade (USA) b. 1972
			Herbager (FR) b. 1956
			Miss Swapsco (USA) dkb/br. 1965
	Genuine Risk (USA) ch. 1977	Exclusive Native (USA) ch. 1965	Raise a Native (USA) ch. 1961
			Native Dancer (USA) gr. 1950
			Raise You (USA) ch. 1946
			Exclusive (USA) ch. 1953
			Shut Out (USA) ch. 1939
			Good Example (USA) br. 1944
		Virtuous (USA) b. 1971	Gallant Man (GB) b. 1954
			Migoli (GB) gr. 1944
			Majideh (GB) ch. 1939
			Due Respect (GB) b. 1958
			Zucchero (GB) dkb/br. 1948
			Auld Alliance (GB) ch. 1948

Storm Minstrel (USA) gr. 2001	Storm Cat (USA) dkb/br. 1983	Storm Bird (CAN) b. 1978	Northern Dancer (CAN) b. 1961
			Nearctic (CAN) br. 1954
			Natalma (USA) b. 1957
			South Ocean (CAN) b. 1967
			New Providence (CAN) b. 1956
			Shining Sun (CAN) b. 1962
		Terlingua (USA) ch. 1976	Secretariat (USA) ch. 1970
			Bold Ruler (USA) br. 1954
			Somethingroyal (USA) b. 1952
			Crimson Saint (USA) ch. 1969
			Crimson Satan (USA) ch. 1959
			Bolero Rose (USA) ch. 1958
	Colonial Minstrel (USA) gr/r. 1994	Pleasant Colony (USA) br. 1978	His Majesty (USA) b. 1968
			Ribot (GB) b. 1952
			Flower Bowl (USA) b. 1952
			Sun Colony (USA) b. 1968
			Sunrise Flight (USA) dkb/br. 1959
			Colonia (URU) b. 1959
		Minstrella (USA) gr. 1984	Minstrel (CAN) ch. 1974
			Northern Dancer (CAN) b. 1961
			Fleur (CAN) b. 1964
			Flight Dancer (USA) gr/r. 1968
			Misty Flight (USA) ch. 1955
			Courbette (USA) gr. 1957

Key -

gr:grey   b:bay   ch:chestnut

dkb/br:dark bay/brown   br:brown